Abundant Light

Abundant Light

short fiction by
Valerie Miner

Michigan State University Press • *East Lansing*

Michigan State University Press
East Lansing, Michigan 48823-5245

Printed and bound in the United States of America.

10 09 08 07 06 05 04   1 2 3 4 5 6 7 8 9 10

LIBRARY OF CONGRESS CATALOGING-IN-PUBLICATION DATA
Miner, Valerie.
Abundant light : short fiction / by Valerie Miner.
p. cm.
ISBN 0-87013-719-0 (pbk. : alk. paper)
I. United States—Social life and customs—Fiction. I. Title.
PS3563. I4647A64 2004
813' .54—dc22
2004012331

Cover design by Erin Kirk New
Book design by Sharp Designs, Inc., Lansing, MI

g **green** Michigan State University Press is a member of the Green Press
press Initiative and is committed to developing and encouraging ecologically
INITIATIVE
responsible publishing practices. For more information about the Green Press Initiative
and the use of recycled paper in book publishing, please visit *www.greenpressinitiative.org.*

Visit Michigan State University Press on the World Wide Web at *www.msupress.msu.edu*

Abundant Light is dedicated to my students
at the University of Minnesota,
Arizona State University,
and the University of California, Berkeley
with gratitude for what we have learned together.

Contents

Abundant Light

SHE SAT BY THE STUDIO WINDOW, SUN BAKING HER SORE NECK. STAINED FINGERS turned knots in a silver thread. Only a few grey strands, but each one a marker of time between them. Time seeping slowly, as air from a slightly pricked tire. Porous, malleable, transient, real. Did such time erase what lay behind?

They had agreed over the phone to meet tonight in the dining commons of the large arts centre. Ridiculous place, really, when they might have had a decent dinner in town. But they had made the suggestion simultaneously—neat? sentimental? romantic?—to rendezvous at a cafeteria like the one where they had met as students, half the continent away and almost thirty years before.

~

THIS MORNING, Jeanne was vaguely conscious of risk as she posted the sign at reception: "Ride needed to Calgary Airport. Phone Jeanne Davies, Artists' Studio #6." Would some weirdo call? Maybe she'd get a driver who would talk nonstop to Calgary. She had never imagined Ted, not consciously. After all, Canada was a large country. And this was a vast arts complex, filled with musicians and dancers and actors in repertory companies, as well as writers and painters working solo at the adjacent colony. Why would Ted be here? He lived in Toronto, for Christsake. Well, she thought he lived in Toronto. He used to. She didn't even know if he were alive. No, of course he was alive; she would *know somehow* if he weren't. Jeanne posted the notice because she needed a ride. Simple.

Now she should take a shower, do something with this mop of hair. Instead, she just sat in the sun wondering how she had brought on this imminent encounter. She had never been good at taking hints, and yesterday the universe had given her a massive premonition.

AS SHE SET OFF hiking the day before, the trail was miserably mucky from recent storms. Still, she told herself, maybe the Rocky Mountain air would open her imagination for those last canvases. Forward into the early summer afternoon she trudged, heavily sprayed against mosquitoes (she liked the French Canadian term for bug repellent, *"contre sauvages"*), carrying a book in her backpack to ward off loneliness, and harboring confident thoughts to fight against the fear, if not the existence, of bears. The seven-mile hike took her up one thousand feet, to the edge of cliffs, across fast-washing creeks and along steep switchbacks. She didn't gain artistic direction; however, she did forget about the grizzlies for fifteen minutes at a time and felt absorbed, challenged by the terrain. A gulp of fresh air, a respite, is as good as a breakthrough, she told herself; this would help her start fresh in the studio. The northern mountain light would be long and bright this summer evening. Throughout the afternoon, she had seen only two other hikers: an old woman walking swiftly along the creek trail, and a middle-aged man resting with his lunch at an overlook. She had nodded cordially to each, reluctant to break the cleansing silence. The woman had not even nodded in return. Browny-grey mud caked strange shapes on her boots, socks, cuffs. Relaxed, she approached the last half-mile with a buoyant smile.

Then they appeared, the mirage people. The permafrost yuppies. Two women, daisy wreaths in their dark curls, wearing long pink flowered gowns. Behind them were three men in grey suits, one carrying a baby. Then a flushed fellow in a tuxedo, clutching female shoes in one hand, and with his other offering support to an ivory-gowned, veiled woman, who lifted the hem of her lacy dress to reveal hiking shoes. On second glance, she noticed the bridesmaids' brown boots.

Jeanne hoped they had brought bug spray. The baby, in particular, seemed vulnerable. She supposed this ritual was no stranger than getting married in a hot-air balloon, or in the ocean thirty-five feet below the surface, wearing matching Aqua-Lungs. Truthfully, it was the getting married part that unnerved her—although she didn't know why, since she had done it twice. Maybe the baby had been conceived at this very spot (at a dryer time) last summer. Or maybe the best man had brought his offspring as a fertility talisman. Jeanne told herself not to stare. Still, the image remained embossed on her brain. All evening, she reviewed the wedding photograph in minute detail, down to the maple leaf in the groom's lapel. Painting was hard going that night, so she spent the time stretching canvas and cleaning brushes. Not until she lay awake for an hour did she realize that this was July thirteenth, and if she and Ted hadn't split up decades before, they'd be celebrating their twenty-fifth anniversary. Right then, she should have decided against posting the sign. She could have booked a damn bus to Calgary.

All night after the hike she lay shivering under thick covers in her well-heated room. Tears streaked down her face. What was going on? She had a lucky life in California. A lover she loved and who loved her. Two grown kids, who were healthy, happy, and good company. A rising reputation as a painter, a secure teaching job. Her life was a small sanctuary in a world of wars, starvation, homelessness, carjacking, AIDS, cancer. Yet she felt over-whelmed by grief. Surely not about Ted, this man she hadn't talked to for ten years, hadn't seen for over twenty. *She* had left *him*. The decision to divorce, like all decisions in their life, had been Jeanne's. The right choice— for her and, she hoped, for him. Then, why this weeping? Maudlin anniversary nostalgia? She should get some sleep, embrace the precious opportunity to focus on her work, and finish the paintings for next month's show.

THIS MORNING, remembering yesterday's resolve about getting on with things, she tacked the ride sign on the big bulletin board near the registration desk. It was such a long shot that Ted would see it, that he would be at the arts centre. Inconceivable, really.

Dinner line at the cafeteria was crowded with the cast of *Carmen*—people whose appetites matched their large voices. The cook had run out of egg-plant parmigiana and was about to serve the last of the chicken. Shifting from foot to foot between two gregarious tenors, she hoped she wouldn't see Ted in the line. So much for her careful plan to arrive at the designated corner of the dining room first; she had spent too much time primping and reassuring herself. (Should she have worn the turquoise shirt that brought out the green in her eyes?) Jeanne had amazed herself modeling outfits in front of the mirror for half an hour. Returning to the present, she snagged a chicken dinner and walked to the appointed table.

Empty—good; she took a long drink of water. Checking her watch, she noticed she was five minutes early. The hard-won chicken would be freezing by the time he arrived. But she had no intention of greeting him with her mouth full.

Occasionally, over the years, she fantasized about his life. She worried he might have stayed alone, growing more and more eccentric with his guitar and bird photographs. Did he still get up before dawn on the weekends to settle his tripods near nesting sites? On the other hand, she worried he had met some harridan (who easily could have been her older self if she had not met Carey and learned the happy side effects of humility). Of course, he could have met Ms. or Mr. Right. If he had found a good partner, would she feel a little jealous? Yes. More than a little. Mostly, though, she was curious. What did he look like? Was his red hair now grey? Did he still have the beard? Had he stopped smoking? Was he writing plays? Did he have children? Who was this man to whom she had once promised the rest of her life?

Maybe she should have bought a carafe of wine. She needed to relax. No, the cheap wine would only make her speedy. Eyes closed, she felt how tired she was from her almost sleepless night.

"Mind if I join you?"

She looked up to a slightly faded version of his former self. One could say that his youth had been a slightly vivid version of his current self. Emerging from her reverie, she caught similar disappointment in his eyes.

"Not at all!" She stood. They both reached into a quick, congenial hug.

"Long time no see." He shook his head nervously.

"So how are you?" She was racing. "What are you doing at Banff? How long have you been here?"

He smiled, erasing his familiar irritation at her impetuous barrage of questions.

She had been an unusual girl. Unique. He fell in love the first time she flashed that brilliant smile and said, "Hi there," in her open American accent. A Californian come to snowy Ontario for university. A scholarship girl, an orphan, who earned expenses in the cafeteria where he, too, served breakfasts because his famous architect father thought it was character-building to work one's way through school.

Now, Ted reminded himself to sit up straight. Lately, Monique complained about his hunched look. He was beaming at Jeanne, but that was

OK; she was still someone to beam at. Fit, beautiful in an elegant, middle-aged way, although he admitted he missed the youth—more her youth than his. She was just as attractive as he imagined his wife would be at forty-five.

"What are you eating?" she asked, to break the silence. He was staring so closely, she felt like a museum exhibit.

He prodded the meal curiously with his fork. "Beef medallions, I think they called it. They were out of chicken." Now how stupid did that sound?

"Yes." She blushed at her prize. "There was an early run on it. Would you like half of mine?"

He laughed, noticed his shoulders releasing, his stomach. "Just like old times, eh?"

"Pardon?" She always loved his rueful, upside-down smile.

"Jeanne arrives early. Jeanne snares the best dinner. Jeanne offers to share it with tardy Ted."

They laughed together. Impulsively, he took her hand, although he never did anything impulsively. Soon each was on the edge of tears from melancholy laughter.

"Well, how do we catch up on all these years?" he asked. "I mean we've had a couple of conversations over the decades, but there's the great unknown. When did I last see you—eight, nine years ago?"

"Try twenty-one"—she shook her head—"at Sandra's funeral."

"Poor Sandra," he murmured. "At least we're not dead."

"Not close to it, I hope." She peered at him meaningfully.

"No bad news from this quarter!"

They returned to their tepid dinners at the same moment. Around them, the huge cafeteria erupted in conversations, banging plates, screeching chairs.

"So how's Corey?" he tried, after a couple of mouthfuls.

"Carey," she smiled. "He's fine. Good health. Great spirits. His magazine just won a big design award." What would Carey think about this reunion? Would he feel threatened? Amused? She was afraid that in her recollections, she always framed Ted as a bit of a buffoon.

He blanched, as if there was something off in the dinner, but quickly recovered. "And your children?"

"All grown up now," she said wistfully. "Almost grown. Jennifer is starting medical school, in an accelerated program, and Brian works downtown with 'at risk' youth, finishing up in psychology."

"Downtown?" Ted asked. He wondered, would she think him a lush if he bought a carafe of that foul red wine to the table?

"San Francisco." She was taken aback that he didn't know. "We've all stayed in the city." How chance this meeting. They might have lost one another forever, without addresses, phone numbers.

"And you? Are you still in Toronto? Writing plays?" She felt oddly shy about asking if he had a lover, a wife.

"Toronto, yes, still Toronto." He picked around the plate, but couldn't stomach the food. "I'm doing more directing than writing these days."

She was nodding with a distracted air.

He sighed heavily. Why hold back? "My wife, Monique, was more successful as a writer."

"Was?" Her voice grew concerned.

"When the kids came, she shelved her plays for a while. You know . . ." He remembered what a passionate feminist Jeanne had been. Maybe Corey had raised their kids. "But she teaches the odd workshop, and plans to return to writing once the boys are in high school."

"They're young, the boys?" It sounded like an accusation, but she *was* startled by these big differences in their lives.

"Yeah, Clay is eleven. Ronnie's nine."

This wasn't what she imagined at all. They were drifting further and further apart with each exchange.

Ted noticed that although she had only eaten half her treasured chicken, she seemed finished with the meal.

"How about a walk to town?" he suggested. "I know a nice wine bar in the village where we can get a decent zinfandel."

She shivered at his recollection of her favorite wine. However, toward the end of their marriage, she was consuming quite a lot of it. The fresh air would feel good after a long, dead day in the studio.

He drummed his fingers on the table, an old habit.

She surprised herself by saying, "No, I'm in the middle of a project. I should stick with the muse; she's been fickle lately."

He inhaled sharply, as if someone had belted him in the stomach.

Noticing his chagrin, feeling her own, she asked, "Do you have any other free nights before I leave?"

"A couple." He tried not to sound too hopeful.

"Well, why don't we go out for a real evening—say Friday or Saturday?"

"Yes," he said evenly. "How about Friday?"

Ted walked straight back to his room, intending to turn in early because he'd had a restless sleep. Instead, he found himself taking the sylvan path down the mountain and into the village. Banff was more like Disneyland than a town, transformed by trinket shops and candy stores and restaurants. Japanese couples came here to be married, and traffic was often stalled on the main street while a black convertible carrying the veiled bride and her black-tuxed groom stopped for photographs in front of a particularly Wild West façade. Still, he walked to town every couple of days for the exercise. He supposed he could be climbing the Rockies in his spare time, but he didn't feel sure-footed enough to hike alone, and it had been hard to make friends at the large and often diffuse arts centre. Especially since he was an artist-once-removed, a director from a small theater back east, not really a composer or a poet or a painter.

Long walks often reminded Ted of Jeanne because that's how they came to know one another—strolling at night after studying, around the U. of T. campus, sometimes up to Bloor and as far west as Bathurst. Their first kiss had been in front of Hart House on a profoundly frozen February night. He knew as he escorted her home that evening that he wanted to marry her more than he would ever want anything in the world. He was surprised when she said yes, and surprised again when his family's reactions were so mixed. His alcoholic father adored her; his mother was suspicious of her absent family. His brothers thought she was a catch. Largely oblivious to these responses, he felt grateful he won his shot at heaven.

Ted found an outdoor table at the High Country Wine Bar—away from the noise and in sight of the waiter. He ordered a salade niçoise, as an antidote to that poisonous beef, and a carafe of zinfandel. He considered asking for two glasses, but that would be getting carried away. He drank in the blessed light that lasted forever this far north.

Ted raised a silent glass to the students in his workshop, pleased that the rehearsals were going well. He was a decent director, a good teacher. On the whole, he was glad he had accepted the month's commission here.

It was a nice break, and the salary would cover Clay's summer orthodontia bill. He missed Monique and the boys, but he phoned every other night to the holiday house Monique's family kept on Cape Breton. Monique was a much better match for him (his mother told him so) than the flighty American painter who ran off with a rock singer two years into their marriage.

Two years of marriage. He poured himself another glass. Two years as lovers in university before that. How could someone disappear so completely after being as close as two humans can be for *four years?* When she left, he simply refused to believe it. He waited. Even after the divorce, which she got easily and promptly down in California, he waited. Then one day, Monique moved in. That's how he remembered it. Or didn't remember it. His closest analogy was that he had awakened from a coma, a little older, a little depleted. Monique, a determined woman, slowly revived his will.

Finishing the salad, he felt better, as if the simple, fresh food had purged him of the assembly-line mystery meat. Downing the second glass of zin, he considered how he *had* grown up: he had surfaced from moodiness, earned a fair living, made a variety of friends, was a successful husband and father, and a semi-successful theatre director. Ted's architect brothers worried about his fiscal security, but also subtly envied his "avant-garde" life. The family believed he had forgotten Jeanne, but she returned at odd moments—sometimes for days, sometimes not for months. Yes, he had moved along with his life, and the small hole in his heart was invisible to everyone else, even to himself most of the time.

He wanted another carafe, but the waiter was busy inside. Ted noticed he was the only person dining alfresco. People strolling along the sidewalk clutched sweaters and jackets tightly around themselves. He put a twenty-dollar bill under the empty carafe and walked through the moonlight up the hill to his small but perfectly adequate room.

She managed to make a reservation at Le Bistro d'Or, the hottest restaurant in town. By chance, the owner knew her work. He promised a quiet table.

Ted had wanted to walk down the mountain together, but she made up an excuse about needing to be in Banff early for a gallery appointment. She hoped this wasn't transparently false. Ever since Jeanne suggested dinner, she'd been having panic attacks. What was the point? What was left to say? Well, she could say, "Good-bye." She had neglected that twenty-three years before.

The maitre d' greeted her warmly, led her to a corner booth. She sat with her back against the wall. Carey teased her that she needed to keep an eye on things, but actually she always chose the wall seat because she was getting a little deaf. She also made sure she picked a table with good light so that she could lip-read.

Jeanne studied the menu; perhaps knowing her order would make her less flustered when he arrived. What was going on? Some guilt, that's for sure. Some confusion about rules and roles and relationships. Who were they to one another now? Echoes? Memories? Friends—no, they could hardly claim that. But he was still part of her. She thought about him every few months, and occasionally, when she was giving a slide lecture, opening an exhibit, she kept half an eye on the door, wondering if she'd recognize him as he walked in.

He approached the table with the maitre d' and she took a long drink of water.

They were both standing, greeting each other with formal hugs. Seated, they caught up on the "news" of the previous days.

The waiter arrived with a bottle of champagne, "Compliments of the Manager."

Ted looked impressed. Jeanne was horrified. She must have given Georges the wrong impression. Surely she had explained she was meeting her *former* husband.

Once the waiter filled their glasses, she was so discombobulated that she forgot what she had planned to order and was forced to put on her reading glasses again to review the menu.

Ted watched her carefully, picking up the anxiousness, which in turn calmed him. She really shouldn't be embarrassed by the glasses. He tried, cheerfully: "Monique talked me into bifocal contact lenses a few years ago. They work a treat."

Puzzled, she said awkwardly, "That's nice." And when the waiter returned, she ordered the halibut, a salad.

He had wanted the same thing, but quickly switched his order to mountain lake trout.

They sat in uncomfortable silence until he remembered. "I'll show you my photos if you show me yours."

She smiled. "You first!" she laughed, and reached over for pictures of two handsome boys playing soccer. "The older one, the taller one, he looks quite like your brother John."

Ted beamed. "Exactly! It's uncanny. And Ronnie looks like Monique . . . oh, here's one of the four of us."

"Monique is very pretty," she said instantly. Young, she didn't want to say young, to notice young. The fresh-faced brunette with the big brown eyes was clearly the genetic model for their attractive younger son. "I see what you mean about, uh, Ronnie."

He grinned, intrigued by this peculiarly intimate moment, introducing his former wife to his wife, all the while aware that he didn't feel particularly "former" about Jeanne as they sat across from one another in this posh restaurant, sipping good champagne.

Proudly now, she offered photos of her offspring. Did they start with the kids' pictures because they were less complicated than the spouses'? Were they? (Thomas and Marie—she could still remember the names of the children they planned to have together and what they would look like: Marie short and fair like her, Thomas taller and with Ted's olive complexion). Focus on the present, she reminded herself. Here, now—your own real, beautiful children. Jennifer in her bridesmaid's dress at a cousin's wedding. Brian, already prematurely grey like Carey, in his blue work shirt and jeans. Great, smart, kind kids. How had she been so lucky? Ted was asking her something.

"Three more years of med school," she said, "then the residency and so forth. Who would have imagined my wee Jennifer a surgeon?"

The salads looked like complete meals, sixteen different varieties of field greens topped with roasted pistachios, chèvre, and yellow light-bulb tomatoes.

Ted carefully salted and peppered his salad before taking a taste, and she noticed that this habit, which used to drive her crazy, was endearing because she could imagine him doing this at age six or seventy-eight. Truly, she had been an intolerant bitch during the last years, relentlessly critical of who he *wasn't*.

He glanced up to see her watching him. "Great salad," he said to calm her stricken look. Just change the subject. Why hadn't he thought of this twenty-odd years ago? Maybe they would still be together. Before the idea carried him further, he asked,

"And Corey, you have a picture of him?"

Shyly, she held out a photo of the two of them in the back garden, surrounded by midsummer bloom.

"Carey," he corrected himself. Then, "I'm glad you're happy."

"I've grown up a lot."

He nodded, discomfited by the closeness, and dug into the mountain of field greens. Where *were* the fields with all these greens?

"I wasn't really ready—when *we* married." She took a long drink of champagne.

The light-footed waiter materialized to fill their glasses.

"Ready?" he asked in spite of himself. The appetizer was a little rich for him—why did they put cheese in a perfectly reasonable salad? He chewed dutifully.

"Ready for the kind of understanding and compromise and patience a good marriage requires."

"You make marriage sound like a spiritual discipline," he laughed.

She was full of seriousness. "I guess I just want to say I'm sorry—for my 'behavior' in that last year. For the way I left."

The last *year* . . . he had always wondered how long the affair with Claude had been going on. He had never imagined a whole year.

She continued apologizing—making amends, she called it—but he could hear nothing except the roar of loss from the first months after she vanished. He recalled his quixotic schemes to win her back, as well as his less voluntary fantasies. Like the one about Claude driving them into a tree on the qew, and how after Claude was buried, Ted would bring Jeanne in her wheelchair back to their safe flat on Robert Street.

Someone had finished his salad, all the pistachios and chèvre. The waiter replaced that empty plate with an entrée of trout steaming over corn and peppers.

She paused before starting her halibut. "Want to trade bites?"

"Yes," he laughed, as he fixed a side plate for her and she did the same for him.

"To our friendship!" She raised her glass hopefully.

"Yes," he said, regarding her with a familiar yet new admiration. It was hard to open those heavy old doors, and she was doing it gracefully. Yes, he did want a truce with this beautiful, cosmopolitan, mature woman.

After tasting his fish and her own, she declared, "You made the better choice. That's delicious."

He didn't say, you forced me to do it. Nor did he offer to trade dinners with her. He smiled at his impulses and his restraint.

"What's so funny?" she asked.

"Oh, us," he laughed. "In some ways we haven't changed at all."

"Speak for yourself. I've gained ten pounds." Now *why* had she said this?

"You were too skinny," he parried chivalrously. He hadn't noticed this at the time, but she looked trim enough now, so it must have been true.

"And half of that in wrinkles." *What* had got into her; she hated coyness. Besides, she actually liked her face now. She understood she was reaching for some errant intimacy. It was impossibly sad to grow so separate from the man with whom you had been one—or as near to one as you ever got with anybody in your life. After Ted, she had lost that endless optimism. Oh, she loved Carey all right, but she had clear boundaries. And tonight—maybe it was the wine, the good food, the private table—she ached for that risky part of herself.

"Well, you'd look pretty strange without them—a forty-five-year-old woman and no wrinkles."

She liked him for not denying the lines or saying they added character. Ted had a knack for succinct truth. She laughed.

"Now it's my turn to ask what's funny."

"I was always glad you couldn't lie."

"I'm happy you were grateful for something," he said in spite of himself.

"Oh, oh." She was stricken. Although Ted had turned mean and uncommunicative in the final months, she knew she was losing a fine, gentle, smart man. "No, no," she said remorsefully. "Your music. Your birdwatching. Your intelligence. I was, am, grateful for all that."

He blushed—for the first time in his life, he reckoned. Maybe it was a male hot flash. He took a long drink of water.

"Are you still playing the guitar?"

"Sometimes. On a Sunday afternoon, if we're not in production. I pick it up once in a while."

"In production. Yes, tell me about your theatre in Toronto—and more about what you've been doing here with the repertory training."

The conversation evened out. Play productions past and future. Dreams of building a classy, comfortable space for the company outside the warehouse district. For her, solo exhibitions coming up in Chicago and New York. A fellowship to Bellagio.

"You're a great success," he smiled over coffee, glad she had declined the second bottle of champagne. "I've followed your career, as best as one can from up here. Went to your exhibit in Yorkville three, four years ago."

"Three." She was flattered, disappointed. "But you didn't attend the opening. I would have loved to see you."

He shrugged, unwilling to reveal how terrified he had been, how he had waited until the exhibit's last day, then forced himself to go. "I loved what you're doing with lines of light. Apparently everyone does. You're in the big galleries. Winning prizes."

Sometimes she wondered how much of her success came from preying on convention, but it would sound like false modesty to demur now. Instead, she turned back to him. "And you're still dreaming the dream of the perfect theatre. It's great for your company that you're stretching and scheming."

"What would really be great is professional fundraising. Not my strong suit."

As they finished their coffee, a reflective quiet draped between them.

He swallowed hard and asked, "Your new paintings. Do you have any up at the studio here?"

"Yes," she brightened. She had always loved to show him her work. Was she imagining, misremembering, that he had been her best critic, both generous and honest? "Want to drop by on the way back to the dorm? I have some chamomile tea."

He laughed. "The paintings are more appealing than the tea."

Ted felt happy. Why had he fretted about tonight? He'd had a splendid time. And viewing her paintings in the studio made up for his cowardice at the Yorkville gallery. It would be like those early days, which until tonight he believed he had to forget. But surely all the past is part of one's present. You don't lose moments or people. Despite your best efforts.

Silvery light on the mountain path made her realize how long they had talked over dinner. She breathed in the scents of dirt and pine, and concentrated on the pleasure of stretching her muscles as they climbed to the arts centre. This evening, which she thought would make her feel old, on the contrary had revived her.

Their ambling silence was mutually soothing, and as they reached the centre, each was startled by electric lights from dorm windows, voices of

other strollers. They hurried past the housing block to the darkened artists'
colony trail, unlit to foster the privacy of the fellows.

"Oh, dear, I don't have my flashlight," she said.

"That's OK," he answered, "we'll just walk carefully."

Within a few feet, he stumbled. She reached for his hand; he reached
for her hand. Although it was unclear who made the gesture, they each held
on, alone and together.

She felt right, he thought—her strong, calloused, small hand. He was
back in front of Hart House on that frigid February night.

A painter notices hands, and Jeanne had always been attracted to Ted's
long, thin fingers, the mass of palm. Carey's hands were among his few dis-
appointments—thick, unlike the rest of him, the short fingers halting
abruptly at his chewed nails. She gulped the cool, wild air, regretful there
was only a week left of the residency. She hadn't allowed herself to think
much about time until now. She pretended residencies were ever expand-
ing, and this optimism sustained her work.

An almost-full moon broke through the canopy of fir trees; now he
could see the path. He was good at following paths, rarely strayed.
Conscious that they were still holding hands, he thought how he had never
been unfaithful—with Jeanne when they were married, or with Monique.
He was a one-woman man. Yet now he ached to hold Jeanne in the old
ways, to enter her, to sleep wrapped together in each other's limbs. How
could this be infidelity? It was, if anything, a kind of memory. Jeanne had
made him who he was to Monique.

Her studio was at the end, by the forest's edge. She enjoyed the semi-
solitude, the closeness of the wild noises large and small—hawks, elk,
woodpeckers, foxes, maybe bear. What else could make that lumbering
tread—only a bear or a ghost.

Carey had teased her about the seclusion of her studio, about going
off to a residency altogether. Didn't she own a beautiful, light-filled work
space in the most elegant city in the world? Now that the kids were gone,
what interruptions did she have? She couldn't explain the motivation she
gained at a colony, where art was honored as labor, where nobody bothered you if you worked until 2 or 3 A.M. or through the night. Anonymous
in each new colony, she had the chance to start out as a fresh person. This
same kind of opportunity had drawn her to a strange Canadian university
years before.

At least she had remembered to leave on the deck light; she hated fumbling with locks. Just as she inserted the key, she heard him say something.

Jeanne hesitated before saying, "Pardon?" Knew that if she carried on, he'd be in the door, arms around her, within seconds. But she was trying to break her old manipulative habits. "Pardon?"

He cleared his throat in what he reckoned was a familiar bronchial noise. Irritating, but what could he do about his long-retired smoking habit? "Jeanne"—he dropped her hand and put his palms on her shoulders—"I think it might be best if I saw those paintings in the clear light of day."

She looked into his familiar eyes and found an unfamiliar determination. Perhaps she would be grateful to him tomorrow.

"May I come by in the morning? Or Tuesday?" he asked.

Something turned in her. A meanness or shrewdness or fear or kindness, it was hard to tell. "No, no, I'd rather have you see them properly hung, in an exhibit space. Any chance you'll be in New York next fall?"

"I might be." He put his arms across his chest, thinking how he had seen her work and herself in so many states of disarray. Still, he understood.

"I'll be opening at a gallery in Chelsea. October third. Carey's coming. Maybe you could bring Monique?"

"Maybe," he said numbly. And then, "Do you still need that ride to the airport?"

"If you don't mind." She felt sad, shy.

"It's easy," he nodded. "My flight is a couple of hours later. Shall we leave here about ten?"

She smiled, too choked up to speak.

"Should I drop by earlier to pick up the paintings?"

"No. No, thanks. I always ship the canvases. It will be just me and my suitcase."

"See you then." He leaned over and kissed her forehead.

"See you then!" She waved and ducked inside her studio.

———

THEY BOTH worked hard that last week. She completed the exhibit paintings and started on several others that might turn into a new series: images based on night sounds—real, imagined, remembered, hoped for.

His company flew through the final rehearsal, and both performances were enthusiastically received. After the first, the centre director invited him back for the following summer. He surprised himself by saying about this coveted prize, "I'd like to think about it." Both nights he peered out into the audience, hoping to see her face.

That last morning, the rains were too heavy for conversation as they packed the car. Driving along stormy mountain roads was tricky, since he was used to flat Ontario highways. He knew she had driven to the Sierra for decades of family holidays, and was glad she didn't offer to take over. It wasn't a macho thing, staying behind the wheel, it was just that the car was insured in his name. For the first twenty miles, he couldn't tell whether her silence was from fear or discretion, but he appreciated it nonetheless.

The winds abated as they reached Calgary's outskirts. All the things he had wanted to say or ask were coming back to him. Questions about her family. About mutual friends long disappeared from his life—from hers, too? He wanted to tell her that he wished he were more successful but he was happy enough. Feeling eager to get home, he realized this was the story to tell himself.

Jeanne thought she knew why he hadn't come into the studio, but it took all her willpower not to ask.

They checked in at separate airlines and agreed to meet at the airport café before her flight. Halfway through his latte, he worried that she had simply vanished again. That's what it had felt like two decades before. She had been so fast during their days together. Landing in his life, fluttering around his family, friends. Sure, he always knew he couldn't hold on to her—that he'd have to enjoy his twenty-four hours, or forty-eight hours, or three months—and he was gratified that she had stayed for a few years. Then, poof! She was off with Claude. Gone to France. Back to California. Married. Kids. A butterfly in someone else's garden.

Jeanne raced toward his table. "So sorry to keep you waiting. I knew I should have shipped *all* the canvases, but I didn't feel quite finished with that last one, you know."

He nodded.

"And I wanted it on the plane with me. They gave me such shit, excuse me, about checking it as baggage."

"You won, of course."

"Of course." She took a sip of his latte and sighed.

She was wearing a turquoise cotton shirt that perfectly matched her eyes, her earrings. He couldn't stop staring.

Emboldened by his admiration, she asked, "Why didn't you come into the studio that night?"

Spontaneously he answered, "Because I didn't want to lose myself again."

"Is that what I mean to you?"

He shrugged.

"Will we ever see one another again?"

"Of course." He offered her another sip, then finished the latte. "I'm afraid of ghosts."

"What?" She heard them announcing her flight, but couldn't leave with this enigma. Words. He had always caught her with words, describing her, prescribing the nature of their relationship, their future. She had needed air. He had never understood that if he had left the window open just a crack, she might have stayed.

"That's your flight," he said.

"What do you mean?" she persisted.

"I'd rather have you in my life as a person, even a geographically distant person, than as a memory . . . haunting."

She grinned, grabbed her gear, and together they hurried toward the gate. They kissed on both cheeks, and up the ramp she strode, her left shoulder drawn down by the heavy garment bag.

He watched Jeanne propel herself beyond fatigue. The harsh airport lights made her appear drawn, pale, and he could imagine what she'd look like in another twenty years. He hoped they'd see each other before then.

At the runway entrance, she swiveled, dropped one bag, and blew him a kiss.

Greyhound, 1970

BELLA WAS GOING TO HER NIECE STACEY'S WEDDING, IN A ROUNDABOUT WAY—
traveling from Vancouver to Detroit to Florida to San Francisco by
Greyhound. Quite a trip, the clerk had said.

She knew what he was thinking: quite a trip for an eightyish woman,
but he was too polite to mention her age. People were like that about old-
ness—as if it were something you yourself hadn't noticed—and in certain
ways that was right, because she felt more aware of others being younger
than of herself being *older*, which didn't stop her from using a senior citizen's pass. On the other hand, she sometimes did feel old in the sense of
tired, in the way of being a veteran. Her brothers Douglas and Keith were
veterans right after World War I—fifty years ago—but a woman's duty
(marriage, childbirth, widowhood, grandmotherhood, the death of an only
child, the rearing of a child's child) went undecorated. You were meant to
keep going. Maybe that's why the Greyhound ride felt comfortable. Her
whole life had been the same story: you got on the bus and kept going.

She glanced through the window at the brownish grey land and tried
to convince herself she was truly riding through the high desert of
Southern New Mexico. Evidence stretched before her: uninhabited land;
sleek Winnebagos; hot, dry, dusty air whenever the bus door elbowed open.
Hard to imagine that a lass from the Edinburgh tenements would be riding the coach through the Sonoran desert as a blue-permed cowgirl. This
was the America she had dreamed about—vast, unsettled, physically
uncomfortable, cinematic, thrilling.

Pathetic: she was being as sentimental as those Americans who pictured
all of Scotland to be a Highland summer morning, minus the rain. In fact,
she and her sisters had settled in New World cities just as dark and crowded
as the Edinburgh they escaped, as if they had shifted addresses from one
end of the street to the other.

Then again, this was a holiday, time for a little fantasy. And it was a treat to travel by bus, so high above the ground, rolling on these tall, sturdy tires across the Southwest. Looking out the coach window was much more intense than watching a movie, but not the Wild West—not quite the real thing.

What was the real thing? Take family—Stacey was technically a half-niece, someone she hadn't met until the child had grown to ten or eleven, and whom she saw once a year these days. Yet there was something about the girl—spunk and intelligence mixed with an all-too-familiar self-doubt—that went straight to this auntie's heart. Clearly, Stacey overwhelmed her fretting mother, who might have done better with a more feminine lass, one who would marry and raise four children and live close by. Maddie had wanted a dutiful daughter, and what she was dealt by the nature of her own hard, brave life was a wild card.

Perhaps with this new young one, who according to Maddie was about to marry the *wrong* man and emigrate to the *wrong* country, Bella could be of use. Surely everyone had told *her* that she was crazy to leave her family for marriage with a piano tuner in the far reaches of Canada. If it hadn't been the life they'd planned, it had been a damn sight better than suffocating in Auld Reekie.

"Excuse me. Is this seat taken?"

New passengers boarding. She hadn't noticed. One of the advantages or liabilities of old age was that you weren't always where you were supposed to be—even when you were there. Looking about, she observed the bus filling. There were other places he could sit, but she hadn't paid for two seats.

"No, not at all." She shifted the heavy brown handbag to her lap.

"Whew, thanks."

He was sweating, over-ripe with sweet men's cologne or deodorant. A waxy musk.

She glanced out the window at the pinkish brown bus depot in the miniature adobe town.

"Where are you headed?" His friendly, energetic voice was like the wind, and she gripped one side of her seat.

"San Francisco," she answered economically, inclined to turn back to the window and resume the rest of the journey in solitude.

"Nice town," he grinned, sweat still dripping down his temples.

She couldn't help herself. "And you?"

"L.A." he shrugged.

Los Angeles frightened her—a science-fiction kind of place with palm trees and traffic jams (which had seemed mutually exclusive phenomena before she visited L.A. for the first time). Bella had always felt grateful none of her large family had settled in Los Angeles.

"On business," he said apologetically.

She was forgetting herself. "Oh yes, L.A.—I have to transfer buses there."

Something wrong with this conversational rhythm. She reached for the beat. "What sort of business?"

He sighed and rested his head back against the high seat. "Toys. I work with Toyland and I'm going to a regional training conference in Anaheim."

"I guess they have to train people carefully to assemble some of those complicated trains and planes."

"Thank you," he said somberly.

Puzzled, she reviewed what she had said and, finding nothing to make a person grateful, she calculated that she'd have at least 750 miles to L.A. seated next to this slightly off guy. In a minute, she would look around and see where she might move at the next rest stop.

"Most people, when they hear I work for Toyland," he was continuing in an urgent but sane voice, "say, 'That must be fun,' or 'Bet you never wanted to grow up.' In actuality, toys are both big business and big responsibility, what with monitoring the toxicity of paints and subliminal violence. It's an interesting job, and sometimes an important one."

"Of course," she nodded reassuringly. What about her brought out such volubility in complete strangers?

"I'm forgetting myself." He extended his palm. "I'm Tony. Tony Montale."

She shook his firm, dry hand. "Bella Ferguson."

"You Italian?" he asked eagerly.

Vaguely sorry to disappoint, she admitted, "Scottish. But," as if this might make her more interesting, "I live in Canada." Why was she having a hard time getting this exchange into focus? "Italian?"

"Well, I'm Italian, you see, and *Bella,* well, it means 'beautiful.' It's Italian."

"Isobel," she smiled.

"Italian or no, it's a proper name for a pretty lady like you."

She regarded him quizzically and then, afraid to cause upset, said, "Thank you."

"On some kind of vision quest?" he grinned.

"Vision quest?" The very words made her laugh. Looking for her glasses came to mind.

He laughed too. "Yeah, it's a kind of inner-discovery journey. A lot of hippies come to the desert to find themselves."

"Well, no, I rather suspect that one of my misfortunes is that I've never really lost myself."

"I know what you mean. Solid, steady, reliable. Me too."

He made her sound like an industrial refrigerator, and she felt compelled to soften the image. "I'm traveling to my niece's wedding. Near San Francisco."

"If you're going from British Columbia to San Francisco, how did you wind up here, in the Southwest?"

He did ask a lot of questions. "I'm on my way back from visiting one sister in Detroit, then another in Florida."

"Your family Catholic?"

"Pardon?"

"Four girls. I just guessed. I come from a big Catholic brood myself."

She couldn't tell him the whole story. Fourteen or fifteen children. She didn't *know* the whole story about her parents. No one did. Forbidden love, abandoned children, tragic deaths. Maybe someday it would be discovered. But what was the point? The brothers and sisters were all fine, thanks, getting along better than anyone might have predicted, ignoring who was a half-sister, who was a whole brother.

"Not Catholic," she said, and to prevent further questioning she found herself telling him about how she and Nan and Chrissie and Maddie had all immigrated to North America separately, but had found one another again, through letters, phone calls, prayers. They were a different family now; it reminded her of reknitting a sweater, adding room here and there to accommodate the expansiveness of life lived.

"That's great," he answered with implacable cheerfulness. "I know just what you mean; my grandparents, they immigrated here from Calabria."

Bella nodded courteously as he described his grandparents' hardships in New York, his parents moving west.

She hated when people took her identity and claimed it as theirs because of grandparents. How *could* he know what it felt like to immigrate to tiny, wet Victoria after a rich, overcomplicated life as the eldest child in a huge urban Scots family? How could he know what it was like to pin your hopes on a dreamer like her beloved, occasionally impractical Tommy?

For some reason she was telling Tony that Father had been right. Piano-tuning in the wilderness was a daft plan. How many pianos could there be in a village like Victoria? But she had found a job housekeeping for a widowed Presbyterian minister who fell in love with her accent (did she have an accent still?), and between them, she and Tommy, they paid rent on a sweet flat with a view of the harbor and the Empress Hotel. The truth was that their modest life would have been *much more* modest if they had remained in Edinburgh. There would have been no window on the Pacific, with all its stormy drama.

They were beginning to feel settled. Then, within six months, she discovered she was pregnant, and Tommy developed some kind of desperate cancer and he died, and the minister couldn't bear a shrieking child around the place. So a month after Peggy was born, Bella found herself taking in other people's children to pay the rent on their now cavernous flat by the grey sea.

Bella glanced at her seatmate, who was sitting straighter, his eyes wide, asking her to continue. A nice man.

Peggy was a bright child, with all of Tommy's music and some of her own willfulness, and together they made a kind of happiness in the harbor flat. During the twenties, Bella learned that her sisters had come to the States. No one had heard from Keith in New Zealand, or Douglas in . . . now where had Douglas gone? Archie wrote occasionally from England, promising to visit.

Silence between them. The whole coach had gone quiet.

Tony nodded, encouragingly.

By the time Peggy was in high school, Bella was able to afford a little stone house a bus ride away from her job at Crown's Department Store. This itself would not have happened in Scotland. There, an unschooled widow with an artistic child could never afford a house. Peggy wouldn't have gone to a conservatory. It was a good world there in Canada—not perfect, but *very* good.

Bella didn't know why Peggy married the mad dentist—a kind man, but given to fits of mania. After the red-haired boy was born, when Peggy named him for her never-seen father, Bella allowed herself to dwell on life's compensations.

How long was it before Peggy developed her father's cancer? 1947.

"Nineteen forty-seven?" Tony asked. "For sure, by then there were medical advances."

"Hmmm, well," she nodded. "By that time the only doctoring Peggy would accept was from God."

No, no! Bella had screamed at her dying daughter, who had every reason to live. How can you be a Christian Scientist if you're married to a bloody dentist? Dying had nothing to do with virtue, she pleaded; she'd seen in Edinburgh that death often was more related to poverty or ignorance or luck. But just as Tommy had sought answers in the New World, Peggy had faith in the next world. She, too, left Bella.

Now, she noticed the toy man had averted his eyes. She was blathering; her throat seized in humiliation.

"Sorry," she said.

"No, no," he insisted, tears rimming his brown eyes. "You're a brave woman."

"Not brave at all. You just do what you have to do."

He opened his mouth, but she forestalled protest because she *did not* want to inhabit these old stories. "Tell me about *your* family," she urged. "Why did they leave New York?"

"Adventure." He shook his head, smiling in a way that showed Bella he would not press her further, that he was—like most humans—more interested in his own tale.

"Were they cowboys?" she joked.

"As a matter of fact," he nodded, glancing out at the darkening landscape, "my father eventually owned a little ranch with pigs and sheep and four cows. The cows were my favorite." He looked pensive.

"Why?" she prompted.

"They're smart, you know. People think they're stupid, but cows are smart."

She smiled, touched.

"I remember the terrible day Dad sold Tess. I was heartbroken, watching her being hauled off in that truck. Later, the butcher told us, he stopped for gas in Logan—that's about five miles from our house. The darn cow found her way out of his truck and back home by early evening. After that, she became our longest-lived milking cow."

"Yes," Bella nodded to this appealing man she almost hadn't allowed to sit next to her. "I've always liked cows. Can't say the same for bulls. But cows."

He talked about the ranch going under, his own failure to get a college scholarship, his first job at a Toyland store in Santa Fe, his gradual, steady promotion within the company. And now he was heading to L.A. to train as regional manager.

"Never could get used to flying, but they won't know I came by bus. Not that there's anything wrong with buses," he quickly recovered. "I just mean—as a businessman you're not supposed to be afraid of airplanes."

"Of course," she sympathized. "And you don't like driving?" How could he be a regional manager without a car?

"No, don't mind it, not at all. I just needed some time to review charts, get some rest. Thought the bus would be better than driving for that."

"Then I should let you get to work, so you'll be prepared."

He looked relieved, disappointed. "Guess so."

The next morning, as they rolled into L.A., he was handing her a blue and pink business card. "Stop over in New Mexico next time you visit your sisters. My brother's bought himself a small ranch outside Deming. I'll drive you out to visit with some of his smart cows."

"Aye, I might do that," said Bella, sad to see him disappear, and at the same time gathering her bags and her wits and locating the right bus to San Francisco.

"Good luck at the training!" she called.

"Good luck at the wedding," he waved back.

———

NUMBER 17 was eerily empty for a daytime bus between two California cities. She chose a window seat in the middle of the bus. No one would bother her here.

Bella did notice an Asian woman sitting several rows toward the rear— from Asia, not North America; you could tell by the compact way she occupied her seat. Yes, this would be a good spot. Bella liked Japanese and

Chinese and Korean people. Similar to the Scots, they appreciated reserve, respected space.

She closed her eyes, tired from the cramped position in which she had napped all night. Tony had slept with his legs fanned open; a man needs his room. Her hair would be a mess; she'd get it shampooed and set before the wedding. She pictured Stacey's long dark hair and pink skin—many adventures between that face and hers.

Would Maddie stop worrying about Stacey, about her "staid" fiancé, about her risky work as a journalist? Maddie had tried not to interfere, but she couldn't help urging Stacey to consider a job at the telephone company, where her Uncle Danny's children had found success. Maybe Stacey was one of those daughter/mother echoes, choosing a quiet man to deflect her mother's choice of a noisy one. Well, it didn't bear thinking about; Stacey knew her own mind.

Placing a clean cotton hanky on the headrest, Bella leaned back with her eyes shut. She felt grateful that Stacey had *someone*, however long he lasted. Surely she wished as much for her own red-haired grandson, whom she thought of as her boy now. How often, when she was bringing up Peggy, she wished she could be given another chance to do things better. Yet raising a second child was the last thing she expected from the 1950s and '60s. Perhaps young Tom saved her from going cuckoo with loneliness. Certainly he kept her busy, working that much harder at her job, racing home to fix nourishing meals. People treated her like some kind of saint, although she was simply doing what needed to be done. And the rewards she got back in the person of her sweet, loyal grandson! He wasn't intellectual like Stacey, but smart in practical ways. And he had dreams— including a wacky one of becoming a bush pilot, the Canadian West's equivalent of a city fireman. That ambition, she prayed cautiously, he would grow out of.

"You will excuse me."

A voice from behind. If Bella closed her eyes again, the speaker might vanish. Amazing how a bus journey—simply sitting in a comfortable seat and watching the scenery go by—could tire out a person.

"You will excuse me." A gently insistent tone. "Madame?"

Of course Bella would excuse her. Politely she turned and answered, "Yes, dear?"

The pretty woman smiled shyly. "Are we almost in San Francisco? How far to San Francisco?"

"No," Bella responded kindly. "We've just passed Santa Barbara."

"How far more?"

"Well"—she studied the uncomfortable traveler—"I'd say it's a good eight hours."

"Eight?" She held up eight slender fingers before an incredulous face. "*Eight* hours?"

"Yes, dear."

Necessity overcame the young woman's shyness. "But what about the eating? Do they serve lunch and dinner on the bus?"

Bella watched her carefully. Sometimes peculiar people rode the buses. Also, she had learned to deal carefully, evasively, with disturbed customers at the department store. No, something else was happening here.

"This is your first Greyhound trip?"

She nodded.

The well-dressed woman was perhaps in her early thirties.

"No, they don't serve food, but they will stop several times at cafés for us to buy meals." The only way to deal with these foul restaurants was to carry your own food, and Bella's sister had packed just enough for her to make it to San Francisco. The fruit and cheese were an extra burden to lug around—ultimately, though, quite worth the weight. Bella had been saving the best two apples for today.

"When is the stop? The next stop?" The woman was breathing hard.

"Let's see," she looked at her watch. "It's 10 A.M. now, and I would guess noon. Maybe two hours from now."

The traveler opened and closed her mouth in silent astonishment.

Bella noticed that twisting around like this was too much for her eighty-five-year-old body. She heard herself saying, "Would you care to sit next to me, dear? It might be easier for chatting."

Once the willowy woman was seated, Bella successfully pressed an apple on her. She declined the cheese.

Bella bit into her last apple. Maybe she would buy a tuna sandwich for lunch, after all. God wouldn't poison her the week of Stacey's wedding. Time passed. Kyoko talked about her biochemistry lab in Yokohama, about how she had always dreamed of visiting California. The bus made several stops. Bella dozed.

"You will excuse me."

Bella had had this dream before.

"You will excuse me."

Bella opened her eyes to find a strange lady beside her. Oh, yes, the scientist from Japan.

"This is San Francisco." The other passenger regarded her cautiously. Bella herself was the stranger now.

"Where we get off," Kyoko persisted.

"Yes, yes," Bella groped to the surface. "Oh, yes, Maddie is getting married." Maybe she should stop her while there was still time.

"Is that Stacey?" Kyoko continued relentlessly.

Right, her niece—too late for Maddie, too late for their whole generation. Dutifully, Bella squinted out the window. Waving back at Stacey, she watched the lass's face relax.

The woman smiled. "I take picture of you two together for my memory book. No, I take two pictures, one for you and I will send."

Bella, who had finally arrived, stood grinning next to her niece in front of the San Francisco Greyhound Station.

Several days later, on the very morning of the wedding, Bella and Stacey sat talking among the shabbily genteel furnishings of Mrs. Simpson's apartment. Maddie always made the right sort of friends. Something about her—an air, a dignity—appealed to people like the widow of Judge Simpson, who probably never before had a friend who waited on tables. So, of course Mrs. Simpson would be *delighted* to have Maddie's sister use the flat while she was on vacation. Mrs. Simpson had sent a ridiculously expensive wedding present before leaving town, and had filled the apartment with flowers. Very nice, but a little overdone.

So far, Bella was glad to be here. She knew she had been a big help. Moral support for both mother and daughter. Mediating. Cataloging wedding gifts. Checking on the hors d'oeuvres and champagne for the modest afternoon reception.

And now, on the wedding day, she was reassuring her niece that jitters were normal. Why, she remembered the tremors about her own marriage, not to mention the earthquake around the wedding of Stacey's grandparents. No, not to mention this. She had never even talked to Maddie about those times. And although at this age Bella could afford a trip into memory,

Maddie resolutely continued to reside in her damn cheerful imagination. Aunt and niece sat in the soft, early-morning June light, drinking hot tea and eating gingersnaps together. It felt a little ceremonial.

"Marriage is such a big step," the girl said.

As pretty as Peggy at this age, but with different coloring.

"I mean, the rest of my life."

Bella nodded and, to keep from talking, bit another gingersnap.

"We've been going together for three years, to make sure we don't make the same mistakes as our parents."

Or your grandparents. Bella was silent.

Impatient for her aunt's reply, Stacey sighed warily. "So, do you think you can be sure?"

"No," Bella shook her head. She still felt stiff from the journey. Might this be her last Greyhound tour? She would miss them. Maybe not. Once she got home, she'd sit in bed for a long time, reading and sipping cocoa. But now she had a life before her, not her own but Stacey's, and the lass was unaccountably relying on her for wisdom. She thought about the cow leaping out of that truck and heading back to a long life on Tony's farm.

"No, you can't be sure"—she smiled at beautiful, eager, worried Stacey—"but you can be open to surprise."

"Surprise? What kind of surprise?"

"I don't know. That's in the nature of life, isn't it—surprise?"

Disappointed, Stacey checked her watch. "I should start my hair; it will take hours."

Bella nodded, pleased with the wash and set she got yesterday.

"Will you help me with the veil when I'm ready?"

"When you're ready," Bella said, pouring herself a cup of the hot tea, looking forward to the photo Kyoko would send of Stacey and herself next to the Greyhound coach.

They were wrong, those relatives who told her to forget the piano tuner. They loved her, but they had no imagination. She bet they never met a cowboy toymaker or a Japanese scientist. There were losses either way—staying or going—but she suspected the memories were better on this side of the Atlantic.

Veranda

CARRYING A CUP OF TEA, REBECCA WALKED OUT TO HER NEW VERANDA. SHE hoped the outside air would revive her. Professor Das hadn't mentioned the traffic or the graveyard. Her grey-tiled veranda hung over a loud, congested lane and offered a generous view of the Tolleygunge Christian Burial Ground. What did Das do? Sit in this wicker rocker and count interments? This afternoon, Rebecca was exhausted, jet-lagged, hot, still shaking from the hour-long bumper-car journey from the airport. This wasn't traffic; it was automotive roulette. What had she got herself into? Already she could tell Calcutta was a city where she couldn't walk and couldn't breathe. Apparently, she *could* be buried conveniently. She sipped tea, listening to the grackles and mynahs arguing.

"A veranda," Subendu had said. "You must get a place with a veranda. To watch people, the storms, the astonishing skies." Thus, when Professor Das offered to exchange his flat on First Lane, Russa Road South, for her condo in Chapel Hill, she had agreed. It was so neat; she and Professor Das would trade classes and apartments. Nothing else about moving from North Carolina to West Bengal for nine months was neat, so she had jumped at the veranda flat. Subendu was right about the extraordinary golden light in Calcutta.

After arriving from the airport, Rebecca had tried to nap on Das's hard mattress. Sun and heat seeped through the opaque windows. Above her, the ceiling fan whispered, *You can't lie here all day. You can't lie here all day.* She hadn't felt this listless, this overwhelmed since those long months following the accident. Although five years had passed since Garrett and Andrew disappeared, she could still be gripped by moments of paralysis. She had looked at the photo of her husband and son on the rickety cane bedside table, and could almost hear Garrett teasing her. "Well, if you're going to teach next week, you need to get acquainted with the city."

Now, from the veranda, she could hear someone in the adjacent court-yard bathing loudly, splashing water, sighing and humming. Another neighbor was clearing years of phlegm from his throat. Rebecca was a rational, mature person, and she knew it was too early to judge India, Calcutta, herself. But she was steeped in a familiar irritation with her graduate advisee, Subendu, who had "sent" her here. The man was nothing if not persistent. Pushy in a charming, altruistic way. Perhaps his confidence came of being a returning student, a thirty-year-old computer programmer now pursuing a Ph.D. in English literature.

"My mother says it is time to get a wife, not another degree," Subendu laughed as he sat in Rebecca's tidy, bright UNC office. "But I said a knowledge of literature will cost less and be more satisfying in old age."

Rebecca nodded, lost for response, and preoccupied by the stack of forty unread papers from her honors class.

He didn't register her silence as he finished chuckling about his mother. Then he leaned forward, tapered fingers tapping to the cadence of his words. "I am enjoying your course, Professor." His tone was almost flirtatious, provocative in some enigmatic way.

"Thank you," Rebecca said warily, because experience told her something difficult would follow. She hadn't slept well the previous night, and she was especially unprepared for Subendu's esprit today. He was a bright, handsome, thin man with fine features and rich brown skin. She smiled to herself, thinking that his mother obviously knew he was a good catch.

"But I am failing to understand how you can teach Tagore and Devi and Satyajit Ray if you have never known our monsoons or walked our streets."

She nodded in agreement. She wouldn't defend herself with the award-winning book on postcolonial tropes. He was right; you couldn't fully comprehend a country's literature until you had visited. Suddenly she realized there was nothing she would like more than going to India. A shocking thought, since for the last five years even the short daily drive to school had seemed an impossible journey. Every time she left the house, she felt she was abandoning Garrett and Andrew again. She should have been in the car that spring morning, shouldn't have bowed out of Saturday errands to correct essays. If not for those damn papers, she would have been squashed under the container truck where she belonged, with her beloved little family.

"The light!" Subendu exclaimed in his soft, Bengali accent. "Nowhere in India, nowhere in the world, will you find this brilliant, gentle light."

She enjoyed his accent. Differently inflected English was what had drawn her to postcolonial studies. Although she valued the political significance of the field, her real joy was in the music of the distinct Englishes—Jamaican, Kenyan, South African, Irish, Sri

Lankan. Their mutual language was so supple—the different vocabularies, idioms, accents, cadences. She had simply followed the voices.

"Golden Bangla," he was saying. "And the light in which the bride is best presented to the groom."

"The what?" She laughed, then consulted the wall clock above his head. Fifteen minutes to her next class.

"Calcutta is a jewel." He savored the nostalgia.

She recalled Garrett's big plans. A year in India. He dreamed of dramatic storms over the Bay of Bengal. Then back to the U.S., to save for another sabbatical—a year in Tanzania or Mozambique. Somewhere south of the South, where their little family might blend in.

Subendu described the sweet softness of mid- to late afternoon. "Konay-dekha alo . . . like candlelight in the afternoon. The light of the bride, they call it. Everyone looks more beautiful then. Professor, I think you must visit Calcutta."

"You're right," Rebecca heard herself say. "You get me a plane ticket and I'm off."

The next week, Subendu dropped by with the email address of Dr. Das, who was seeking a teaching exchange with an American professor.

Chanting—loud chanting—thundered from a microphone at the nearby Hindu Temple. Then she heard an amplified call to prayer from a local mosque. Grackles and mynahs and bathers and honking horns and propagating clergy. Rebecca retreated inside, firmly shutting the door to the veranda.

Dr. Das had left pages of careful directions in tiny script about how to turn on the two-ring gas cooker, where to kick the very dented fridge as it misbehaved, which windows to open in the morning, how to close them again against mosquitoes at 4 P.M., where to switch on the inverter for hot water. He had also drawn a map to the university.

THE FIRST MORNING of classes, she stood on the sidewalk beneath a cloudless sky while women, turtled under black umbrellas, glanced sideways and walked by, murmuring. About her? Why was she so self-conscious? Women murmured all over the world. Das had instructed her to stand in front of his block of flats and hail one of the bicycle-rickshaw drivers who congregated at the corner. "Give them no more than six rupees to convey you to the Metro, Professor Green. Anything more is highway robbery." Perhaps Das taught a class in hyperbole. She was learning to modulate his voice in her head. "Lovely veranda with a view," he had emailed her. "Quiet flat with all modern conveniences." Rebecca waited and waved to the three men wearing torn sports shirts and blindingly white *lunghis*. After fifteen minutes, she picked her way along the broken pavement toward their station at the edge of the graveyard.

She selected the newest rickshaw and climbed aboard with her heavy briefcase. *Feet on the footrest, Subendu had instructed her, hands on the sides, gripping tightly.* And whoosh. At first she felt as if she were flying. Then they hit a pothole. And another. Space flight. They passed single-family houses. Blocks of flats. Cardboard hovels. The stink from garbage dumped at the corner was ripe, even this early in the morning. As they approached the main road, she noticed a pharmacy, a photocopy shop—each a one-room storefront. Across the lane were tiny shanties closed to the street with a blanket or bamboo blind, the roofs made of tarp or old plastic cement bags. Swoosh! The driver with his impossibly skinny legs was pulling them into four lanes of roaring coaches, lorries, cars, auto-rickshaws. Most terrifying were the buses, as they bore down through the city, passengers spilling out doors and windows.

At home, Rebecca hadn't been frightened by traffic in five years. Each road excursion had been—at least unconsciously—an opportunity to rejoin Garrett and Andrew. But today, she held her breath as the rickshaw driver cut horizontally though swarming vehicles, pausing only twice to postpone the afterlife. When he halted in front of the Metro station, Rebecca stepped down cautiously, paid the driver, and proceeded toward the subway with her spine thoroughly realigned.

Using the Metro couldn't be much different from riding the London Tube or the New York subway, she assumed; but as she waited for the train—and for her small body to renegotiate its relationship with the ground—she noted that the walls were beautifully decorated with line drawings of local buildings.

The women passengers were immaculately attired in vivid, intricately patterned saris or *salwar kameezes*. She glanced down at her already-wrinkled blue blouse and the flowers wilting on her Laura Ashley skirt, wondering if such untidiness would affront the students. Reflexively, she raised a hand to her damp, curly red hair, a disheveled contrast to the long, oiled braids of the Calcuttans.

Other doubts pestered. She sat straight against the bench—at least they might appreciate her good posture—and pretended to read, while she heard her colleague Mark asking, "*Going for a little cultural tourism?*"

He explained that such teaching was a form of neocolonialism. Mark worked on images of movement in Ken Kesey and Jack Kerouac.

Most of her colleagues found the trip odd. Several said, "Well, maybe this is just the sort of diversion you need."

At the family reunion, Mother offered a different opinion. "India? I can understand, yes, for your work. A short trip. But nine months? And why Calcutta? It sounds like an impossible city—hotter, poorer, more crowded than the others. What about New Delhi? Isn't that the capital? Wouldn't they have more amenities there?"

Daddy leaned over. "I just don't know about your going alone. Calcutta's where they have that Black Hole. And I read the place is run by Marxists."

Of course there was nothing they could do. She was thirty-five years old. She was a widow. She lived alone in Chapel Hill. They hadn't approved of her Black husband, and were kind, but distant, to their biracial grandson. She had stopped listening to them years before.

Family opposition was quelled when Cousin Julia announced over strawberry shortcake that her sister-in-law, Vivian, was a financial manager at the HSBC Bank in Calcutta.

"What a coincidence," Mother declared with relief, as if Vivian might protect Rebecca from pythons and Bengal tigers.

"No, not really. Vivian was always a nut," Julia shrugged.

Rebecca realized that most of today's insecurity came from loneliness. She resolved to call Vivian tonight if the phone was working. She had also promised Subendu to ring his family, and Dr. Das had left an annotated list of congenial Calcuttans who might enhance her social life.

Exiting the Metro station, she was now perplexed by Dr. Das's map to campus.

"Excuse me," she asked a young woman in a chartreuse *salwar kameez*, "which way do I go for the university?"

The woman regarded her blankly, said something in Bengali, and smiled.

"You turn right here. Then walk past the Hospital for Tropical Diseases . . ."

Rebecca looked up at the tall man wearing a starched white shirt and a *lunghi*. He might have been Subendu's cousin; the keen eyes were so familiar.

He cocked his head, waiting.

"Oh, yes," she exclaimed to him, to the map. "I get it now. Thank you."

Rebecca maneuvered through the crowds, a navigation complicated by a broken sewer which everyone tiptoed around. Subendu had warned her to wear closed canvas shoes, but even in sandals, her feet were baking. The traffic noise and sewer stench and bustling people rattled her concentration, and she almost tripped on an old man sleeping in the center of the pavement.

At the next corner, two women and their children sold chapatis, which they heated over an open hibachi. She felt too tired and hot to eat anything. Suddenly the pedestrian choreography split in two, people walking on either side of the chapati stall.

As Rebecca reached a huge government office, she heard a voice.

"That's it, right again, and then left on College Street."

The man in the *lunghi* from the Metro. Had he been going her way, or had he followed her to ensure she hadn't got lost?

"Thank you," she said again, and although she loathed sentimentality, felt as if she had been blessed in some way.

The pavement on this secondary street was less crowded, allowing for hand-wringer machines where men squeezed juice from sugar cane. Four stalls of sunglasses and toothbrushes. Three more sleepers. She couldn't comprehend the street napping. Although this country exhausted her, she found it difficult to sleep at night in her *bed*. Impossible to find a peaceful moment in the city. Perhaps there was *too much of her*, a typical Westerner usurping physical and psychic space—and *too little of her* in the way of spiritual resources to ease physical discomfort.

Rebecca warned herself to concentrate on walking. Finally, College Street. This road seemed more welcoming, with its huge stands of textbooks in Hindi and Bengali and English.

~

ON THE NINTH DAY, the phone suddenly functioned at 5 A.M. The first call, of course, came from her fraught mother. Rebecca explained everything was fine. She liked her teaching, although there were two more courses than Dr. Das had indicated. Yes, yes, she would phone Vivian. Indeed, her apartment door had several strong locks.

Her mother's worried silence was excruciating, even half the world away.

"I've signed on for a home e–mail account," she reassured her.

"E-mail!" Mother sniffed. "I want to hear my daughter's voice when she's off in Calcutta, of all places."

Of all places.

Rebecca couldn't retrieve sleep, so she made tea and toasted a slice of bread on the daredevil electric hotplate. Sitting down on the veranda, she was puzzled by lines of white cloth festooned across the grass. She recalled the snowy backyard of Garrett's graduate studio apartment in Providence. Now she noticed yards of red and yellow and green. Sari lengths, of course. Someone had told her the *dobhi wallahs* dried their laundry in the cemetery. They had transformed the bleak field into a modernist painting. The loud horn-like noise startled her, and she noticed three water buffalo grazing near the rickshaw corner. Further east, a boy escorted several goats. At the far end of the burial ground, near the ramshackle high-rises, she made out a group of older kids getting in a soccer game before the day's fever. A pair of tawny cows with majestic attitudes sauntered through their game, and the boys gracefully played around the sacred animals. Rebecca sipped her morning tea, rocking back and forth in Dr. Das's wicker chair, wondering if her pleasure were a kind of betrayal. Garrett and Andrew would have adored this cock-crow carnival, and they would have been much more ambitious about exploring the city than she.

Her first e-mail came from Subendu. How had he discovered the address?

"Remember to drink lots of boiled water," he said.

The next day, he wrote about the early rains in North Carolina. Didn't she find the rain gentler in Calcutta? And when was she going to visit his family?

She would reply once she had met them. Meanwhile, she explained how busy she was with her courses in eighteenth-, nineteenth-, and twentieth-century American literature. Although she hadn't studied these areas since undergraduate days, Indian colleagues expected Rebecca to teach *her* literature. OK, she had said, if they didn't mind her learning along with the students. They thought she was joking.

Subendu was busy planning for her return, it seemed. He had started a small study group with two other postcolonial lit students, and with Mira, a feminist poet whose parents came from Gujarat. She would write next week to applaud the value of a study group.

REBECCA WAITED for Vivian at the Grand Hotel's comfortable bar. She ordered a small pot of coffee, appalled by the price until she considered she was here on an American salary. (How was Dr. Das doing in Chapel Hill on his special government subsidy wage? She hoped Subendu was showing him ways to economize, and that her self-absorbed colleagues were stepping out of their way to help the visitor.) She ran her fingers over the lush armchair fabric, marveled at the spaciousness and quiet of this elegant saloon.

"Here we are, Ma'am," the waiter said quietly.

She opened her eyes.

And there was Vivian. Please god, let it not be Vivian.

Of course the tall, white woman with the platinum bob, carmine lipstick, and off-the-shoulder red sundress was Julia's nutty relative. Indians would have a term for their relationship—cousin-sister, or something like that. Rebecca's term was *brief.*

"Rebecca!" Vivian shouted across the marble tables.

There were so few white people in Calcutta that Rebecca never wondered at being spotted for who she was. At the university: the American lady professor. In the neighborhood: the rich *memsahib,* who now paid a regular rickshaw driver ten rupees each morning to deliver her to the Metro alive.

"Rebecca."

It *was* agreeable to hear her name.

Vivian swooped down, planting a wet kiss on her cheek.

Rebecca refrained from wiping off the lipstick with the embossed cocktail napkin. She felt as flustered as a twelve-year-old.

"Truly, truly sorry I'm late," Vivian sighed. Signaling the waiter, she called, "I'll have a Bloody Mary. Better make that a double."

"So"—she leaned forward in a wave of Rive Gauche and peered into Rebecca's blue eyes—"how do you like Calcutta? I can't believe it's taken three weeks to meet."

"Sounds as if you have a busy job," Rebecca said.

"Supersonic!" Vivian laughed. "Unlike most things in this country, which move slower than tortoises. Actually, international banking doesn't really take place *in* India, or any country, rather in a virtual world where everything is due yesterday." She savored a long drink. "But tell me how *you*'re getting on. I couldn't *believe* it when Julia wrote you were living way down off Russa Road South. Are you OK there?"

Rebecca didn't feel she knew Vivian well enough to tell her about the cemetery. She said her flat was convenient to the Metro.

"That's near the Tolleygunge Club," Vivian nodded. "I'll make a dinner reservation for us next Saturday."

"The Tolleygunge Club?" Rebecca dared to insert herself, and although she was simply repeating the voluble Vivian's words, she did feel progress.

"Tennis. Golf. Two great swimming pools."

A swim. After three weeks in Calcutta, there was nothing Rebecca lusted for more than cool water. Her body propelling itself across a pool. Exercise.

"Ha!" Vivian patted her shoulder. "I've seen that look. I've worn it myself. Then we're set. I'll pick you up at seven so we can have drinks in the salon."

Rebecca barely uttered her gratitude before Vivian commenced the next benediction. "Oh, here, I've brought you a few things. I call it the 'culture-shock recovery kit.'" From her appliquéd red shopping bag, she withdrew bran cereal, cheddar cheese, prunes, a large plastic bottle of Diet Pepsi, and a tin of Ibuprofen.

Rebecca's eyes widened. Whenever she craved one of these comforts, she told herself to stop being a spoiled American.

"India *is* the most civilized country in the world, but it lacks a few *habiliments.* And I have a contact at the Embassy commissary in Delhi."

Rebecca sipped coffee and contemplated reined-in Cousin Julia. Obviously she'd consider Vivian eccentric, but Rebecca was finding the woman's cheerful audacity quite appealing.

As it turned out, Vivian had contacts for many provisions.

———

REBECCA ENJOYED her students and was stunned by their courtesy—how they stood to attention in their clean, pressed clothes when she entered the room. How they addressed her as "Ma'am." No danger of being called "Becky" here. How they waited for her to formally adjourn class before gathering together their books and papers. Once they got used to her requirement that they participate in discussion, she could tell that most of them were beginning to like the courses.

Now, if she could only *hear* them. College Street bore even more noisy traffic than First Lane, Russa Road South. Most of the windowpanes were broken, admitting automotive backfiring, honking, and a fleet of swallows who sailed across Rebecca's line of vision, chirping, just as she was making a distinctive point or asking a question. The students were oblivious to these birds. She tried not to be distracted. She reminded herself that Subendu received a B.S. here. Learning must occur. By month's end, she grew used to ambient noise and detected a low buzz of discussion in the classroom. Not a roar, but definitely a buzz.

SUBENDU SAID his family lived in Hindusthan Park, in a large, third-floor flat. Unaccustomed to the early dark of tropical nights, Rebecca got lost and arrived thirty minutes late. Hurriedly, she ran a comb through her tangled red curls before climbing the stone steps.

A large, grey-haired woman in a light blue sari welcomed her at the door. "*Namaste*, Professor." The woman's face betrayed relief. Had she expected Rebecca to corral her into a big American hug? "Please come in."

As Rebecca slipped off her sandals, she tried not to notice Mrs. Ghosh observing her. She thought she looked presentable. The White Box Laundry washed and ironed her clothes better than she ever did at home, and she was partial to this yellow cotton dress.

Mr. Ghosh set his beer on the doily and stood to greet their guest, tenting his palms before she might even think of extending hers for a handshake. The trim, bald man looked stalwart, but frail. Subendu had explained his father's heart condition required early retirement from a high civil-service post.

"Welcome Professor. Our errant son has extolled your virtues as a scholar and teacher."

Rebecca blushed. "Delighted to meet you, Mr. Ghosh."

"What may I offer you to drink—a Scotch? A fresh lime soda?"

"A-actually," Rebecca stuttered, because most Indians she'd met didn't drink alcohol, "I love Indian beer—that is, if you have another bottle."

"You are most welcome to a lowly beer." He tilted his fine head. "Cartons we have in the pantry—don't we, Sanganmitra?"

His wife rolled her eyes at Rebecca and frowned impatiently. "His prescription for heart trouble."

Rebecca recognized Subendu in each of them—the mother's coloring and features, the father's build and determined disposition.

Suddenly a pretty woman appeared with a glistening brass tray. She set the bottle and a glass before Rebecca, as well as a plate of fried, salted lentils.

"Let me introduce Debarati," said Sanganmitra. "She is the wife of Subendu's younger brother, Sukemar, who is right now out of station on military duty."

Kashmir, Rebecca reckoned, but didn't ask because of the terrible headlines. She concentrated on the invisible "hs" of Bengali names, mysteriously pronounced "Shanganmitra, Shukemar, Shubendu, Shunrit."

The two younger women exchanged smiles. She remembered that Subendu rued his brother's conventional choices of early marriage and an army career; but in bright, beautiful Debarati, he'd acknowledged Sukemar's luck in the lottery of arranged nuptials.

Over dinner, and a second bottle of heart-healthy beer, Mr. Ghosh asked, "So why would a fellow with a fine job in computer programming return to university for literary study?"

Sanganmitra glanced sharply at her husband, whose eyes were fastened on Rebecca. She offered her guest another helping of subtly spiced *aloo gobi*.

She wasn't offended. She understood the man's genuine puzzlement about his son, the successful emigrant, opting for such immaterial gains. She recalled that Sanganmitra had been a concert sitar player, and devised what she thought was an inspired response. "Perhaps he finds some spiritual satisfaction in the art of literature." No long Calcutta conversation had passed without mention of the next life, the previous life, the auspicious horoscope, a favorite god. Rebecca savored the cauliflower.

Sanganmitra beamed.

Debarati looked doubtful.

Rebecca wondered if she could ask the recipe for the piquant eggplant dish.

Mr. Ghosh moved directly to his other curiosity. "Do you mind if I ask why you never married?"

"Sunrit!" his wife sighed, although Rebecca knew she was also wondering.

Rebecca was used to this. For a few months here, she had continued to wear her ring, but that had provoked even more unbearable questions.

"I lost my husband and son in an auto accident five years ago."

"Ah, a widow," Mr. Ghosh said sorrowfully, closed his eyes, and sat back.

Sanganmitra took her hand. "We are sorry about your loss."

Rebecca knew that although suttee was still practiced, often coerced, sophisticated people like the Ghoshes would oppose it. She herself understood grieving wives voluntarily throwing themselves on their husband's burning biers. Some to avoid the stigma of widowhood; some out of sheer anguish. Back in the U.S., she often wondered why she was still alive, what her purpose was. Since coming to India, she now recognized, she had been so distracted and overwhelmed that days went by when she didn't think of Garrett and Andrew. This insight made her both sad and grateful.

After dessert, Mr. Ghosh insisted on escorting Rebecca to hail a taxi. Although she felt sure he was more vulnerable, she accepted his chivalry and bid farewell to Mrs. Ghosh and Debarati. Her host turned out to be an expert caller of cabs, and before she could stop him, he paid her fare in advance.

"No, no." She rummaged through her purse to reimburse him.

Clearly accustomed to being the commanding gentleman, he raised his hand, then took hers in a surprisingly intimate gesture. "Subendu asked us to care for his distinguished professor. This is my happy duty. We look forward to seeing you often at our home."

"Thank you; thank you again." She blinked as the cab sputtered and clanked away. At evening's beginning, she was relieved to be completing an obligatory visit. Now she felt pleased at the idea of returning to Hindusthan Park. These sweet strangers offered a sense of family she hadn't felt in years. Taking a deep breath, she warned herself once again against sentimentality, and coughing, she warned herself against taking deep breaths. She was here to teach, to collect texts for her American classes, to explore her discipline. At thirty-five, she was too old to get adopted. Rebecca did wonder how the gracious Sanganmitra and the courtly Sunrit wound up with their cantankerous Subendu.

The following morning, she sent him a short e-mail reporting on the visit. Perhaps now he would stop pestering her with benevolent advice. Before she logged off, he'd zipped back a reply asking what they had served for dinner.

⌒

THURSDAYS WERE her break from the university, and she always began with tea and toast on the veranda. This morning her heart sank as she caught sight of her first funeral procession. Normally, she overlooked the few graves and concentrated on the neighborhood sport and labor and socializing. A tall man in Catholic or Anglican vestments was followed by pallbearers carrying the casket—and a small troupe of family? friends? Just as they reached the freshly dug plot, a soccer ball flew over them. The player ran past the mourners, scooped up his ball, and kicked it fifty yards back into the game. No one looked bothered—neither the player nor the members of the funeral procession—as each ritual proceeded according to tradition.

Rebecca shook her head and raised her arms in a wide yawn, appreciating, as she had not three months before, the luxury of having a flat with a veranda all to herself. She was almost one-third through her exchange, and she mused about lessons learned: *Patience*—patience everywhere with the traffic, power outages, bureaucracy. Still she *was* flabbergasted at the prospect of visiting three different post office windows to mail a letter. *Generosity*—at the frequency of colleagues' dinner invitations and the small gifts endlessly pressed upon her (a sandalwood necklace, a miniature leather box, a ceramic trivet.) *Privilege*—she anticipated disjunction between American and Indian lifestyles, but she'd had no idea of the simplicity with which people could live. Not just the street dwellers, but her new university friends who shared tiny apartments with extended families. And *Otherness*—how interesting to be called a "foreigner" (none of this polite "visitor" for the Indians; she was unequivocally a foreigner.) How disconcerting to be stared at, and humbling to have people make assumptions about her politics because of her race. How curious that every woman she came to know would ask her conspiratorially, "Have you ever thought of wearing a sari?"

She glanced back at the graveyard now, which had once again assumed a familiar busyness, with laundry being stretched out to dry, water buffalo and goats and cows grazing. She could tell the day would be sweltering, and she shivered in anticipation of swimming with Vivian at the Tolleygunge Club that evening.

REBECCA ARRIVED early and settled on a red brocade couch in the Club's air-conditioned salon, a room packed with postcolonial contradictions. In the far corner, six teenaged girls, two in saris and the others in capri pants and т-shirts, giggled and drank Coca-Colas. The crisply uniformed waiter brought her a bar menu which included pizza, *samosa*s, and tea and jam. Two Sikh men walked through, wearing golf caps over their turbans. She was so distracted, it took her a minute to register Vivian's presence.

"Wake up, sister, before the pool gets too cold for swimming."

Rebecca smiled wanly, reluctant to be rescued from her cool respite and the marvelous parade. She couldn't imagine water getting cold in this hot, hot city.

Fifteen minutes later, she was grateful for her friend's insistence. The swimming pool was delicious; her muscles relaxed as they hadn't since she arrived in India. The swimming itself was a little dodgy, because the other bathers didn't seem to believe in lanes. Just like Indian driving, she thought, as she navigated around zigzagging bodies. Afterward, she and Vivian chatted at the darkened poolside. Her friend waved and nodded to half the people lolling on chaise longues and plastic chairs.

She knew why she enjoyed Vivian; she just wasn't sure what Vivian saw in her. This independent, exuberant woman had a few "expat" friends, but hung out mostly with Bengalis. She liked India; she enjoyed Indians; yet she was indelibly American in her clothing and accent. Her enthusiasm for Calcutta was contagious, and her adventurousness quite inspiring.

"Sounds like the Ghosh family liked you."

Rebecca blushed. "They were very respectful to the visiting professor."

"To *Subendu's* favorite professor."

Rebecca shrugged.

"So when are you going back?"

"Actually," Rebecca paused, "they've invited me to dinner at the end of the month."

Vivian nodded knowingly.

⌇

THE MONTHS PASSED more swiftly, temperature rising, light lasting a tiny bit longer each day. Her students now talked so vociferously that some afternoons she failed to notice the swallows sailing back and forth over their brimming, nodding, shaking heads.

Life felt more manageable, more pleasant—great fun sometimes. Yet it was never easy. The simple tasks of home—commuting, cleaning, shopping, cooking—were hard work here. Although she had followed Professor Das's insistent advice and hired young Anita to wash the ever-dusty floors and bring supplies like milk, yogurt, and mineral water, Rebecca herself shopped for and prepared her meals. (Vivian's international pals told gruesome stories about gastroenteritis and fifteen types of diarrhea, so Rebecca was determined to eat fresh, clean food.) Still, it was two Metro stops to the Lake Street Market, and a long slog back from the train station, balancing the vegetables on the bicycle rickshaw. Afterward, she needed to wash each eggplant and carrot and tomato with soap before soaking the vegetables in diluted bleach and rinsing them with boiled water and storing her purchases in Das's surly fridge.

Sometimes the emails between Das and herself read like dispatches between hopelessly lost intergalactic voyagers. She queried him about the pokey ceiling fan, and about whether the eerie, almost translucent geckos were harmful. He questioned her about the "fluff" setting on her clothes dryer (she had never used it), and about how much food one brought to a potluck.

One day he wrote, "I must tell you the most charming story. As I was driving your car with an American friend in the passenger seat, he suddenly screamed, 'Das, Das, that was a stop sign.'

"'Yes, of course,' I answered calmly. 'In Calcutta, where traffic is much heavier, we only stop when another car is approaching.'

"My friend instructed me to stop each time I see the red sign. For a country so preoccupied with efficiency, this seems a very queer custom."

Rebecca responded judiciously, explaining that stopping wasn't a custom, it was a *law,* and suggested that he call the number on her AAA card for a brochure about North Carolina driving regulations. She told herself not to worry about the car, the insurance policy. Generosity—hadn't she learned generosity here?

Subendu's emails were less suspenseful, always brimming with advice. Had she visited Tagore House? The National Library? The Tea Auction Centre? Each week he assigned her a different venue. A film at the Nandan Cinema. A play at Kala Mandir. Exhibits at the Indian Museum and the Academy of Fine Arts. And how could it be true she had never stopped for a pastry at Flurry's?

She reported modest progress in her Bengali language class.

Excellent idea, he zipped back, although he would have recommended a different tutor.

By post, Subendu sent thesis chapters, some of which arrived and some of which didn't. Not to worry, he said; she could read the undelivered drafts when she returned to North Carolina. His scope had expanded to include poets from Gujarat as well as from Bengal—a fascinating balance, he said.

BY MARCH, true heat had set in, and Vivian suggested a weekend trip to the Darjeeling Foothills. Of course Vivian, of boundless energy, didn't mention that after the flight to Bagdogra, they would journey three hours in a van—up, up, up to 6,000 feet, to Darjeeling itself.

All was forgiven when they reached the impossibly quaint Windermere Hotel, where their Victorian room was decorated with chintz curtains and velvet furniture. A worn couch slumped before the fireplace. The room, quite chilly at this altitude, was heated by a coal fire. At night, a Nepalese woman brought flannel-covered hot water bottles, and at 7 A.M., awakened them with "bed tea" to rouse them for the hearty breakfast waiting downstairs. At 4 P.M., tea was served with cucumber sandwiches and cakes. Dinner included a Western supper followed by a full Nepalese meal.

In the dining room, the women talked about American and Indian politics, about their very different jobs. Vivian was eager to hear her friend's shifting views of Calcutta.

"The Ghosh family has been very kind," Rebecca said.

"You've visited them fairly often," Vivian smiled.

"Yes, Mr. Ghosh is a hoot. His wife exudes endearing, strained tolerance of her unruly husband. They're devoted to each other, and Debarati is sharp, funny."

"Sounds like you're falling in love with them."

"Oh, I'm too old for romance—of any kind." Rebecca sighed.

They walked forever that weekend. Rebecca loved peeking through the dancing mists at tea plantations, terraced farms, and a kind of Sikkimese-Nepalese architecture: peaked tin roofs finished with elaborate filigree.

Vivian mused, "You can see why it took the English so long to exit this spectacular country and return to their puny back gardens, swapping memories of the Raj over gins and tonics."

They hiked up and down the hills, enjoying the refreshing interval from Calcutta's weather as well as the cheerful profusion of camellias and magnolias. "And the giant rhododendron trees!" they exclaimed simultaneously. This friendship with Vivian had become as close as it had once been implausible.

———

REBECCA HAD LEARNED to bring a small gift each time she visited the Ghosh family, but these tokens hardly reciprocated their hospitality. Since she couldn't entertain in her flat—with a rudimentary vegetable stir-fry, or her Indian version of pasta primavera—she invited them to be her dinner guests at the Grand Hotel. They demurred for weeks before accepting. They chose April second.

Not until Rebecca was fixing breakfast that morning did she realize it was the sixth anniversary of the crash. She dropped on the couch and sobbed. How had she *forgotten?* In past years, she would anguish for weeks before the anniversary, and spend the day itself reading through old letters from Garrett and birthday cards from Andrew. Now, these relics were a universe away, neatly stacked in the bottom drawer of a desk being used by Astronaut Das.

Damn. Damn Professor Das. Damn Calcutta. Damn, damn, damn Subendu for sending her here to this rich, difficult, absorbing land that allowed her to forget. The anger, however misplaced, felt good. Overwhelmed by a sudden ache, not just for husband and son, but for her whole American life, she let in a flood of self-pity and miserable longing. *Quiet*— her huge desire for silence was ridiculous in a country where one billion people lived on land two-thirds smaller than the U.S. Talking, talking: people were always talking outside her windows, from 5:30 A.M. until dark. Well past dark. And construction! Drills. Jackhammers. Bulldozers. Rebar reached out everywhere, antennae to a better life. *The News.* Calcutta papers carried few international stories, even from other South Asian countries. Her shortwave rarely picked up the BBC. The conservative Voice of America made her want to throw up. She also missed her bed, her bathtub (sans geckos), an armchair by the garden window where she read every morning in the relative *quiet.*

She would give 10,000 rupees to walk down the street to her favorite *coffee shop.* She was so weary of sweet, thick chai. This woke her—the ridiculous nostalgia for a latte exposed the tangling mire of homesickness. Resolutely, Rebecca rose, pulled on a light cotton dress, and followed broken pavement to a flower stall on Prince Anwar Shah Road.

Standing amid brilliant yellow and orange garlands, she noticed people noticing her. Westerners didn't shop here. They patronized stands with arrangements of cut flowers.

The young florist tensed and held his one good eye intently on the fresh blossoms he was separating from stale ones.

She lifted a rope of beaming marigolds, and one onlooker actually gasped with surprise. "Two of these, please," she said in tentative Bengali.

The diffident florist grinned at her, then selected the freshest, longest garlands.

Rebecca strolled through the cemetery gates, toward no specific destination. She noticed a recently covered grave, as yet unadorned, unidentified. Here, she placed the marigolds over rich dark brown dirt, closed her eyes, and spoke to Garrett and Andrew, her sweet adventurers. How they would have relished Calcutta neighborhood markets and the daily parade along Chowringhee. Garrett had it all planned. India, Southern Africa. The next sabbatical would be in Chile or Australia. They'd be in their sixties by the third trip, she'd said. He'd thrown up his hands in that sassy Garrett way, declaring, "Hey, honey, we'll be steaming along in our nineties." Rebecca never doubted him.

When she opened her eyes, morning noises deluged her. A cluster of women stood talking under their sensible parasols. Would she ever remember to carry an umbrella, which offered such versatile protection? Down at the street corner, the bicycle-rickshaw men joked and laughed together. Animals bleated and mooed and barked.

The loudest sound, however, was the expressive squeak of wheels rolling up behind her. Rebecca steeled herself for the outstretched hand, the face set in angry pleading. When she glanced at the legless man on the wooden scooter, all she found was respectful curiosity.

"*Namaste-ji,*" he called, rolling along in the direction of the rickshaw drivers.

⁓

THE GHOSH FAMILY clearly enjoyed the hotel food—and the entertainment. Rebecca hadn't expected sitar and tabla players.

"Tagore songs," Mrs. Ghosh nodded approvingly.

"Sanganmitra used to specialize in Tagore's music," Mr. Ghosh reminisced. "I stole a great artist from Bangla's music lovers."

Mrs. Ghosh blushed and gazed at her plate.

Wordlessly, they listened until the end of the set.

Then Debarati asked Rebecca—as if this were the most original question on the subcontinent, "Have you ever thought of wearing a sari?"

"Oh, yes," Sanganmitra clapped. "You would look stunning in a dark green or a deep blue."

Rebecca shook her head shyly and had the sinking feeling she wasn't going to escape this round. Indian women were right; their form of dress was much more becoming. *On them. On her*, however, the sari would look like a Halloween costume.

"Let me take you to New Market next week," Sanganmitra said. "I have a man there. The lightest silks. The truest colors. And he will give me a good price."

Debarati reached for Rebecca's hand. "Oh, yes, I shall come too. We can stop afterward for tea at a charming place I know."

Mr. Ghosh smiled and flexed his shoulders. "You may count me out of this particular expedition."

Sanganmitra *tsked* affectionately.

Mr. Ghosh shook his head in mock condolence. "Once Sanganmitra has made up her mind, there is little alternative but to follow. That is why I have become such a quiescent, well-behaved man. She does this to everyone in the family."

Family—Rebecca's breath caught. Of course he meant family and friends. This was one conversation she would not report to Subendu.

TOGETHER, THE THREE of them ambled into New Market.

"Madam, Madam," a grey, wiry man called to Rebecca. "I am an official guide. Allow me to escort you."

"No thanks," Rebecca tried.

Sanganmitra dismissed the man in lilting Bengali, her bracelets clinking as she waved him away, and Rebecca knew those steel magnolias in Chapel Hill had nothing on her friend. Together, they walked past stalls of shoes and shirts and kitchen appliances. As they slithered deeper into the steamy, mercantile warren, Rebecca longed for the Air-Conditioned Market on Shakespeare Sarani. But she knew the prices and selection were better in this jammed shopping center. Hot, muggy, the air thickened as they infiltrated New Market's deepest recesses. Would she ever acclimate to Indian temperatures? She tagged after her friends, lost in a reverie about heat.

She had tried to accommodate to the weather, but heat was relentless in mid-April. Every morning she awoke in a steam bath. A cool shower relieved her for an hour of reading. Then, clothes would be drenched in sweat. She bought even lighter clothing, but still she boiled, as if the fire were coming from inside her. Eventually Rebecca understood why Subendu had insisted she set a departure date before late May. Last summer in North Carolina, she had opposed his idea, planning to travel after the school term, to achieve a sense of the larger country. Now she appreciated that she had so much to absorb about Calcutta that the best idea would be to spend the summer sitting in her back garden, organizing photos into an album, rereading the books she had discovered. And remembering. She had the clear impression that she wouldn't have truly visited India until she returned home and began to contemplate the smells and sounds and hues and tastes and temperatures.

Sanganmitra was one tough shopper. Yards and yards of exquisite silk ran through the hands of the three women: saris with elaborate patterns, feathery textures, dazzling turquoises, teals, mauves, scarlets.

"This one." Sanganmitra fingered a finely embroidered light silk. "This one would be a perfect wedding sari."

Rebecca resisted a rush of pleasure, then tumbled back into that strange, completely inappropriate erotic dream about Subendu. Oddly, the next day his e-mail mentioned a visit to Calcutta next month. Why was he coming? He himself said the pre-monsoon period was the most difficult. It made more sense for him to visit his family next fall for the *puja* celebrations.

Composing herself, Rebecca agreed the sari was pretty. She finally decided to purchase the simple white and gold lengths. She would wear the fabric once as a sari to please Sanganmitra and Debarati. Back home, she would turn the gorgeous material into curtains, a radiant memento of her short visit to Calcutta.

Of course, she could not stop Sanganmitra from buying the finely embroidered azure silk. "As a present for our new friend."

Graciously, Rebecca thanked her, thinking the "wedding" fabric would be a splendid gift for Mother, a perfect match for her blue eyes.

"Perhaps you will wear a sari to dinner when Subendu comes."

"His dates are settled?"

"Two weeks from now," his mother grinned proudly. "It has been three years since the last visit. Sunrit says I badger him about marriage and settling down. But I have learned my lesson. Not a word of chastisement have I uttered in letters, on the phone these last eight months. Oh, it will be so fine to see our elder son."

Unnerved by a weakness in her chest and arms, Rebecca saw him in her flat again, leading her to Das's bed. Finally, finally kissing her, sighing on top of her.

She shook herself. "Yes, I'm sure he'll be glad to see you. At the university, he would speak fondly about all his family." *At the university*— she situated the institution firmly between herself and this seductive household.

Rebecca fought back the faintness, her imagination. Still, why would he come to Calcutta now if not to see her in his world, if not to . . .

"It's getting hot in here," Debarati declared. "Shall we go to tea?"

As they exited the cavernous market, Rebecca blinked at the afternoon light: a soft, golden radiance that wrapped everything—cracked buildings, pot-holed streets, crowds of pedestrians—in a gentle suffusion.

"What a lovely time of day," Rebecca exclaimed.

"Yes," Sanganmitra agreed. "*Konay-dekha alo.* This is our special light. The light in which the bride is best presented to the groom."

"Exquisite." Rebecca recalled Subendu's elaborate description last year. Remembered Subendu's fine, intelligent brown eyes. She thought she saw Sanganmitra wink at Debarati. Rebecca pulled herself together. "The tea shop, is it nearby?"

———

REBECCA EXPLORED the small library of the Tolleygunge Club. Not much of a library, really—just a few shelves of popular novels and magazines—but it was a quiet nook off the main salon where she and Vivian could have an uninterrupted beer before supper. She had to talk with someone, and Vivian had become a fine friend these last eight months. She would miss her verve and irreverent wit, and most of all, her extraordinary common sense. Yes, Vivian would know what to do.

"What to do about *what?*" Vivian inquired over dinner. "Either he comes or he doesn't. Either you fancy him or you don't."

Rebecca lowered her voice in hopes that Vivian might do the same. "Maybe I'm making this up. We've never had more than a cordial—some-times not-so-cordial—*academic* relationship."

"But he's just five years younger. You're a stunning woman. Why wouldn't he fall for you?"

"It's so improbable. I never thought of him as anything but a student—at least not consciously—until a week or so ago."

"Why don't you just wait and see. If you're both into it, what's the problem?"

"His family. I've come to like them, respect them. I don't want to create offense."

"Honey, you are one prime catch for the Ghoshes, especially if they've given up on him marrying an Indian girl. The question is, do you love this guy?"

"Love . . ." She took a long gulp of her third Sandpiper. The whole evening was a fiasco. Once she waddled out of this refrigerated club, she'd be back in sizzling Calcutta, bloated by beer and brewing a hangover for class tomorrow.

"Yes, *love.*" Vivian waited.

"He's smart, attractive. In some ways, a very considerate man, always sending solicitous emails inquiring how I'm faring. But . . ."

"But what?" Vivian fiddled with one of her kaleidoscopic Rajasthani earrings.

"I still feel married to Garrett."

"Excuse me, Rebecca." Vivian's voice acquired a new tenderness. "Your husband died quite a while ago. I don't want to intrude, but from what you've told me about his open heart and liveliness, he wouldn't *want* you to spend your whole life in mourning."

Rebecca was strung between tears and fury. Not anger at Vivian, exactly, more irritation with herself. This conversation was ridiculous. Heat had zapped her brain cells. Or maybe she had a touch of malaria. She needed to slow down and take care of herself. In a month, she reflected, she would be weeding in her garden, would be making curtains from that luscious white and yellow fabric.

———

THAT WEEKEND BROUGHT the rains. Pre-monsoon storms, she was told. They looked like monsoons to her. Spring could be wet at home, but she'd never witnessed such downpours in her life. Caught in one as she left the Park Street Metro station, she arrived at the hair salon drenched and shivering.

The beauticians flew into action. One woman gave her a robe, took her clothes, and while the other snipped and clipped, she carefully restored Rebecca's blouse and shirt with a hairdryer. They lent her an umbrella, yet she was soaked again by the time she reached the flat.

Rebecca checked her email, but there was nothing interesting. Some university memos and a query from Das about whether he should trim the kudzu. "A very impressive, almost Indian vine," he commented. Nothing from Subendu. However, he was arriving the next Thursday, so what was the point in writing?

The skies opened every day, and despite her newly purchased umbrella, she arrived at the university looking like a wharf rat, while her colleagues and students, male and female, appeared dry and fresh. Women on the Metro still looked crisp in their fresh cotton saris.

———

AS THE PHONE RANG on Thursday evening, she jumped. Calm down, she scolded herself. She didn't know how she felt about this man. Or how *he* felt about her. Her mouth was dry as salt when she said hello.

Debarati's voice. Subdued. Concerned.

Had something happened to him? Probably just a delayed arrival. In his cockiness, he could have missed the flight.

"Yes, yes, hello Debarati," she said with forced brightness.

"I'm ringing on behalf of Subendu," she spoke softly.

Why wouldn't he call himself? Jet lag? Perhaps he'd gone to bed.

"Did he have a good flight?" she asked, growing more uneasy.

"Yes, yes." Debarati's voice was shaky, tearful. "They did, but both of them are travel-worn now. Oh, Rebecca," she sobbed, "this is not what I thought. I believed you and he . . ." She steadied herself. "He said he wanted to surprise us with Mira, and that he succeeded in doing."

———

RETURNING FROM SUBENDU's engagement party, she noticed how fresh the sari still felt against her moist skin. Vivian had offered to accompany her to the festivities, to meet Subendu's Gujarati-American fiancée, but she couldn't imagine Vivian and the Ghosh family in the same room. During the evening, Rebecca felt both relief and loss. She was grateful her reluctant heart had been opened again—by the dream, by the Ghoshes' expectations. She tried to let the gratitude carry her through the evening. Everyone was a little stiff, and she left early, against polite objections. Rebecca unlocked her gate just in time, it seemed, because the night sky was roiling with black-grey clouds.

Rebecca walked out to the veranda. The rains had started in full force now. Thunder. Lightning. Next door, several telephone wires sizzled like holiday sparklers. Then more clouds, and great clamoring shots of light across the ceiling of the world. Mr. Ghosh had predicted a cyclone. She watched sheets of water racing down First Lane, the clouds flying south toward the swirling Bay of Bengal. Reaching for her camera, she started flashing her own lightning into the black night. She peered through darkness and reckoned this was the first time she'd seen the cemetery vacant of living souls. Rebecca listened for neighbors' voices and televisions and record players, but the roar and whish of the storm prevailed.

Quiet, of a sort, for the first time in nine months. A lonely quiet. She missed clicketing rickshaw wheels, munching water buffalo, chirping swallows, buzzing students, murmuring women in their rustling saris, whining sitars, the dawn-time whoosh of Anita's rag, the surprising whispers of *"Namaste-ji"* from cordial strangers.

She looked down the street and noticed large groups of people gathered on verandas everywhere. Whole shelves of people who, like her, were waiting, watching this fierce tempest of death and life. A veranda; you must get a place with a veranda, he had said.

Playing Catch

RICHARD DUMPS DEAD TOWELS ON THE GREEN-TILED BATHROOM FLOOR. Sprinkling the tub and sink with Babo, he recalls how his Mom always used Babo. "Bring me the Babo," she'd say in that soft, Irish accent. A very definite sound, her Babo. He likes the reliable can. Oh, he's sure there are more powerful products these days, with antibacterial protection, plus a little aromatherapy. Even though Rose won't be staying here, he'll swing her by the house to show off the new basement and the back deck. A long swig of juice, and he remembers his sister isn't coming for two weeks.

Earlier that afternoon, after Richard says goodbye to Rose on the phone, he goes to the fridge for a glass of grape juice. Not great for his diet, but he craves the tart sweetness of it, always has since childhood. He pours a large glass, then gets distracted by photos on the fridge door. That Christmas picture of Mom and Dad must be twenty years old. The house in Sacramento. Rose is in the photo, too, sitting in the middle—a pretty girl, but smartness was what marked her. She would go far. You could see determination in her face, even then.

He sips the juice slowly, thinking that Rose doesn't understand why he couldn't or didn't want to follow her. Richard finished his wandering vicariously, listening to their parents' tales of emigration from Ireland, struggles in Boston, adventures in California. He's content to have his destiny shaped by the previous generation. Rose, though, is always tossing the ring to a farther world. Did he and his sister share *any* genes? Mom used to joke she picked up the wrong baby girl from the hospital. Later, of course, she was proud of her talented daughter. Of course.

He lets a long sigh run through his body, wondering why he's so agitated. So Rose is coming to San Francisco on one of her biannual trips.

It's just a visit—"to catch up," she says. Rose never intrudes, always tacks a get-together to an exhibit or painting workshop, so it doesn't feel like a momentous reunion. They—there are lots of "theys" who admire his sister's work—put her up at a posh hotel, buy her meals.

Meandering around the house with his half-glass of juice, Richard remembers he wasn't very hospitable the one time she stayed here. A middle-aged bachelor gets used to his ways. What he hated most were the long talks at night and her endless questions. Rose is always trying to figure out their family, as if insight could change history. He found her questions boring. No, more than that—painful, disturbing. Everything was over now —their parents' fights, divorce, deaths—and he had survived to create a pretty successful life. Looking over the living room, he considers how he's finally made this into a real home.

Anyway, this time she's hoping he'll be free on a Saturday, so she can buy lunch to celebrate his promotion and maybe walk in the park before her plane leaves for New York at 5 P.M. A whole afternoon? Of course, he says, yes, yes, can't wait to see you.

DRIVING TO THE GALLERY, he regrets that he didn't catch her exhibit. But the paintings were only up a week, and work was crazy, with lots of evening entertaining. He supposed he could have taken one of the Japanese clients to the show, but they're such formal, private people. Sometimes Rose's paintings—at least the ones she was doing ten or twelve years before— were pretty intimate. He remembers people making love, and vivid images of breasts and other female parts. On the phone, Rose said not to worry about attending the show; the important thing was that they'd have time together to catch up.

Parking downtown is a bitch. He goes around and around her damn block trying to hang on to his temper. She'll understand if he's a few minutes late. It would be bloody typical: as her "Irish twin," he was born ten months after her.

EACH YEAR, the nuns would greet him expectantly: "You're *Rose's* brother, aren't you?" Sister's enthusiasm would wane by Christmas, and that was fine with him. He could just get by with his mediocre grades—except in math, where he excelled far beyond Rose, which is why he works in IT. "We each have our own gifts," Mom always said.

They were lucky with this loving mother—some said "saintly woman." It was terribly unjust that cancer took her so quickly after the divorce. Rose handled all the hospital arrangements. He was tied in knots at work that year. Besides, he didn't know how he could have faced his mother during the chemo and after. If Rose was the brain, he was the sensitive one.

Finally, he lands a space, four blocks from the gallery. He's sweating and stops for a bottle of mineral water as he hurries toward the place. Amazing, really, that his sister wound up in this hot international arts scene. OK, he does well enough, in middle-management already. He's a decent, solvent guy who, if he doesn't observe the family religion, still conducts civic duties, practices kindnesses. For the last two Christmases, he's played clown at the children's ward, has had those kids in hysterics. Maybe some of Rose's artistic temperament has worn off on him.

She's always living in her imagination, Rose. His personal imagination isn't such a friendly place, even as an adult. Even though he long ago let go of his anger at Dad for batting them around, for breaking Mom's arm, for deserting the family. Live and let live; otherwise you go crazy.

When they were little and slept in the same room, Rose would tell stories at night. He picked the subject—Hopalong Cassidy, or The Lone Ranger, or The Cisco Kid—and while it could take Rose a while to rev up, her stories were OK. So OK it was hard to sleep. One night Mom caught them, and that was the end of Rose's storytelling. He was sorry about that.

There she is, standing outside the gallery talking to a wild, red-haired woman in a see-through flowered dress with a tattoo snaking up her right arm. The gallery owners inevitably look more artsy than his sister, in her short, dark hair (he guesses she dyes out the grey, nothing extravagant, just back to her girlhood color). Trim as always, usually wearing black, and a little silver or turquoise jewelry. She's an attractive woman for thirty-eight, but what strikes him is her smartness, the steady focus and depth of those green eyes.

Eyes that are now on him, masking worry with relief and fondness. She watches, arm waving broadly, smile brimming.

Big hug.

"Hey, Lindsey," she exclaims, "this is Richard, my brother." She regards the art dealer expectantly.

He knows Lindsey sees a plump man in a green polo shirt and jeans. Not her type, he can tell. His sister *never* gives up. Once she asked hopefully if he'd like to meet some of her gay friends. His "no" must have been emphatic enough because Rose never mentioned this again. Maybe he *is* a little lonely, but life is less complicated this way. And he has to admit, Rose is getting better at not pushing things.

Rose kisses Lindsey, who is thanking his sister for a first-class show.

"Very successful." Lindsey turns to Richard, asking pointedly, "Did you manage to catch it?"

"No." He ducks his head—what a dumb gesture. "Work's been chaotic."

Lindsey studies him as if searching for some family resemblance between the edgy artist and the computer nerd. The snake on her arm is about to strike. Then she nods noncommittally. "Of course."

As they walk to his car, Rose wheeling her compact black airline bag behind her, he wants to apologize again for missing the exhibit. No, he was clear enough in front of witchy Lindsey. His shrink has explained that sensitive people apologize too much.

"Lindsey recommended this great trattoria near Golden Gate Park. That's where we're walking, isn't it?"

His heart sinks. He knows all about those new Italian places, oily and spicy and herby. He's never had a cosmopolitan stomach.

She catches his downcast expression. "Did you have another idea, Ricky?"

No one calls him Ricky any more; the old name feels sweet.

"Well, first I kind of want to show you how I paneled the basement, and there's a new deck out back."

"I'd love to see what you've done, sure." She looks seriously at him.

"Then there's this deli I like—good salads and simple pastas, but on the other side of the park, on the way to the airport. I thought we could walk around, have lunch, and be all set to take off."

"I feel launched already," she laughs. "Sounds like a plan."

SHE ADMIRES THE BASEMENT, notices how clean, kept-up, the house is. He feels a little weird about not inviting her to stay, but she gets put up at the Hilton, for chrissake.

Golden Gate Park is buzzing with rollerbladers and cyclists and joggers. He's been dreading the walk because Rose is a lot fitter, but today she strolls placidly, asking him questions about his job. The fog has lifted on a damn near perfect afternoon. Richard doesn't feel tired, hardly notices the time passing. He helps her with the names of some computer graphics folks. They tell family stories, catch up on news of their cousins in Donegal.

"I've been dating a lighting designer," she says.

"Oh, yes?" He steps aside, the speeding cyclist just missing him.

"Nothing too serious, but fun, you know."

He's not going to get caught. If he asks for more details, she'll start quizzing him. Gently, politely—but all the same, he doesn't want any of that. "Maybe we should turn around now," he suggests, "so we'll have time for a relaxed lunch." A relaxed lunch—it's something Mom would say.

Soon they're driving to the restaurant. He turns on the AC to cool them through the inevitable San Francisco parking marathon. They ride around, scoping out possible places. Time passes. When they do find a spot, it's five or six blocks from the deli, and they hurry along.

"Half a carafe of red," Rose says to the waiter when he brings the menus.

Richard frowns because she's not much of a drinker. He hopes she doesn't need the courage to say something difficult.

She gets a little looser, and he realizes that these exhibits must be stressful, no matter how many you've done. He'll catch her next show for sure.

"Do you remember Dad's driving?" she asks.

"You mean tailgating other cars at ninety miles an hour?"

"Ninety? No."

"Oh, yeah. A miracle he didn't get arrested."

"Or that we didn't get killed," she winces.

Richard is starving. The salads are taking forever.

"Well," he shrugs, "altogether we were lucky to escape the family alive. With him smoking three packs a day and Mom smoking one."

"Guess that's where I get the chronic bronchitis," she says.

"You, too?" he asks. "I didn't know."

Finally the salads arrive, and they dig in. He's annoyed by the bits of cilantro and artichoke hearts, picks around them and then grumbles, "I thought I ordered Chicken Fennel Salad."

She observes him curiously. "Actually, I heard you say, 'Chicken Fiesta.'"

He continues excavating. "I'm a little dyslexic. Took a test last year. Of course I'm a highly functioning dyslexic."

"Of course," she grins, her cheeks flushed from the wine or the sun.

A few beats later: "It doesn't surprise me. I am, too. Dyslexic. Always screwing up the letters. Why I went into visual work, I think."

"Yeah?" He wonders how he could know so little about his own sister. Pretty crummy if this is their only shared gene. That wine is tempting, but it would wreck his stomach.

"Yes," she says. "Dad, too. That's why he dropped out of school. He wasn't stupid. He just had trouble reading."

Whenever she brings up Dad, he stiffens. Now he scrambles for a new topic, which is difficult after four hours of non-stop talking for a man who lives alone. He knew a whole afternoon would be too long.

She's emptied the carafe and eaten her salad.

As he finishes picking out all his chicken from the fiesta, he thinks her trattoria would probably have been a better choice.

Quickly, she scoops the bill. Then, "Congratulations!" Rose pulls out a fancy wrapped package.

A picture—he can feel the frame. He steadies himself to say something nice. Finally it comes to him. "How thoughtful," he declares, hoping to open it in private.

"Oh, do look," she urges, excited.

The silver frame holds a photo of the two of them in the backyard: Rose twirling in a turquoise tutu; him sitting on the grass behind, hugging their dog Bruno. Since he inherited the family photos, he wonders where she got this one. He's going to cry. Instead, he reaches for her hand, mumbling, "Thank you."

THEY HEAD OUT to the car. It's a half hour to the airport, and he likes to be on the safe side. San Francisco people drive like lunatics in hot weather.

She looks happy, hums some Italian tune.

Perry Como? he wonders. Frank Sinatra?

Now that the visit is almost over, Richard wishes it could be a little longer.

Then the oddest thing happens. This *never* happens to him. The car isn't where he left it. His mind spins to theft insurance, then to finding Rose a taxi to the airport.

"Hang on," she says brightly, "didn't we park on that street, 'Walter Drive?'"

Dubious, he follows her. The car is nowhere. It's hard to lose a metallic purple Mustang. This car stands out in a crowd, an emergency. An unusual make for a computer nerd, his colleagues point out. He tells them he comes from an artistic family.

"OK," she asserts, hands on hips, "we're two smart grownups. We can do this. You take that street and I'll take this one."

"And we'll meet back at the deli?"

"Right, Watson." She's still mellow from the wine.

Walking up the street, he wishes he had worn something lighter. What a ridiculously hot day to lose your car. This is why he prefers ramps—you record the stall number and the elevator location on the little ticket. Richard exhales and loosens his collar. No Mustang here; lots of Lexuses and Saabs and BMWs. San Francisco is getting too bougie, he sighs— actually, because of people in his field. Kids straight out of school earn salaries three times larger than Dad saw in his whole life. Tattle Street, he thinks, or Tawler? All right, one more inspection on each side of the road. Then he'll go back and discover that Rose has found the car. Typical.

It was a freezing February afternoon when he lost the glove walking home from school in Boston. Rose took his hand to keep it warm, she said, as they traipsed through mountains of Massachusetts snow back toward St. Martin's. Halfway there, she spotted the red glove. Someone had put it on the fence post—no doubt making it more visible—but he never would have seen it, eyes to the ground.

Approaching the deli now, he has the oddest feeling. It's about losing Rose some day. He doesn't want this to happen. A bizarre anxiety, since they hardly ever see each other.

There she is, pacing in front of the café, and he thinks how hot she must be in that black outfit.

She spots him. "No luck. How about you?"

Richard doesn't panic. Who would steal a Mustang when you could have a BMW?

They've still got time to make her flight. So they split up again and try the cross streets. Their next rendezvous is the same. The deli guy points them to a taxi rank three blocks down and over two.

Richard reassures himself. He'll get her settled in the cab, then roam these damn streets until midnight if he has to. Tomorrow he can send Rose's bag DHL to New York.

Then he sees it, his car, just where he left it on some street called Wattles Road, not a very San Francisco address. Why did he have to park on Wattles Road?

OK, they're safely back in the Mustang, and the AC is going full blast.

Rose starts laughing. Really guffawing. She's hysterical, but seems to be breathing OK.

She notices his distress. "Don't you see?" she manages between fits of giggles. "This proves we're related."

"Hungh?"

"The dyslexia—both of us, we both lost the car." Her eyes are tearing.

"Oh, right," he laughs, to keep her company, but his mind is on the airport. He wants to make that flight. His place isn't large enough yet, for company. Although now that he's finished the basement, he's been thinking about a little guest cottage in the garden. With a birdbath outside.

She settles down by the time they enter the freeway.

Really, they have plenty of time—he's sure.

She's telling him about her collaborative show in Chelsea, a multimedia event with dancers, actors, writers—something about homelessness.

He finds it a little hard to follow, but he's sure the show will be significant.

Richard hears the planes roaring overhead and spots the airport turnoff. He considers how he used to resent her, as if she were showing off being so radical and famous. Going to college in Paris. Winning prizes. Mom said she was very proud, but she also felt a little left behind.

They swoop up to the Departures curb, and he sets out her bag.

She thanks him for the ride.

He thanks her for the lunch and the fantastic picture.

"You know, you're welcome to stay with me at the loft, any time." She smiles affectionately, none of that lost-car mania in her eyes. She always does this at the end of a visit, invites him to New York.

"Thanks," he says, head down. "Sometime would be great."

She nods, a little disappointed. No guilt-tripping, though.

He doesn't mention the guest house with the bird bath, because that could take a while.

"The dyslexia thing"—she shakes her head—"that was so funny."

She's always had a sense of humor, always been a good sport. As he's thinking this, standing mute amid the honking horns, she reaches over and gives him a big hug.

Rose's hair smells a little minty—like Mom's, he notices, hugging her back.

Then she rolls her suitcase onto the sidewalk.

"Bye," she waves, grins. "Don't lose any more cars."

He almost says, *Don't lose any little brothers*—but he doesn't, thank god—what a stupid line.

Instead, he waves back and calls, "Catch you soon!"

Something Special

THEY PULLED UP BY THE OAKVILLE GROCERY AND CAFÉ ON A SILVER HARLEY. Rather, they sashayed to the curb, which is a movement you might not associate with motorcycles. The muscular, grey-bearded man drove; the thin blond woman sat behind, holding onto his small belly. You noticed their black helmets gleaming in late-afternoon sun.

She hopped off, waited by the low patio wall. He was settling the cycle, like a bee honing its stinger into flesh. The loud strong engine left a hole in the soundscape; not silence exactly, but some powerful absence.

Unbuckling her helmet, she shook out blond curls of different lengths. No sweat. You noticed that on a hot evening after a hot day. Beneath her overalls, she wore a bright pink string T-shirt, and when she raised her arm to point, you saw the shaven pit, the firm muscles, the pleasant angularity of her figure.

Now he stood beside her in jeans and a white T-shirt, looking pleased with the parking space, with her. Maybe he was anticipating the items behind the glass of this gourmet deli—roasted asparagus, *haricots verts* with shitake mushrooms, rosemary roast potatoes. Maybe he was deciding between a chilled Sauvignon Blanc or a light Pinot Noir. Leaving their helmets on the bike, they walked hand-in-hand toward the big door of the grocery.

Another couple arrived on the patio, finding a table in the shade with their brown-bagged dinner. He sat down first, taking out his Diet Pepsi and her unearthly green Sprite, a container of potato salad . . . Shuffling toward him, she stopped to take all the natural, undyed beige napkins from the condiment table. Heavily, she limped in a black shirt and baggy black pants, releasing a grateful sigh as she lowered herself into the blue net chair.

"I have lots of napkins," she said seriously, as if this man had been spilling food for forty years. They were in their early sixties, just five or six years older than the motorcyclists—all of them white, all of them able to afford Oakville Grocery prices—but you knew these two wouldn't have much to say to one another.

"How come she"—meaning you, sitting alone with a glass of zinfandel while your partner waited inside for a double espresso to fuel the long drive home—"has a tray and a real glass?"

His voice lowered discreetly. "Because they got their dinner 'for here,' and we got ours 'to go.' Better *this* way. They have to return the tray, the glass, inside."

She nodded, forked a red potato from its bed of mayonnaise and scallions.

Two families emerged with nouveau pizzas, searching hopelessly for napkins.

You looked away.

How long could it take to make a double espresso? Maybe Pat was scrutinizing the dessert shelves, too. That could take time.

The motorcyclists reappeared with a large brown bag. You wondered if their bike had a storage bin.

He put the helmet on her, pausing while she removed her sunglasses. Then he tugged the straps and clicked the buckle. After helmeting himself, he sidled onto the bike, keying the ignition. The glittery machine wiggled back and forth. Everyone in the café courtyard was watching, the napkined and napkinless alike. She picked up the grocery bag, gracefully mounting behind him, put one arm around their dinner, the other at the side of his waist. They disappeared up the street, heading north.

The motorcyclists seemed happier than the rest of you, somehow. Happier than the Diet Pepsi Man and the Sprite Lady, and the messy-fingered families, and you with your half-glass of decent zin.

They seemed to know something special, which they would savor quietly over dinner, together.

The House with
Nobody in It

THE HOUSE NEXT DOOR WAS UP FOR SALE AGAIN. A LARGE CORNER LOT IN ONE of the city's most pleasant, convenient neighborhoods. Lawns were mowed and nicely framed by oak and maple trees. Bluets graced yards in spring; hostas bloomed in early fall. People respected your privacy and were always ready to help dig your car out of the January ice. So where were her new next-door neighbors?

WHEN THEY FIRST MOVED IN, Tamara had expectations about neighbors, modest hopes. She thought maybe someone would drop by with a small pie or cake. Perhaps an older woman, a long-time resident, from whom she could learn a thing or two. Then maybe they'd exchange the occasional "Yoo-hoo," over the back fence.

Instead, silence greeted their arrival. Practiced tolerance from the Lutheran parents on the north side, who didn't care for two lesbians living in plain view of their six children. Their first conversation with Mrs. Olsen ended abruptly when she learned that Joan was not Tamara's sister. The house on the other side was virtually silent. The retired army couple didn't notice that Tamara and Joan had different bodies from those of Mr. and Mrs. Lancaster, who had lived in their home for the previous twenty years. Within months, the colonel had entered a nursing facility and his wife returned to their children in Duluth. The house lay empty for a year while the kids, who were busy having grandchildren of their own, decided what to do with it. Joan told Tamara she was developing an unhealthy obsession. After all, they had each other, their families, lots of friends and colleagues. Why was she so hung up on neighbors?

BUT TAMARA FELT SAD about the vacant place, oddly lonely. And it kept coming back to her, that earnest Joyce Kilmer poem she had memorized in the fourth grade about "a poor old farmhouse, its shingles broken and black . . ." Get over it, she told herself; clearly Milton Avenue was no place to recapture childhood memories of sidewalk fraternity: families chatting over fragrant piles of burning autumn leaves; neighbor ladies joining Mom on the front porch for lemonade on a scorching July evening. Tamara wasn't much of a gardener, but she cherished scenes of Dad trading recipes for tomato sauce over the back fence as he tended his plot of crimson beefsteaks. She thought back often to those early days, when things were as they were meant to be.

FOR A WHILE, Tamara continued to take the absence of neighbors personally. At the age of forty, this was the first house she could afford as a college teacher. Once she recovered from the shock of earning enough money for a down payment, and managed to repress her panic about impending floods in the bathroom and storm-drunk trees smashing the roof . . . she began to look forward to having neighbors, to being a neighbor.

"For Sale." Finally, the son from Duluth decided to sell. All summer, that sign guarded the next-door lawn, through the bluets and lilacs and hydrangeas, well past the end of the roses. Week by week, they speculated about who might buy the place. Tamara toyed with organizing a small welcoming party. Dozens of people trooped through Sunday Open Houses. In late September, the place was still up for sale. Mr. and Mrs. Olsen started talking to Tamara occasionally, on the sidewalk, about realtors and potential buyers. An empty house was bad for property values, they said. Apparently the older couple had let it go to seed, in the understandable neglect of people who were losing their vision and sense of smell. Milton Avenue wasn't an area where people bought a fixer-upper. The bungalow was peculiar—a little pea-green wooden structure in the midst of large brick or white-stucco Edwardian houses. Maybe years ago, Tamara thought, a young Colonel and Mrs. Neighbor had built it as their dream house. Maybe their dreams foundered.

Another year passed. By this time, the Olsens were talking to them at least once a month, and together, over their meticulously groomed back hedge, they ruminated on the strange spirit occupying that bleak corner house. Tamara wondered if it were haunted by the proprietorial ghost of ancient Mr. Neighbor, still stalking those elusive dreams.

Tamara admitted she had become a bit of a busybody, staring out the south window through the increasingly dense summer branches, optimistically inspecting realtors and their clients.

One day, Joan grew exasperated. "Relax, we have nothing to complain about after two years of almost complete silence next door. If we're lucky, the spooky house will stay on the market, and peace will prevail!"

Tamara admired Joan's self-containment. Maybe it had something to do with running her own physics lab. Still, sometimes she missed the finer points of an argument.

"Silence," Tamara intoned, "is not the same as peace."

TAMARA WAS FIVE when Arthur Snider moved into the big yellow house kitty-corner to them. They used to walk to school together, and one afternoon by the gym, he proposed. As their early years of betrothal passed, she and Arthur spent more and more time playing dolls in her sunny living room. Practicing for their future together. Dad told a puzzled Arthur to go outside and throw a ball. He delivered Little League leaflets to Mr. and Mrs. Snider. But Arthur was content indoors, playing with the dolls and Tamara. Dad grew nervous that Arthur was a bad influence on her brothers, and he banned Arthur from the house. The engagement fell through. Years later, she learned that Arthur had joined the Navy, had married someone else. Her father could only hope for such respectable sons.

ONE OCTOBER MORNING, when there were still enough red and gold leaves to allow you to peer through the maple branches without being obvious, Tamara and Joan watched two movers carrying furniture into the green bungalow. Boxes of books. Then suitcases. A floor lamp. Later that afternoon, a young man joined the movers, and together they made a dramatic ceremony of wrestling the realtor's sign out of the lawn. From her living room, Tamara clapped at their success. "Neighbors! *Enfin!*"

Joan shook her head, concerned. "Aren't you getting a little melodramatic? I mean what is your thing about neighbors? Most of the time I understand you, sweetie, but really, we can barely keep up with our social life as it is."

Melodramatic, Tamara thought—just the word her mother used to describe her. Maybe that's why she taught Homer and Virgil. What was life without a little melodrama? "I don't know," she confessed, vaguely hurt. "Ever since I was a kid, I thought it was part of the well-lived life. Someone to love. Our own house. And good neighbors."

"Well," Joan cautioned. "Wait and see. Don't get your hopes up."

Next morning, they were wakened to what Tamara eventually learned was alternative rock. OK, she thought, you need something to keep up your spirits when you move. She remembered the panic of two years before— suffocating in corrugated cardboard and styrofoam chips.

The music got louder at lunch. Joan rolled her eyes. "Your neighbors!"

"Don't be silly," she said, "they're settling in. They'll turn it down."

They waited a week. A long, loud, sleepless week.

The following Saturday—a suddenly frigid, grey afternoon—they bundled up and carried a tray of Joan's never-fail mocha-pecan brownies next door. The first thing they noticed was how neatly the juniper had been trimmed. Unusual for a rock band, Tamara thought.

Walter greeted them at the door.

Beautiful Walter, red curls haloing a perfectly oval face, Tamara noticed. Circular gold spectacles surrounded his sapphire green eyes, and his skin had the sheen, the softness, of her grandmother's pink satin bed jacket. She and Joan were surprised, relieved, to discover he was the bungalow's sole occupant.

Walter's voice swelled with goodwill. "I hope you'll let me know if there's any way I can be neighborly. If you go out of town, I could collect the mail, feed your cat."

Dumbly, Tamara marveled at his sweet openness. And she hoped Joan wouldn't launch into her diatribe about how not all lesbians loved cats, how she herself was fatally allergic to the animals.

He smiled, serving them coffee in fifties retro Melmac mugs.

"Thanks," she nodded, preoccupied, wondering how a twenty-five-year-old could afford to purchase a house. "And vice versa."

Joan, meanwhile, went straight to the point. "Your music . . ."

Softly, Tamara kicked her under the blue linoleum table.

"Your music . . ." Joan's tone lifted. "Do you think you could reduce the volume?"

Affliction invaded his seamless face. "Of course," he frowned. "I'm terribly sorry."

Joan smiled primly.

Right before their eyes, Tamara thought, they were transforming from renegade queers into decorous matrons.

"You see, the bedroom is on your side, the south side of the house," Joan continued.

Tamara could tell, just by looking at him, that everything would be all right.

"Thanks for mentioning it. Really." He refilled their cups. "If I slip up again, just come over and I'll cut the volume. Promise?"

"Yes," Tamara laughed. "I'm sure this'll take care of it."

Pensively, Joan sipped her black coffee.

"What kind of work do you do?" Tamara asked, moving the conversation along.

"I've bought into a bakery," he was pleased to tell them. "Specialty breads, brioches, croissants. I'm training now, in the kitchen and shop. The Prairie Pantry—have you heard of it?"

"Oh yes!" Tamara recalled their delicate apple tarts. The Prairie Pantry was the city's best bakery, and Walter seemed adorable in his vocational fervor. She didn't have any twenty-five-year-old friends; he might be a very interesting neighbor.

WHEN TAMARA'S FAMILY moved to Seattle, Dad bought an Irish Setter, "to make the family complete." Rudie was a sweet puppy, energetic and friendly, but he grew up to be the terror of passing drivers and bicyclists. Tamara tried to train him, took him for walks, whispered about good behavior to him at night. The rest of the family gave up, so he became *her* dog. She hadn't loved like this since Arthur Snider. But the infractions continued. Their paperboy refused to deliver the *Post-Intelligencer.* Rudie also liked to dig up gardens. They got several official warnings. One day, Mrs. Miller across the street spread hamburger meat mixed with ground glass around her azaleas. Two weeks later, Rudie came bounding back from the vet's, and Dad found him a nice home in the country.

A WEEK PASSED before they heard again from Walter. Eleven-thirty the following Saturday night. Walter and his guest Dave Matthews, or Iggy Pop.

Tamara had bought a few CDs in the spirit of cultural education, but at this volume, couldn't tell the difference.

"It might be Marshall Crenshaw," she said to her wide-awake partner.

"Why do you care about the particulars?"

"I'm a scholar; I'm only trying to understand . . ."

"What you need to understand," Joan grumbled, "is that we have an inconsiderate neighbor. I trust you're making the most of this cultural opportunity." She climbed out of bed, pulled on her jeans, and headed next door.

Tamara lay beneath the blankets, feeling guilty that Joan had gone alone. After all, she was the one who had prayed for neighbors.

Time passed.

Iggy Pop got louder. Tamara grew worried, for what did they really know about Walter? Maybe this was his M.O. Maybe he lured innocent neighbors to his house late at night and then chopped them to pieces. Maybe he wasn't a twenty-five-year-old cherub, but a cannibal disguised by clever plastic surgery.

Still buttoning her sweater, Tamara raced outside. When she reached Joan, her partner was pumping Walter's doorbell.

"No answer?" she asked brightly.

"Probably can't hear it ringing above that racket."

"Well, let's go in."

"What, are you crazy?"

Joan had just suffered through *Sweeney Todd* at the Ordway Theatre for her mother's birthday.

Maybe Tamara *was* crazy, entering the lair of the local baker/butcher, but she was also furious.

His door was unlocked, not remarkable in wholesome Minneapolis. Walter was nowhere within the excessively neat rooms of the ground floor. Electric guitar vibrated from below.

Shaking, Tamara opened the basement door and shouted down, "Walter."

Nothing.

"Walter," in her most piercing voice.

The stereo volume decreased slightly. Scrambling up the stairs, he grinned. "You sound like my mom."

Tamara stood there, glaring at the enemy, who thought she was his mother.

"The music . . ." Joan said calmly. "The music is very loud. We can't sleep."

"Oh. Oh, no." He seemed more troubled by Joan's announcement than by having his house broken into. "Oh, right!" He ran downstairs and turned it off.

"Sorry about that," he called, walking up the steps. "I guess I got a little carried away celebrating; I baked my first batch of *palmiers* this morning."

Tamara could understand how that could rev a person up.

They left for home, carrying a white sack of sticky *palmiers,* three of which Joan had to consume before she could get back to sleep.

———

TELEPHONE CALLS were no more successful than doorbell ringing. They put notes in his mailbox. These would make a difference for a day or two and then . . .

Kapow at one A.M.: Smashing Pumpkins.

Tamara did have to wonder at his eclectic taste.

Two A.M.: Public Enemy.

Maybe the music made him alert for his early-morning baking shift.

Three A.M.: Pearl Jam.

That night, Joan called the police. Tamara felt terrible, as if they had just turned her younger brother in to the Stasi. But as Joan pointed out, they required sleep to remain employed.

Rigid, Tamara waited in bed for the cops to pull up. Slamming their car doors, they walked heavily to Walter's little green house. Thud. Thud. Thud. They knocked firmly. Ice-T answered. Eventually, the police abandoned the front door and moved around the house, rapping on each of Walter's windows.

Soon—well, soon something happened, because the autumn night was restored to that familiar semi-silence. Once again they could hear buses snuffling down nearby Hennepin Avenue. And the pleasant rattle of their old refrigerator, Marge.

"At last," Joan whispered, rolling over to sleep.

Stiff, wakeful, Tamara lay beside her. Before morning, their neighbor had stabbed them to death with a silver cake server. He repeated this grisly double murder the next night and the next.

In real life, several days after the cops, Walter rang the bell and handed Joan a sack of fragrant caraway rye rolls. An amends for slipping up. It was so easy to get lost in the world of music, he said.

Throw away the bread, Tamara told Joan. There was no telling what he had put in it.

She shrugged. "Well, if you don't want any, this should take care of my lunch for a week. I love caraway seeds."

Joan survived. So did Walter and his midnight jam sessions.

Never was Tamara so happy to see November as that year. With great relief, she watched their neighbor install his triple-glazed storm windows. And she accomplished the annual chore herself with particular speed and dexterity. Quiet had returned to Milton Avenue. Quiet of a degree.

Storm windows: evidence of how insulation leads to insularity on the prairie, considered Tamara. Up and down the block, every autumn, otherwise sensible people climbed teetering ladders to replace summer screens with the glass barricades. Once windows were hung, hibernation began. Every year, after the fifteenth of November or so, there was no more smelling the neighbor's dinner. No hearing the boy across the street practicing his seven A.M. trombone. No eavesdropping on revealing family arguments from back gardens. As the snow rose and the temperatures dropped to thirty, fifteen, seven, below zero, then slipped steadily into the minus teens, you saw less and less of your neighbors. Occasionally, you'd notice someone under hats-coats-mufflers-mittens, chipping at the ice on their front porches, or scuttling between automobile and house, or race-walking a dour dog. If there were an ecumenical hero in Minnesota, it was the postal carrier, who needed an advanced degree in acrobatics to negotiate their slippery sidewalks. Holiday tips in mailboxes were always generous. State records revealed that for the past one hundred years, no Minnesota dog had ever bitten a postal worker between the months of November and April.

Walter rocked on, of course. Most nights, with the aid of a white-noise machine and industrial earplugs, they found sleep. Three times they had to call the police. Generally, though, their windows and Walter's muffled intercultural exchange.

TAMARA WAS BEGINNING to realize she had always had bad neighbor karma. Could she somehow be the source of the problem? She used to wonder this about Mrs. Woods. When Tamara was twelve, she babysat next door for cute twin boys, Steven and Sebastian. Mrs. Woods was the first person she had met who had gone to college, and Tamara spent many happy afternoons listening to the young mother reminisce about the good days at Rochester. She had been studying to become a concert pianist, then suddenly found herself on the other side of the country, married, with two small boys and no time to think, let alone play the piano. Tamara's mother didn't understand how she was babysitting if Mrs. Woods were in the house with her, talking, talking. She wasn't interested in her neighbor's college stories. Didn't the woman have errands to run? Tamara thought Mom seemed scared of Mrs. Woods; definitely she didn't like her. Still, it was with a gentle, concerned voice that she broke the sad news to Tamara: Mr. Woods had found his wife in the sunroom, dead from an overdose of tranquilizers.

⌣

THE LONG, RAW WINTER on Milton Avenue was, as they say in the Upper Midwest, a genuine season.

Spring bloomed late, and Tamara was so happy to see the crocuses and narcissus that she waved warmly to Walter the first time she saw him in May.

He waved back reluctantly. In fact, his whole being seemed more hesitant, older. The skin was pale, the eyes dull.

Down came their windows; up went his music. For several weeks they seriously discussed moving. Sleeplessness was interfering with their teaching. What else could they do? Well, this was eco-conscious Minnesota, Joan laughed. Maybe they could file a noise complaint and have Walter extradited to Manitoba.

Joan had another idea. An inspiration. Since Walter couldn't live without his music and they couldn't sleep with it, they might compromise. They would offer to buy him a pair of classy earphones. Why did it take so long to think of this? Tamara wondered. Maybe in the way of older people, they just assumed he would come around to seeing the reasonableness of their position. The earphones could cost two hundred bucks, but they would be worth it. They put a note in his mailbox.

The June evenings were stretching to luxurious lengths. Snowplows were a dim fantasy. At twilight, the evening after Joan's inspiration, returning from a walk, they spotted Walter trimming the juniper.

"Hi there!" Tamara called.

"Hi," he returned neutrally.

"Did you get our note?" she asked.

Joan searched the pinkening sky in exasperation with Tamara's impatience.

"Oh, yeah." The tone was vague.

"So what did you think of Joan's idea?" Tamara ignored his shuttered eyes, defensive shoulders.

Clip. Clip. He concentrated on the juniper.

"The earphones," she tried cheerfully.

"Won't work." He swept clippings into a green garbage bag. Like everyone on Milton Avenue, Walter was tidy.

"Why not?" She was annoyed by his categorical dismissal.

"I don't do earphones," he muttered.

"But, but," she stammered, pulling away from Joan, "you do noise!"

He glared at her.

Joan's face grew anxious.

"Look . . ." Walter extended his hand, as if to calm Tamara, then withdrew before making contact. "Look"—a laissez-faire nineties tone—"I know my music bugs you. It's not your thing. And if I were you, I'd call the cops, too."

"What?" Tamara shouted across the generations.

Joan tugged at her T-shirt. "It's getting dark. The mosquitoes . . ."

"Hey, it's a moot point, anyway." He spoke loudly and slowly. "You only have to put up with it for a couple of more weeks. I'm moving. The bakery business isn't for me."

"But—"

"Come on," groaned Joan, "we've been wasting our breath." Now, Tamara followed, understanding that homicide would cancel her recently earned tenure. She went to bed early with a double brandy, resolute to get a few hours rest before the evening concert.

———

MR. HAWKINS WAS RETIRED from fifty years as an engineer on the Southern Pacific Railroad. When Tamara's dad ran off, Mr. Hawkins became the ideal neighbor for Mom—doing little repairs, clearing out the garden, taking her to the grocery store because they didn't have a car. "Anything to be of help," he always offered, saying that it made him feel useful in his old age. So when Tamara missed the school bus one morning, he was the obvious person to call. Three miles to the high school—they had gone halfway—Tamara realized what Mr. Hawkins was doing with his hand on her thigh, moving it higher and higher. What a weirdo. She jumped out and walked the rest of the way. That night, Mom was astounded, infuriated by her story, and she warned Tamara never again to talk to him. She was terribly upset with Mr. Hawkins, but also, Tamara knew, with her daughter, because he had been such a wonderful neighbor.

———

AS TAMARA was slipping off to sleep, she heard the phone ring. Joan answered in the adjacent room. Her voice was cool, as when she talked to her older brother. It was past ten. Who else would call at this time of night?

Walter's lullaby commenced. No, no, far too early. Damn him. She rolled on her side and put a pillow over her left ear.

His racket didn't seem to be fazing Joan. Tamara could hear through the wall that she was still on the phone. Not saying much. The occasional two- or three-word phrase. God, she hoped Joan's brother hadn't had another car accident.

Still clutching the pillow, she wandered into Joan's study.

"Yes, yes." Joan's face was intent, not anxious. "Yes."

She held the phone away from her ear, grinning.

"Is your brother OK?" Tamara blurted.

Baffled, Joan put a finger to her lips. She was still listening, but to what? The only thing Tamara could hear was the *David Letterman Show*, "Live from Next Door!"

"A little lower," she said.

"What?" Tamara mouthed silently.

Joan held up a hand for her to wait.

"Yes, that's it," Joan said. "Maybe a little lower?"

Something strange, thought Tamara.

"That should do it."

Tamara noticed the music had stopped.

"You're welcome. Thank *you*, Walter."

"Walter?" she asked when Joan hung up. Her partner burst out laughing. "Yes, yes." She drew long breaths. "He called to do a 'sound check.' Said, 'I don't know why I never did this before. Tell me when you can't hear the music any more, then I'll mark that on the volume control and keep it as my max.'"

"What? Do you think it's because we offered to buy the earphones?"

"Don't ask," her eyes widened. "Just be grateful." Waiting a beat, she smiled. "He said he wanted to be neighborly."

It was a simple thing, Tamara ruminated—the brandy doing its work, making her feel profound as well as sleepy—a simple thing being considerate. Why had it taken them a year to offer the earphones, that long for him to think about the sound test? And the Olsens—would they ever get beyond those stiff backyard conversations? How could they be neighbors if they inhabited different universes?

She toddled off to bed with her pillow. At three A.M., sure enough, she was wakened.

Joan's sweet, warm body snuggled around her. The silence was eerie. Tamara strained to hear the buses juggling along Hennepin Avenue and, finally, fell back to sleep.

After that, they saw Walter two or three times, long enough for a nod, a wave. Tamara watched him wistfully on moving day, his turquoise T-shirt vibrating against that red hair.

ONE AFTERNOON, at the end of summer, Tamara saw them walking up their sidewalk. Right away, she could tell who they were. A young couple, tentatively carrying their new responsibility. She holding a pie; he with his hand lightly at her back.

"Hey, Joan," she called down to the basement, "come see this."

She arrived, breathless, lugging a suitcase up from the storeroom.

"Do you see what I see?" asked Tamara.

Amazed, Joan nodded.

They rang the bell. Tamara answered, soberly assuring herself that they were no apparition. Joan had seen them too.

"Hi," the woman began.

"We're the Morgans." He extended a firm hand, pale and feathered with fine black hairs. "Sally and Roger, your new neighbors."

Stupidly, Tamara stared at the pie. Wasn't this her role? Had they misread the script?

"Oh," Sally said wryly, "you must be wondering. We won a raffle at church. Six pies—blueberry, cherry, raspberry, peach . . ."

"Isn't this apple?" Tamara concentrated on real, physical evidence.

"Yes, Dutch apple, and we couldn't possibly eat them all, so we decided to share them as a way of meeting our new neighbors."

"Neighbors." Joan recovered first. "Won't you come in?"

"Yes, yes." Tamara woke. "What am I thinking? Please come in for some coffee and . . . pie?"

Nervous, blushing, Sally entered. Roger tripped over a crate of books in the hallway.

Wordlessly, they surveyed boxes and suitcases stacked in the dining room.

"You're not moving, are you?" Sally sounded stricken.

"Oh, just for a year," Tamara explained guiltily, "for our very first sabbaticals!"

"We were really looking forward to neighbors," Sally sighed.

"It's actually just for nine months," Tamara jumped in before they could take their pie and leave. "Joan's brother will be in and out, doing repairs, painting the interior. We'll be home next summer. Here, have a seat."

Reluctantly, almost suspiciously, the Morgans complied, perching on the edge of a drop cloth thrown over the couch.

"Oh, it's so sad," Sally said, "a house with nobody in it."

"Caf or decaf?" Tamara asked, determined not to let them get away.

Back Home at the Driftwood Lodge

I DRIVE WARILY THROUGH THICK FOG TOWARD THE COAST. GRETCHEN IS peppering me with questions. She leans over, so close that I can smell her cinnamon gum.

Work's hectic, I tell my sister; lots of people drifting in from L.A.

I'm straining to remember what our rental-car guy said about the exit to Glass Beach.

Yes, the girls' art classes are going well. I wipe one nerve-sweaty hand on the car seat and grip the steering wheel more steadily.

She's always like this at first: rat-ta-ta-tat, full of curiosity. I'm grateful for her interest, yes. I need to discuss a couple of office problems with her, but maybe when I'm holding a glass of chilled wine, with a view of something besides the murky highway. All summer I've been fantasizing about the Driftwood Lodge. Spacious rooms overlooking the Pacific Ocean, gourmet organic meals, friendly staff. Homey, according to the web site. "Homey"—not a word I'd use with Gretchen.

My sister and I vacation together every two years. Leaving partners, children, dogs, jobs behind for five days, a week. It's a priority for each of us, which shocks some people. "A *week* with your *sister?*" Sally asked me at work. "Don't you go nuts?" Other friends find our tradition admirable, enviable. Well, what can I say? We're close.

In childhood, Gretchen and I were allies, the relatively sane daughters of party parents. Oh, it could have been worse. Dad always brought home a paycheck, and Mom usually cooked a form of dinner. I suppose if it weren't for Grandma keeping an eye on domestic melodramas, we'd have turned out differently. But she loved us unconditionally and taught us to rely on one another. These days it's hard to get together, with Gretchen's medical practice in Duluth and my job liaising with Tucson's homeless services, so we plan each holiday well in advance.

She's finished the questions now—maybe we'll return to them at dinner—and is describing her hospital's new surgical wing. Just what she'd hoped, yet she's getting bored with work. I used to think Gretchen was brighter than I; really, though, she just has an impatient intellect. She can also be a wee bit rigid. My husband Roger calls her "Gretchen the crank." I do laugh at some of her e-mails, like last month's diatribe about the inanity of self-help books. She's a highly principled, energetic woman with a laudable indifference to other people's opinions. Right now, Gretchen is complaining about a colleague who resigned from her planning committee. Out of the blue, she sniffs, mystified.

I'm half-listening, partially because I'm concentrating on the road, partially because I'm excited to be back in the Northwest. I remember the Driftwood as a handsome building with a wide front porch. According to the website, the back deck is forty feet from the beach. During our family's Seattle period, we came camping up here on the Olympic Peninsula three or four times. Our parents used to stop for drinks at the elegant Driftwood bar. Gretchen and I played pinochle for hours in the corner as Mom and Dad chatted with fancy people. I recall those evenings as happy respites from our ragged, rainy campsites. And I've always thought of the Driftwood Lodge as the height of stylishness, so when Gretchen agreed on it for our vacation, I was floating for weeks.

⁓

"LISA, HONEY, the place may have changed in thirty years," my husband suggested softly.

"Yes, yes." I was edgy. "*I*'ve also changed since the age of seven."

"You're definitely cuter . . . and taller." Roger whistled as we walked out to his cactus garden. He's refused to introduce nonindigenous plants to the desert, and his garden *was* splendid.

⁓

IT'S FIVE P.M. by the time we reach Glass Beach. The sun has finally appeared, and there are hours of light left on this summer evening. Village shops are shutting briskly.

Gretchen tugs open the heavy beveled-glass door of the Driftwood Lodge.

I can almost hear the ginny tinkle of Mom's laugh, and am faintly disappointed to find an empty saloon. Those little red velvet chairs are still there—and the marble tables perched on filigreed wrought-iron legs. The liquor cabinet is impressively stocked. Muted lights shimmer on the Jameson (Mom's favorite) and a series of other Irish whiskies. Six vacant wooden stools face the untended bar.

Gretchen rings for service at the immaculate front counter.

I stare at red block letters on a nearby door: "Private."

A small man, wearing rimless glasses, pokes out his head and regards us skeptically.

All those years ago, the place was run by a jovial young woman who sneaked three cherries into our Shirley Temple cocktails. This guy would be her age. Her brother, maybe. When I'm more relaxed, I'll ask about the woman.

"You must be the Carlson ladies." He glances from one of us to the other, adding with exaggerated discretion, "Sisters, would it be?"

Gretchen nods curtly, submits her credit card. "You don't seem to be very busy," she says, in a voice that could be interpreted as abrupt if you didn't know her.

"Oh, we're quite full," he laughs. "But one of you"—he scrutinizes Gretchen's Visa card—"yes, it would have been the *other* lady, made a reservation two months in advance."

I smile thinly because I did book the rooms before Gretchen had technically agreed on the Driftwood. I knew I could cancel. Now, partially to forestall further discussion of my prescience and partially because I don't believe he is "quite full," I say, "We requested the quietest rooms available."

"All accommodation at the Driftwood Lodge is quiet. Tranquility is the signature of our inn."

Gretchen studies her manicured nails. The purple isn't what I would have expected, yet it suits her.

He scans our registration cards. "Duluth!" he exclaims to Gretchen. "I've been to Duluth. Went there last January for a philatelist convention."

Gretchen, who loathes Minnesota winters, stares at him incredulously.

"Do you collect stamps?" I ask.

"No." He is distracted by the buzzing intercom.

Philately *is* stamp-collecting, isn't it? I wonder.

"I'll be right there," he grumbles at the intercom, "after I serve our new guests." To us, he explains, "No, no, my son is the collector, and I'd do anything to make him happy."

Handing over the keys, he says, "I believe you'll find these two rooms—directly across from one another—quite comfortable. Please inform us if you need anything. Oh, dear, I've forgotten to introduce myself. I am Arnold Werther, and you must tell me if there's anything we can do to make your stay more enjoyable. The Driftwood Lodge is a homey place."

"Actually," I stammer—not sure whether to address him as Arnold or Mr. Werther, which although it sounds excessively formal, complements his demeanor—"I was curious when dinner is served."

"Dinner, oh my, no, that was—well—'before.' You must have one of our old brochures."

My stomach rumbles for those gourmet meals.

Maybe he hears my vulgar intestines. "In your room, you'll find a list of pleasant local restaurants." He points to the stairs.

We follow his circumlocutionary directions around one stairway and through the saloon. I love the red brocade wallpaper, something out of a Victorian bordello. I see my father's mysterious eyes and Mom's wide smile. They were a handsome couple, and we all knew it. Wherever we went, Mom always carried a pack of cards in her pocketbook so Gretchen and I could entertain ourselves while they drank and made new friends.

"Do you remember?" I swivel to Gretchen, who is a step behind, rolling her green suitcase. Then I notice her staring toward a tall window draped in ivory lace. Before it stands an empty wheelchair.

"For the son, I suppose," she whispers.

I nod; this would go partway to explaining Duluth in January.

At this point, my nostalgia for pinochle matches seems trivial. Yet there was something formative about the *rules* of a game in our otherwise chaotic lives: the intense interaction between us; the security of having adults laughing and talking nearby. No, the moment for mentioning this has passed. Gretchen would complain about how much our parents smoked. She'd call me sentimental yet again.

At the top of the stairs, we find our rooms. At least we'll be spared hotel-elevator rattle. As someone who's worked with homeless people for fifteen years, you'd think I'd be a bit more Zen about vacation accommodations.

"Shall we shower and unpack?" Gretchen proposes. "Meet in an hour to go grazing for dinner?"

She sees herself as the organizer.

"Sounds like a plan."

My compact room pulses with fiercely competing floral patterns. The snapdragons on the flounced valance battle with lilies on the floor-length drapes. My bedspread sprouts an improbable jungle of peonies and carnations and rhododendrons. The rug is all roses. I can feel my allergies kicking in. Well, living in the great Southwest with sweet, indigenous-gardening Roger, I don't see too many pink flowers these days.

The small vanity table with its three-way cosmetic mirror is inviting, as if they were expecting Grace Kelly. Next to the coffee maker, they've set out a packet of cream cookies. Very hospitable, as the website promised. I discover that the bathroom sink and shower are also pink. But clean. This will do fine for a few days.

The view? Now I'm alert enough to draw the blushing blinds and open the window. Ah, sea air—even this sliver of rolling Pacific waves—will help me sleep. This is why I've traveled here. I missed the ocean and my sister.

———

SHE CAME TO NEW YORK a year after I did, both of us N.Y.U. scholarship girls. Our tiny Village apartment barely held two beds, a kitchen, and bathroom, yet it was the scene of wild adventure, avid study, and ardent romance. Oh, of course we argued, but often our lives flowed with intuitive choreography. We each fell in love the second autumn. One week, she'd get the apartment with her lover and I'd sleep at Roger's place. The next week, I'd get the apartment while she stayed with Carol or Aaron or Pat—there was a stream of them until she met Bruce, the crusader. Bruce got us involved in city politics and anti-apartheid work. Still, Gretchen and I always made time for school and for each other—exploring a different Manhattan neighborhood together each Sunday afternoon.

I suppose we thought that would always be our lives—separated at most by the cross-town bus. Gretchen started Columbia Med School the same year Roger got into grad school at A.S.U. He sent me flyers about social work programs in Arizona, and photos of Canyon de Chelly, the Superstition Mountains, desert flowers in March.

One spring night, while Gretchen and I were playing pinochle, I told her I was thinking about leaving.

She fell silent.

"Maybe you could do a residency in Arizona," I suggested.

She winced.

I said that given Dad's heart problems, I'd like to live closer to our parents. They'd been dry for a year by then, had settled in a double-wide trailer outside Santa Fe.

"I don't owe Mr. and Mrs. Martini anything," she murmured, studying her cards, "except for you."

I burst into tears—at our imminent separation, at her uncharacteristically direct expression of fondness—and flung my arms around her skinny shoulders.

Gretchen jiggled free and laid down her hand. "Trump."

———

"YOU ALRIGHT IN THERE?" Gretchen raps on the door. "You get bitten by any of that marauding flora?"

I laugh, opening the door to my sister, who's dressed in her own mode for dinner. Her once blond hair, now attractively streaked with grey, dangles in dizzying coils. The deep blue velvet blouse looks as if it comes from a vintage shop, but she's strictly a sales-rack department-store girl. Her long legs are draped in green crepe pants over black utility sandals. She resembles an aging hippie. Which, in a way, she is. A very accomplished, fast-lane hippie.

"Cleopatra!" I moue. "Please enter and allow me to complete my titivations."

She raises a pale eyebrow.

In truth, I envy her blondness, although Roger says he loves my "auburn mane."

Gretchen smirks. "I don't have all night. Marc and Julius are approaching in separate chariots."

Maybe she's not kidding, because if our Gretchen isn't a fashion model, she is a *bonne vivante*. She says medicine has deconstructed romance for her, that Bruce is a tolerant guy. His ardor is for local politics, and there's a lot to organize in Duluth.

I slip on a black cotton dress, silver beads, and my shawl.

Descending the stairs, I notice the wheelchair has disappeared. Maybe the son uses crutches *and* a wheelchair. I'm glad to think he's that mobile.

We head out to the wilds of Glass Beach, Arnold's restaurant guide in hand.

Drizzle. This might turn into heavier rain.

"I'm going back for an umbrella," I sigh.

Gretchen pulls a windbreaker from her shoulder bag. "I'm OK with this. Umbrellas make me feel like a helicopter." She waits under an awning.

Inside, I hear a woman singing. As I approach the stairs, the song ends. A thin, precise, *a capella* soprano. I guess Arnold listens to opera during his down time.

In the light rain, we study window menus at Joie de Vivre, Brennans, and The Big Fish. I love French food, but Gretchen is dubious about authenticity out here on the Pacific Coast. Does she consider Duluth some kind of cosmopolitan food fair? Fish—she believes in fish. Fish swim in the ocean. Pacific waves crash nearby, so we settle into a cozy booth beneath a net snagged with clam and mussel and abalone shells.

We swap news about our daughters while waiting for the menus and our drinks.

The waiter places a squat red candle between us. Overhead lights dim.

Sipping our margaritas, I consider how Gretchen resembles Dad—the cerulean blue eyes, the firm jawbone. I've stopped in Santa Fe on my way here, so I launch into a report. Best to dispense with parents at the beginning of the evening.

"Dad's doing much better since the bypass surgery." I stare into the flickering candle. "Really, he looks ten years younger."

"Glad to hear it." She licks salt absently from the rim of her glass. "He couldn't have got much worse without dying."

"And Mom . . ."

She moves the candle close to her menu. "Why are these places always so *dark?*" she demands. "Don't they *want* you to read the menu?"

"Mom's gotten interested in local archeology. Goes out on digs sponsored by the university."

"Finally using her brain for something. That's good."

I don't know why I talk to her about them. She never contacts our parents, either on Christmas or birthdays. They should have known better, she says; should have found steady jobs; should have settled in one place; shouldn't have risked their bodies and our lives with alcohol.

"Who knows why you waste your time on them"—she shakes her gold and silver curls—"after the idiot, *immature* choices they made."

"That's one difference between us, Gretchen. I don't believe they had so many choices."

She groans impatiently.

"I see it at work every day. People lose their jobs and are suddenly out on the street. Dad—well, at least he was always *employed*."

"Had to pay for the booze somehow."

I pull the candle close to my menu, then look straight at her. "I visit them for selfish reasons. They're my only parents. If I were estranged when they died, I couldn't stand the guilt."

"Guilt! They're the ones who are guilty. We were innocent children."

That's Gretchen: hot or cold, fast or slow. Guilty or innocent. Loud or silent. With our parents, she's silent, and will be to the end of her days. Roger says I should stop trying to reconcile them all. I have stopped, honestly; I'm just filling her in now.

The expertly poached wild salmon arrives, and we eat greedily for several minutes.

"How's Rona's trumpet?" she asks. "And Cate's soccer?"

Kids are an easy topic with us. The families we've *made*, rather than the one that made us. We often invite Gretchen's daughter Louise to hang out with her cousins. When Tucson temperatures go off the charts, Rona and Cate visit Gretchen at the cottage on Lake Superior. Sometimes I imagine the three girls sharing an apartment near N.Y.U., but Gretchen tells me I'm sentimental, that they'll all head in different directions. I don't know where I got this sentimental streak, but Gretchen does.

"*Mother*—you inherited her romanticism *and* her laugh."

"Laugh?"

"You laugh a lot."

"Really?" I ask, laughing.

When the waiter delivers the cheque, Gretchen inquires, "Where *is* everyone? I thought Glass Beach was a resort town."

"Oh," he yawns. "They came for the Early Bird Specials. Glass Beach is a senior community. Lots of retirees. Some nursing homes. You're the youngest customers we've had all month."

"We'll try not to be too rowdy on the way home," she says.

"Where are you staying?"

"The Driftwood Lodge," I smile. Maybe Gretchen is right. Maybe I *smile* too much, too.

"The Driftwood," he repeats neutrally. "A busy place."

It's still raining as we amble along the vacant streets of Glass Beach toward the lodge. Inside, the velvet saloon chairs are empty. A metal grating has been pulled down to prevent nocturnal pilfering. Shadows from street lamps dapple the scarlet wallpaper. I crave a good, rich port. If I ring the little bell, will Gretchen accuse me of the family weakness? Maybe I'll order one tomorrow night.

Approaching the stairway to our chambers, I notice the wheelchair is back.

My bed is comfortable enough, but always I have trouble sleeping in a new place. Gretchen attributes this to our peripatetic childhoods. Today's events reel through my brain. Everything has gone fine. Flights reasonably on time. Decent rental car. Comfortable rooms. Tasty dinner. I roll over and open the window wider, hoping the sea air will lull me.

The music from Arnold's suite resumes. Mozart. Lighter and gayer than I'd associate with him. Maybe the disabled son is an opera fan, as well as a philatelist.

I am dreaming about the circus—a tall man in a top hat walks through three wheels of fire—then footsteps on the stairs awaken me. Two A.M., according to my watch. I fall back into a dreamless sleep until 5:30 A.M., when I hear more footsteps. I guess Arnold was candid about the full house.

Rain again the following morning. We drive to Port Angeles and take the ferry to Victoria's lush Butchart Gardens. More pink flowers. The next few days pass with little excursions as we putter through the mist, talking about our kids and husbands and jobs and the perfect years in New York. Gretchen keeps me laughing with her tart jokes; this wit is a side of her Roger has never appreciated. Mist and rain are so thick that I imagine we're at sea, headed to that mythical island we conjured as children, deep under the earth's crust, between here and China.

Gretchen does most of the driving because I've been sleeping poorly. She hears nothing in the dark, thinks I'm imagining the night climbers because, as she correctly points out, we've never seen another guest. Guest, I blink; she doesn't say ghost.

Glass Beach. They say that on sunny days the inlets here reflect clearly, and I do remember seeing my face mirrored back one bright childhood morning. On this trip, we wait for sun. And wait. Eventually, under cloudy skies, we explore the beach together, walking briskly along the wet, windy shore. This foggy afternoon I am intrigued by a sign marked with skull and crossbones. The letters are red. "Quicksand—Beware."

I inch closer, examining the puddle beach. Picking up a rock to toss into the mix, I hear her anxious voice behind me.

"Lisa, are you crazy? It's quicksand; see the sign?" She's breathing heavily.

"Sure," I shrug. "I'm not going to jump in. I just want to test it with this rock."

"Don't go any closer." When she's frantic, Gretchen reverts to lecturing mode. "It's not ordinary sand, you know; it's mixed with water, and if you get trapped, if you try to pull out, you're fighting the vacuum left behind. Its viscosity rises with shearing."

I don't want to provoke her, but really, she's going overboard. "Calm down. I know. Cate did a sixth-grade project on this. If you get caught, you lie down on your back and carefully float to steadier ground."

"Fine, I'm sure she got an "A" on her project, but come away!"

"The same way you can float on the Great Salt Lake or the Dead Sea." I'm remembering the paper vividly now.

"*Come away* now."

I should tend to the panic in her voice, but it spurs me forward. I toss the rock. Slowly, irrevocably, it sinks to some invisible place.

"Do you think it's gone all the way down to China?" I turn to Gretchen.

She is yards away now, on the pier, walking briskly toward Driftwood Lodge.

The day before we leave, I wake up exhausted once again. I can't return to my job and family in Tucson worn out from a vacation. After morning coffee and cookies, before Gretchen and I venture out in search of breakfast and a final adventure, I pad down to reception and ring the bell. A minute elapses as I practice my perfectly reasonable request.

Finally, the door behind the red "Private" sign cracks open.

I wait.

A young man appears—Arnold's coloring, but thinner.

"Are you the stamp collector?" It slips out.

"Yes." He regards me cautiously, pacing behind the counter, checking everything, as if I might have stolen a key to someone else's room.

"Your father told us about the convention in Duluth."

He waits, shifting from foot to foot.

"Well, actually, I'd like to speak to your father," I try again.

"It's kind of early." The kid is dubious. "I'll check." He disappears.

I linger, my discomfort magnifying. I remember the wheelchair and realize we've invented the paraplegic son. What else don't we know about this haunted place? Maybe we should find another hotel for our final vacation night.

Arnold appears, atypically rumpled. "Yes, Ma'am?" he grumbles drowsily.

I'm not going to apologize for disturbing his sleep, since I haven't had much rest this week.

"I was wondering"—my most reasonable dealing-with-city-functionaries tone kicks in—"if I might have a different room."

He releases a huge sigh.

Before he can resist, I continue. "You see, I was wakened last night— and the nights before—at 2 A.M."

He's nodding vigorously. Suddenly we're allies. "Yes, I got wakened then, too. Had to let in the guests who do cleaning on the pier."

"And someone wakes me up around five each morning."

"Oh, yes, me too, every day when the retirement-home attendants finish their graveyard shifts. But they go straight to bed. That's why the Driftwood is so quiet during the day."

"I was hoping it would be quiet at *night* so I could sleep." I speak gently, still thinking he'll take the hint and give me another room.

"I sympathize, Ma'am," he yawns. "I share your desire."

Anger morphs into hilarity. I remember Gretchen's comment and restrain a smile. Tact, I reprove myself. Community organizing teaches many useful skills.

"Well, Mr. Werther, perhaps the difference here is that you *own* the hotel and get paid for opening the door at night, whereas I'm paying *you* for a restful vacation."

He looks pensive and annoyed.

"Why don't you give the lady Mother's room?"

Hearing a female voice behind me, I glance over, then *down*, to find a sixtyish blond woman in a wheelchair—*the* wheelchair.

I remember her *clearly* from years ago, sharing drinks with Mom and Dad, the three of them singing tunes from "Oklahoma!" while Gretchen and I played pinochle. Later, Mom told us she had given up a stage career to run the family hotel.

"Hello"—she extends a pale, manicured hand—"I'm Louise Werther. You must be one of the Carlson ladies."

I nod.

"We used to have lots of young, gay guests like you when I ran the place."

Young, gay. I can't wait to tell Roger, who complains about being stolidly middle-aged.

"Then we had the accident. It wasn't really our son's fault; he was a new driver, you see. Anyway, Arnold left the mill to manage here. He decided— wisely, I know—that we'd have a steadier income if we accommodated the retirement-home workers."

"Yes," I say, thinking how pissed off Gretchen will be for missing this installment of the soap opera.

"I had to give up the flower garden, of course. Did you know it was featured in *Sunset Magazine?* But I've tried to compensate by brightening the inn with floral patterns. I hope you've noticed."

"Oh yes—the roses, the peonies," I nod, riveted.

"But here we are, keeping you standing after a rotten night's sleep. We *do* have an extra room upstairs. It used to be ours, before the accident, and now we reserve it for Mother's visits. She's raging around Mallorca right now—wonderfully fit for eighty-five. You might as well have it for the last night. It's got a lovely view of the ocean, when you can see through the mist."

As she speaks, Arthur draws down another key and busily records the transaction in his neat maroon ledger.

Gretchen emerges from her room as I finish moving my clothes.

"What the . . . ?" she begins sleepily.

I take her hand and show her the grand chamber—far from the stairs—with a large picture window. One entire wall is corkboard, which Louise has lovingly covered with photos of the Driftwood over decades, some from well before her time. Women in long skirts with proper gloves. Flappers in fringes and sequins. A blond who looks astonishingly like Marlene Dietrich. Men in World War II uniforms, and their dates in shirtwaist dresses and platform heels. I search in vain for a photo of our parents.

Then Gretchen spots it—a color snap of two girls in the corner, the younger one concentrating on her cards, the other looking worriedly toward the blurry adults.

Filled with wistful melancholy, I sniff. "I bet you won the game."

"Yes," she nods, her eyes on the ocean. "I always win the game. It's what I know how to do." Her left hand grips the brass bed rail.

"Well, you're a smart person." I try to lighten the mood. "But I won't concede you're smarter than your sister," I laugh. "Just different."

"Just different." Her knuckles whiten. "I win the game. I avoid sink-holes, ledges, precipices; walk on firm ground. I sleep through the night." She's weeping now.

I wait, knowing she doesn't want an embrace.

The crying makes her voice almost inaudible. "Then I wake up in the morning, and it's the same damn thing all over again."

I see two little girls, battling imaginary waves in the middle of the earth, and I wonder who saved the other from drowning.

We both stare out the big picture window at the pier, the beach, the quicksand. I think about that rock dropping down, down, making its way to some beach near Shanghai.

Il Cortegiano
of Thomas Avenue

TERESA CONTEMPLATES THE TALL, BRITTLE GRASSES DANCING WITH THE WIND. Yellow, beige? How to describe this not-quite-straw color? Her grandson Al, the budding poet, would have words. What she knows is that this is a memory of Umbria. Umbria. She hasn't called the place "home" in decades, although it's where her beloved parents are buried, where her sisters wait in black dresses around a scarred kitchen table.

No, home is not that long-ago village where she ate dust until she knew she might suffocate. Home is not this lake in the Northern California hills where she comes each summer with Eugenio (Where they *almost didn't make it* this summer. Will it be their last?) Home is the small, sturdy house in Oakland, which her husband Claudio built and plastered and painted in the early 1940s, where she planted olive and lemon trees after cutting down gargantuan maples that blocked the sun. Thomas Avenue. Such a nice American sound to it. Nothing fancy—but respectable.

BOTH SISTERS WROTE approvingly about her living on a *viale* rather than on a simple *strada.* In that era before instant snapshots, she let them believe what they liked. Thomas Avenue was a modest road then, settled by other Italian tradespeople: the Minellis, the Foppianos, the Martones. From all over Italy they came, and she, who grew up speaking an Umbrian dialect, couldn't understand some neighbors. But together, they murmured Latin at St. Martin's Church on Sundays. And they all savored the sunshine of this flat, blank little neighborhood on the east side of San Francisco Bay.

Eugenio and Dacia were among the last arrivals, building a house adjacent to Claudio and Teresa. Her first reaction was uncharitable. Why didn't Claudio have money for both properties? Once familiar with

American privacy, Teresa cherished it more than material goods. A private person, now. She never dreamed of such privacy in Umbria.

~

TERESA LOOKS UP from the grasses as she hears an engine's volume rising with the hill—that dull, heavy noise which confirms an inevitable arrival. Setting aside her knitting, she eyes the horizon. She can predict his exact words, his chiding tone.

"*Buona sera*," he calls, slamming the door of his hulking Plymouth. "You should come down to the lake tomorrow, Teresa. It's much cooler there."

The lake. Boats. Fishing. Men shouting. No, she'd choose her peaceful warm hill any day over such hubbub. What kind of vacation is that? Like Thomas Avenue in the 1970s, before speed bumps.

Teresa smells him before he steps forward, sopping with sweat and lake water and seaweed and frogs' eggs.

"*Cara* Signora Pichetti, once more I have brought home the bacon to Mama."

She laughs, in spite of herself, at his constant mixing of metaphors and relations.

~

ALL THOSE YEARS AGO, she resisted the new neighbors, but Dacia won her over through breads and cakes and cheerful ways. Eugenio Lombrella was overblown then, with his lucky job as a city gardener and his beautiful wife. He loved to play Puccini and Verdi, loudly, on their victrola. Soon there would be five or six Lombrellas, he often boasted to Claudio, who would shrug, then repeat the story to Teresa over a tasty lasagna. Why so many children? he wondered, content with their bright son, Roberto. Claudio, too, was a private person.

~

"VERY IMPRESSIVE," SHE SAYS to Eugenio, watching two handsome trout sway on his lines. Shutting her eyes, she can almost feel the breath in them.

"You OK, Teresa?" He speaks to her, as he often does, in the contradictory cadence of a *solicitous order.*

Of course she's OK. She may wear her eighty years unevenly, but she's still a decade younger than this foolish old man. Teresa ignores the question, declaring instead, "Salad is prepared, Eugenio. Vegetables are ready to boil. The table is set. Tell me when the fish are cleaned and I'll put on my apron."

———

TERESA IGNORED THE BURBLING Eugenio and enjoyed a friendship with Dacia, who also sewed at the ladies' dress company downtown. Dacia chatted excitedly on the bus from work each night. Teresa found her voice restful after a day of buzzing machines. Dacia would have chatted on the way *to* work also, but Teresa, who needed early mornings to herself, carried a rosary as protection. Dacia plainly admired this devotion, and Teresa felt some remorse at her charade. Yet they relished their late afternoon chats. On hot August and September evenings in the common back garden, the women would sit with their feet cooling in buckets as they shelled peas or snapped beans.

———

"CERTAINLY," EUGENIO CALLS, heading to the back-porch sink. He still has enough energy for cleaning the trout before he rests on the deck with a cold beer, watching sun soften the strong, green fir branches. Eugenio sings to himself, pulling out fish guts, chopping off the heads and tails of these two fellows who joined him finally, finally, in late afternoon. The reward of luck and prayer. He shouldn't pray for trivialities, he knows. A skeptic all his life, in recent years he has started to converse with God occasionally. And he's learned to ask questions rather than make demands. Questions about why Dacia had to die so young, about whether he can do anything to lighten the spirit of their only daughter, now a sixty-year-old spinster. Yes, a few requests. Death itself he won't mind so much—but suffering! He hopes to be spared physical pain. And he wants to alleviate anguish for Signora Teresa Pichetti. They both know he's failing—although on balmy, fortunate afternoons, he believes he will catch fish another ten years. Someday, obviously, he will leave her, and he worries because a private person needs others around to disregard.

Still, today is today. He has only coughed twice, and his head has been clear when necessary—driving the car, launching the boat. Sitting on the blue green lake under the hot July sun, his mind drifted—which is natu-ral—back to Napoli and dreams of his own trawler, bringing in sardines each afternoon to the sweaty clatter of the *pescheria.*

⎯⎯⎯

FROM THE KITCHEN, she hears him singing. It's a tiny cottage they've rented for two weeks every summer these last twenty years. You can hear every-thing. Bathroom noises. Doors shutting gently. The tiny roar of the stove's propane flame. He has a robust voice. Even though the words come from Southern Italy, she has heard the songs enough times—from the back gar-den on Thomas Avenue forever—that she finds herself humming along. Teresa savors this time of day when the oak trees cast thick shadows—like the arms of a strong man—across the pale hillsides. And the underbrush captures brilliance from last light. She waits for the tranquility of full evening. It's not that sleep comes easily, but she does enjoy closing her eyes and recalling scenes from a day. She seems to be noticing more lately, as if watching, for something.

Evening in the hills—which are and are not the hills of childhood—this is why she agrees to a creaking cabin year after year, despite the work of preparing, packing, and the suspensefulness of his driving.

⎯⎯⎯

"A MIRACLE," THE DMV examiner described Eugenio's sight and dexterity. "At ninety! They ought to feature you on the evening news."

The DMV man didn't have to travel highways through Oakland and Richmond and Napa County and Mendocino County with the Plymouth speeding for twenty minutes, crawling for twenty minutes—trucks and buses passing them, people craning their necks to identify the erratic motorist. Some vigorously shaking their heads in exasperation, others bran-dishing fists—or worse. Eugenio remained oblivious to his audience, eyes (such as they were) on the road, singing about the *barche* and *onde* of Old Napoli.

Teresa knew she should be more responsible, should suggest the Greyhound. Yet it was his Plymouth that brought them together—him offering a new widow lifts to the Safeway, the beauty parlor, church. At first Teresa accepted from panic, necessity. And continued, she had to admit, out of a loneliness she could never have conceived. Since then, the driving and the riding turned from favor and convenience; their movement together became a kind of communion.

~~~~~~~~

SHE HEARS A RUSH of water signaling the end of his task. He'll leave the kitchen clean for her. Eugenio knows this much. He is a good companion, learning her patterns—not intuiting them as Claudio did, yet learning. Perhaps the difference between a lover and a friend. If only her son Roberto could understand this.

Still, all these years after Papa's death, he is suspicious of Eugenio. Judges their friendship unseemly because of these summer trips, because in Oakland Eugenio sometimes sleeps in her spare bedroom after a long evening of TV. They are simply company to each other in this late chapter. Her grandchildren are even worse than Roberto with their distasteful but affectionate innuendos. Offensive, impertinent. Eugenio's teasing doesn't help. The granddaughters shriek as Eugenio chivalrously takes their soft hands and then—as if it's a surprise each time—tickles their palms with his thumb. Young Al always greets her old neighbor slyly: "Hey Gino, how's it going?" Maybe Roberto is hurt that the kids didn't know *his* Papa, resents their easy ways (too easy) with Eugenio, the only kind of grandfather they've ever known.

Yet if grief is harsh for her, for Roberto, think of miserable Maria, who never married and visits her mother Dacia's grave each Sunday after mass. Teresa used to picture Roberto marrying the dark young beauty next door. Now she's grateful he chose Lenore, a less-emotional woman. Lenore has no perceivable opinion about Teresa and Eugenio's friendship; for this good sense, she appreciates her Anglo daughter-in-law.

Teresa folds her knitting—a sweater for Al when he goes to that graduate school in frozen Chicago—and heaves herself up from the padded deck chair. *Ouuuph.* Yes. She should be walking more, eating less. Even at her age, they say, it makes a difference.

They pass in the kitchen.

She rubs her hands, loosening the joints for cooking. A simple meal. Only simple meals, any more.

Whistling an old Perry Como song, he pops open his nightly bottle of beer.

"*Bella*," he addresses the trout, perfectly cleaned and filleted.

She nods, wondering how long his grip will remain steady with this razor-sharp knife.

SHOWERED AND CHANGED, Eugenio slips into the wooden rocker next to her cushioned chair. He scoots out of shade. Never enough sun. He couldn't comprehend his brother settling in foggy San Francisco. Naturally, his life was thirty years shortened. No, who really understands how the clock is wound? He raises his bottle to the Western hills, then swallows cooling bitterness. Turkey vultures are swooping in circles down by the stone pine. And a woodpecker has returned to the high branches of the live oak, its white and black feathers glimmering. On this trip they have also seen bobcat, wild turkey, deer, skunk. Back on Thomas Avenue, he will dream about the animals long into winter.

"*VIENI A MANGIARE!*" She summons him to the picnic table. Teresa insists on a proper cloth and napkins.

As she serves food, he watches the setting sun color the sky red, coral, purple.

The eating is enthusiastic. And without words.

After dinner, they lean back in their chairs, sipping coffee.

"Let's talk memories again." His tone is eager.

She releases a long sigh. He loves to converse about the old days in Oakland, about two young immigrant couples going to the Paramount and watching movies they didn't completely understand. About the births of Maria and Roberto. The children's school days. Maria's prom dress. Roberto's wedding. Her family, as well as his, that's for sure. Talking. Talking. He likes to recall good times. Never sad things—Dacia's cancer, Claudio's heart attack. Chat, chat, chat: sentimentality feeds his astonishing vigor.

Why be petulant? He spent all day luring those fish, his eccentric bacon. She should humor her good friend. "You go first," she says, hoping to think of *something* when her time comes. *If* her time comes, for he can go on. And on.

"OK," Eugenio announces. "Let's do our *happiest* memories tonight." He laughs to himself, then continues: "All day I've been back in Napoli.

Waiting for Papa's boat . . ." He describes a spirited boyhood. Fifteen minutes later, after the flamboyant clouds have vanished and a red moon is rising in the east, he finishes. "Papa would let me help, dropping some of the catch into my small pail. He'd say, 'One day, you'll grow into a fine *pescatore.*'" Eugenio shrugs, perplexed by his salty tears, grateful it's too dark for Teresa to examine his face.

She watches a scrim of fog lifting from the valley. Soon it will be too cold even for ancient fools to sit outside. She can rise now, and he'll forget she didn't speak. But she holds a single compelling image. "One of *my* happiest memories: this afternoon, sitting on the deck, smelling the grasses and pennyroyal, listening to the hummingbirds and bumblebees murmuring in the sage. Sun lit the oak tree, turning the branches gold, *oro!* It was quiet up here on the hill. And I knew my friend would be returning with fish for dinner. Yes, a very happy memory."

He is weeping now. Doesn't care what she sees as he takes her hand—carefully so as not to stir the arthritis—and brings it to his lips.

Percussion

THE CHEERY, INCOMPREHENSIBLE CAB DRIVER INSISTED ON CARRYING THAT BIG grey suitcase down steep stone stairs to her basement door. Lucky thing, too, because Anna hadn't realized what "garden flat" meant. She had imagined rolling the bag into a street-level apartment, which overlooked a backyard brimming with Scottish flowers.

A girl, twelve or thirteen, was opening the door for them. Not what Anna had expected either. Where were her parents?

"Books!" declared the cabbie, jovially heaving the scarred grey elephant over the transom.

"Yes," she nodded, hoping to please him with her seriousness. And with the tip. Pound coins. Pound bills. Bank of Scotland. Bank of England.

"Here's how the immersion heater for the tub works," the red-haired girl was explaining listlessly.

"No, lassie, you've given me too much," winked the driver to Anna. "That's a tenner. You just owe me five more quid."

The telephone was ringing, the way it did in films. Brring. Brring. More polite than the long siren-squawk of American phones.

The girl shrugged, as if to say, "It's probably for you."

Anna lifted the receiver. "Hello?"

"Hello, this is Susan, Lydia's mum. Is everything OK down there? Is Lydia explaining things fully?"

"Yes, thanks."

"Would you like to come up for a bowl of soup and homemade bread before you start unpacking? You must be exhausted."

"I'd love a rain check, but I wouldn't make great company right now."

The cabbie was lugging down the last of her bags.

～

ANNA'S FRIENDS TEASED HER, but she believed a poet had a right to one phobia. Hers was noise. She required quiet for work, so she lived on the third floor of a widow's house in the more rural side of St. Paul, a choice which doubled her commute. And the year Mrs. Penny remodeled her kitchen, Anna had sought refuge in the public library. Not that she had a lot of time for refuge or for poetry. At Greenwin Community College, she taught five sections of comp—or if she were lucky, four sections and one literature class.

Anna was surrounded by other people's stories: greying Carmelita's struggle to keep her kids off drugs. Nineteen-year-old Arnold's difficulty holding down a job, attending college, and parenting his three-year-old son. Her own mother's dying—an endless and yet far too sudden process.

Basically, Anna felt lucky. She had good friends, a job, a sweet lover, one book of poetry published and another on the way. Amazingly productive, colleagues said, although some seemed to imply "promiscuous" when they said "prolific."

Mother did die in the spring. Her loving, combative, hilarious, melancholy mother died in her own home, in her daughter's arms, during the spring Anna turned thirty-five.

Everything shifted after that. In June, Stephen left. He had seen her through Mother's death—she appreciated that—but he was forty and wanted to sow a few more wild oats. (The clichés weren't his most attractive feature.) So after ten years of togetherness, romance, partnership, Stephen cashed out his modest savings, took an unpaid leave from the high school, and set off across country with his Burmese cat, Edie, in their camper truck. He'd return, he promised, after he got this traveling out of his system.

They had a lovely farewell evening—Chilean sea bass, champagne, opera torte, long talk, good sex. In the morning, Anna realized she wasn't sure she wanted him to come back.

What she wanted was to finish the book. What she craved was time. Distance from other people's stories. What she needed was peace and quiet. And one steamy July afternoon, a miracle occurred: an airmail letter announcing that Anna had won a literary fellowship to Edinburgh for the following spring term. If it wasn't a miracle, it was a fluke. (Anna never won anything, not even from the dollar lottery tickets she bought weekly.) But the award letter spelled her name right and stated very clearly, "full salary replacement and travel expenses." The Overseas Club Fellowships placed few expectations on her. She would be invited to give an hour's reading toward the end of her stay. Otherwise, the time—and the arrangements—were hers. When she saw the "garden flat" listed on their housing sheet, she knew she was going to heaven.

Suddenly it was April, and she had found herself walking from an air terminal into Scotland. As her gregarious taxi driver wove through the pink Edinburgh evening, around the imposing seventeenth- and eighteenth-century tenements, Anna allowed herself to face just what a mistake she had made—flying off to a foreign city set in another century, where people spoke a peculiar language. Staying in an apartment alone. Alone without friends. Without Stephen. Without a mother. Three months. Three months would be long enough to finish the book. Or to go crazy.

YOUNG LYDIA WAS RAPIDLY winding up her introduction to the garden flat. "Leave the window open to prevent dry rot," she advised. "Here's how you turn off the space heaters—take a 5p coin or a nail file."

She led Anna into the stamp-sized kitchen. "Always use the fan here," she said. "And remember that rubbish is collected on Mondays and Thursdays."

Anna tried to focus. However, she was distracted by the high-pitched whirring, her jet lag, the girl's once-removed tone—by something quite wrong.

As Lydia opened the heavy front door, the flat was invaded by buses and cars and screaming children on the street. She looked Anna in the eye. "My mum, she's sorry she couldn't show you around herself, but she just came home from the cancer clinic yesterday."

"I'm sorry to hear that," Anna managed before the girl disappeared, shutting the door firmly.

Anna turned off the fan and the heater and the water immerser and the lights, and sat on an edge of her small bed, looking out beyond the cast-iron bars through a window at the still-rosy sky.

A garden flat. Robert Louis Stevenson wrote *A Children's Garden of Verses* on this street. The fellowship beckoned as perfection, redemption last term when Anna was surrounded by one hundred composition finals. Now here she was, alone in a tawdry bedsit, beneath the house of another sick woman. Mother used to read little Anna one Stevenson poem each night before she fell asleep. She hunched over the lumpy single bed and wept, as she hadn't in months, for her own contradictory mother, for Stephen, for fragmented poems. And for Lydia and the unknown Susan, upstairs.

Tired, she reminded herself. Travel worn. Looking again out the window, she noticed a brick-colored pot of pansies and daffodils tucked in a corner of the stairwell. Freshly planted flowers. For the garden flat.

Her first Edinburgh spring. They said it was unusually warm, but she wanted to believe April was always like this. True, her flat was perfumed and dusted with the tiny, ever-accumulating detritus of urban life. In the morning, she woke to the sound of buses idling at a nearby shop. During the day, she caught the ringing voices of passersby; and, as she learned the language, their increasingly comprehensible conversations pulled her out of work.

The blessed compensation was that she lived across from the Botanical Garden, and everything was budding these days. Each morning, before working, she visited a different section of "the Botanics": The orchard of blossoming fruit trees—delicate white apple and sultry pink cherry. Or the roses—thousands of roses colored coral, peach, bubblegum, silver, blood. She was drawn to the Botanics as much for the human population as for the flowers. Neat, silvery-haired women, wearing long-cared-for tweed skirts and woolen jumpers. What did you call their shoes? Brogues. Then the young women, pushing prams and chatting in that deliciously soupy Scots talk. Every once in a while, she'd see a pair of young monks in long maroon robes. And during the weekends, there were couples—men and women, women and women—nuzzling on the benches or lying on the grass beneath a Douglas fir or a Norfolk pine. On one of the few cold mornings, Anna wandered around the cacti and orchids and brilliantly hued intergalactic succulents in the greenhouse. But most of her ambling was outside: in the rock garden, or among the newly planted Chinese flowers, or around the ever-grinning bed of tulips. She loved the magnificent, giant brown hedge of beech.

Anna wrote every morning after her walk, usually skipping lunch and working until 4 P.M., when she ran errands, cooked a simple supper, and returned to reading and writing in the evening. One night a week she audited a Scottish literature class, and often went out to the pub afterwards with a few friendly folk. These long, northern nights gave her such spirit for writing. Besides, she knew summer school would start soon enough, stealing her thoughts and words for something more lucrative than poetry.

Sometimes Anna wondered if she had Scots blood mixed in with the Ukrainian and Italian streams, because she felt so moved when one of these ruddy, compact people greeted her.

"Mornin.'"

"Hello, there, luv."

"Afternoon, hen."

Lydia swept the stone steps on Wednesdays and Saturdays. The only other time Anna glimpsed her was when the girl brought down mail.

Should she call on her upstairs neighbors? Worried about Susan's health, she wasn't sure of protocol. The Scots seemed formal, fiercely private compared to her own family. Of course, anyone might appear subdued in contrast to her bellowing Sicilian father. Deceased, but still bellowing. She stretched for a more neutral term. Demonstrative.

The first time Anna heard the drums, she thought a nearby garbage truck was compacting trash. Something like that—a temporary disturbance from the street. But when the noise resumed each afternoon, just after Lydia's return from school, she allowed herself to remember Susan's answer to her inquiry about the flat. The woman had mentioned how nice it would be for her musical daughter to have an artist living downstairs. Musical—if Anna had thought about it at all, she would have heard flute or violin, or maybe piano. Music. She had never pictured drums.

Three weeks had passed without a word from either mother or daughter, and Anna was beginning to feel like a pantry mouse—living with, but apart from, the family's daily rhythms. Although Susan's toilet was on the second floor, Anna could hear the flush and gurgle making its way down the cellar pipes at 6 A.M. No bother, because teaching had made her an early riser, and there was always cheerful sun at either end of these northern spring days. Susan listened to Radio 4 news over breakfast, as did Anna. An hour later, though, she could hear Lydia banging around the upstairs kitchen, switching to the loud dissonance of Radio I. Thus, the girl's clanging and bumping and dropping became a cue for Anna's Botanics walk. By the time she returned, Lydia was at school. She pictured Susan sipping another cup of coffee as she reviewed the latest briefs. From neighbors' conversations, which Anna overheard from the pavement above her steps, she had gathered Susan was a labor attorney, working from home during recuperation. Susan had a light tread and didn't play music while working (the sign of an evolved human being, for Anna believed that neither music, nor its close cousin, poetry, should be employed as aural wallpaper.) There were a few daytime interruptions. Kitchen noises. Retching in the loo on the first floor. From Susan's grey pallor and slow gait, Anna guessed she was on chemo. The more she learned about the family from her initially unintentional eavesdropping and then her unabashed straining after conversations, the harder it seemed to walk upstairs, knock on the wooden door, and say hello.

Anna was writing a series of sonnets about gardens. Although the form hadn't visited her for years, she was enjoying it now, and happily concentrating on a tricky rhyme one Wednesday afternoon when an uneasiness settled over her. Fearful of losing the elusive muse, she kept her eyes on the page. Oddly, the pen ran dry, and as she lifted her head to find another, she noticed Lydia staring into her window as she absently swung the broom back and forth along the basement steps.

Irritated by the intrusion, she dug into the desk for another pen and tried to reenter the sonnet, but failed. At least for now. She could sit here, an actor miming poetry, or she could take the opportunity to say hello to the girl.

Tea. She had asked the clerk at Tesco about the best bagged tea, and noticing her accent, he gave her thorough instructions on bringing the water to full boil, steeping the bags for exactly five minutes, and removing them from the pot before pouring. At the time, she had found him half-charming, half-condescending. Subsequently, she was pleased to discover that such tea did taste brisker, fuller. So it was with great confidence that she cracked her window and said, "How about a cup of tea and some cook . . . rather, biscuits?"

The sullen girl smiled thinly at her visitor's attempts with local language. "Well, I'm almost finished. And I don't have anything better to do."

"Right, then," said Anna, taken aback by Lydia's rudeness, disinterest, shyness. "I'll just leave the door ajar while I fiddle in the kitchen. Make yourself at home, when you're ready."

Puttering at the tiny sink, she was struck by how big the girl had appeared on the stairwell—four inches taller than her and maybe twenty pounds heavier. This was her first long glimpse since that confusing evening of space-heater instructions. Anna didn't feel threatened exactly. More unsettled. Lydia's solid, shuffling footsteps indicated she was now roaming around the studio. Not much to entertain her, just books and papers. Anna *thought* she had put her current work away in the drawer.

"Here we are," she announced brightly, carrying a tray to the small coffee table. She was admiring the assortment of chocolate digestives, gingersnaps, and oatmeal squares when her foot caught on a snag in the rug.

Panic drained her face as she sank to her knees. Miraculously, Lydia caught the tray as she descended.

"Oops, careful!" Lydia looked worried. She placed the tea and biscuits on the table, then offered Anna a hand.

"Thanks."

"My, you're what they call 'petite.'" Lydia inspected her curiously.

Anna shrugged.

"And you get all dressed up just to stay home and write?"

"I feel better when I've washed and dressed," she said evenly. There wasn't anything fancy about her grey wool slacks and light blue turtleneck, but she could understand how Lydia, in her strategically torn jeans and overlarge sweatshirt, might consider her dressy.

"Do you take milk in your tea?" Anna changed the subject.

"Yeah, ta. No offense intended." Lydia's voice rose. "And sorry about the carpet. Mum planned to have that mended. Tenant before you practiced his golf swings, chucked up the carpet a fair bit. Ever since Dad died, we've had renters down here." She nibbled a biscuit.

"Golf swings?" Anna smiled with horror. She could not raise real questions—when? how?—about Lydia's father, not yet.

"Oh, yeah, we get some wild cards in the garden flat."

Anna laughed.

"Oh no, there I go again. I don't mean *you*. We've never had a published poetess before."

Poet, Anna said to herself, but did not correct the girl.

Lydia liked the gingersnaps and oatmeal squares, so Anna chose a chocolate digestive, even though she had already eaten her ration for the day.

"Mum was going to fix the carpet for sure, before she got sick."

So many questions, but she settled on the basic "How is she doing these days?"

"Beats me." Lydia turned toward the window, watching the pumps and sneakers and loafers parading along the pavement.

Then, after long silence, "Seems like this chemo stuff is worse than the cancer."

Anna nodded, wondering if it would be helpful to talk about nursing her own mother. Still, she wasn't sure how steadily she could retrieve that memory just now. She waited, sipping brisk tea.

"Womb cancer," Lydia spoke suddenly. "How can you get womb cancer? Mum doesn't smoke. She's a vegetarian. Hey, this is kind of crazy, but I'm an only child. Do you think it's my fault?" Her face went red as her shoulders lowered.

"Pardon?" Anna said. The poor girl needed a counselor. Surely they had them in Scottish schools, or through the NHS.

"Well," Lydia struggled, picking at the crumbs on her plate, "do you think it's because of something I did when I was a baby—in there, you know?"

"No!" Anna answered emphatically. She surprised both of them by walking over, putting her arms around the girl, and weeping softly.

Lydia remained dry-eyed, but allowed Anna to hold her.

"You make a decent cup of tea for an American," Lydia teased.

Gratefully, Anna returned to her seat and poured another round.

"So where do you *go* every morning? Just as I wake up, I see you walking busily down the street like you had a real job, but Mum says she always hears you come back once I've left for school."

She was touched that they knew her rhythms too, and surprised by the pang of loneliness this provoked. "I walk in the Botanics."

"Mum and I used to do that. The fruit trees are smashing this time of year—all those lacy blossoms."

"Yes," smiled Anna, thinking how she had underestimated the girl. "Would you like to go with me, some day after school?"

"Oh"—Lydia blushed and finished her tea in one gulp—"After school's when I practice my drums."

"I know." Anna bit into another chocolate digestive.

"Does it bother you?" she demanded anxiously. "Mum says I have to stop if it bothers you." Her voice took an edge. "Since you didn't complain—the golfer complained big-time while he was wrecking our carpet; he even made a crack in the window—we figured you were OK with the music."

Anna had wondered about the crack (back home, she would have thought gunshot)—had noticed it the first cold night of her stay.

"Well, then," Anna said, "How about a walk on Saturday morning at eight? Three days from now?"

"Saturdays I get to sleep in."

"Those fruit blossoms don't last long. They'll disappear with a good rain."

Lydia rolled her eyes. "Well, how about nine o'clock, then?"

Anna tapped her foot pensively. "Let's compromise—8:30."

"Deal," said Lydia, carrying her cup and saucer to the kitchen. "Thanks for the tea."

"You're welcome," grinned Anna. "Thanks for sweeping the steps."

Lydia shrugged and waved on her way out the door.

A week later, in the morning dark, there was a loud banging on the window by Anna's bed. She opened the door to a bathrobed, barefoot Lydia, talking faster than breath.

"Can you help, Mum wants to know, the taxi's late to take her for the chemo, it's hard to get another this early, can you drive her in our car?"

"Sure," said Anna, before she thought about it. "I'll be right there." As she heard Lydia's feet slapping up the cold stone stairs, she remembered that Scots drove on the other side of the road. A cultural adventure, she decided, blocking further doubts in the face of emergency.

The drive back from the hospital early that afternoon was far less harrowing for each of them than the madcap morning during which Anna had gradually absorbed the rules governing traffic roundabouts.

Susan opened up to her tenant, driver, and—if she lived long enough —potential friend. "I fret about Lydia's anxiety." The big, blowsy woman spoke deliberately. "This is a lot to drop on a thirteen-year-old."

Anna nodded, glanced away from the traffic long enough for a full view of Susan in her sensible grey sweater and slacks—wig slightly askew but red, the same fiery shade as Lydia's hair. For the first time, she realized that Susan was probably the same age as she, maybe a year or two younger.

"I've made arrangements with my sister in Airdrie."

"Arrangements?" Anna responded stiffly.

"Och, now, it's hard to beat uterine cancer. Especially at this stage."

"But the chemo . . ."

"Couldn't go down without a fight, yet at this point, *you* could tell *me* who is fighting whom. There's a *ten* percent survival rate with this stage cancer if you take chemo. I'm on the toxic drip for Lydia—feels like another labor, only this time a lot more protracted and less hopeful than the birthing."

Anna recalled Lydia's sad question about causing the cancer. "I'm sorry," she said. "I hope you beat the odds."

"Me too." Susan closed her eyes for the rest of the journey home.

Their first Saturday Botanics walk proved such a success that they set out again the next week and the next. Anna asked Lydia if she and her mum would like to join her at the Lyceum for a production of Brian Friel's *Translations.*

"Will there be drums?" Lydia asked, intrigued but uncomfortable with the invitation, joking her way out of it.

"I don't know, but there will be a lot of interesting Irish history."

"Irish!" She shook her head and then, thinking better of it, declared, "I'll ask Mum. She likes theater and acting and getting all geared up."

For several days, Anna awaited Susan's reply, filled with doubt about intruding. Of course, she could go to the play alone, or with one of the jolly crowd who went pubbing after class. Yes, she was a little lonely, but she had lots of friends at home and only six weeks left of her fellowship. Seven weeks before she would face five classes of expository writing in the wilting heat of a St. Paul summer. She had enough to keep her busy—a weekend reunion with her cousin Esther, who was studying for her third Ph.D., an engineering degree at Imperial College in London. This visit with dull Esther was for Mother. When she returned from London, she still had to explore Holyrood House and climb Arthur's Seat. And there was so much to write. Lately, she had turned to family poems—about the unpredictable, wondrous devotion between her reserved mother and ebullient father, both of whom died too young. Even to poems about her own childhood: her first visit to the ice sculpture exhibit, weekends sledding with friends in Como Park, glowing yellow maple leaves on the shore of a family weekend at Lake Superior. These poems surprised her because she'd never been given to autobiographical work, and because the Minnesota scenes seemed even more vivid to her at this distance.

Lydia was wearing a lovely purple cotton dress, carrying her mother's white blazer for the walk home.

"Sorry I can't join you," Susan said, her legs stretched out on the couch. "The Lyceum is my favorite theater. But this is a wonderful experience for Lydia."

"I'll enjoy her good company," Anna smiled.

Lydia crossed her eyes and blushed.

"And since you won't let me pay for her ticket, please take this"— Susan handed Anna a tenner—"for a nice treat . . . cakes or pastries after the performance."

"That's not necessary . . ." Anna held up her hand.

"No," Susan shook her head. Pausing for breath, she said, "But it's my way of partaking in the evening."

"Ah, Mum," Lydia whined. "I wish you would *come.* You love things like this."

"Aye," Susan smiled, shifting herself awkwardly on the couch. "But I have to save my energy for Aunt Helen's visit."

"Oh, who wants to see old Aunt Helen, anyway?" pouted Lydia. Then, more gently, "Won't you come, *please?*"

"Not tonight, dear. I'm truly knackered." She looked meaningfully at Anna.

"OK, Kiddo," Anna said. "We better go before someone claims our seats."

"Could they do that?" Her blue eyes widened anxiously as she collected her purse.

"No point in taking chances," Susan warned dramatically.

When Anna turned to wave to Susan, the other woman winked. Ten percent, thought Anna. With that spirit, she'll make the ten percent.

The production began slowly, concerning Anna that this had been a poor choice for Lydia. But the girl was full of arguments and questions at the interval. Afterward, she didn't stop talking about the play through the cakes and tea, the bus ride home. All evening they avoided one topic; still, Anna persuaded herself that Lydia needed a break from worrying.

Stephen's letter arrived that week, bucolic pages about hiking on the Olympic Peninsula and then down in the Sierra. Anna felt grateful for his friendship, but that was it. Clearly his passion had also ebbed, or he would have written sooner. In the same post was a letter from the college asking for her fall textbook order. This would be her thirteenth year of book orders, and she fought an urge to crumple the triple-carboned sheet, with its questions about edition and price and ISBN number, and toss it in her fireplace. Of course it was far too warm—as it had blessedly been since her arrival—for a fire. Instead, she took a midday walk to clear her mind, restore humility, remind herself she was lucky to have a job. You couldn't live your whole life on fellowships.

The trip to Raeburn Place had the opposite effect. As she walked past the elegant eighteenth-century gray stone buildings, she fantasized staying on here through the summer. Through the fall. She pictured Auld Reekie in the darkening of a November afternoon. She would go first-footing on New Year's Day, rewarded with a glass of stalwart single malt. She loved the daily way people shopped here—at the corner grocer's, the fishmonger's, the cake shop. Anna only went to Tesco when she was in a hurry these days. The poetry kept coming as it never had in distracting St. Paul. Why couldn't she stay in Edinburgh, teach at a polytechnic? Surely she could add a "u" to "labor" and an "m-e" to "program." By now she was bloody fluent in Scots talk.

Lydia's drumming sounded louder each day now. Anna dismissed possible implications of this increased volume. When the banging commenced, she stood up, stretched, and collected her carrier bag for shopping. Today, just as she stepped out the door, her phone rang.

Cautiously, she lifted the receiver. Who would call her here? Had Stephen had a road accident? Had she forgotten a line on the damn book orders? Esther—it would be dreary Esther, inquiring about her London visit.

No, this was Susan—Anna discerned this not so much from the voice, which was getting rustier, fainter, as from the even-louder drumming in the background.

"How are you doing?" Anna asked.

"It's a medium day." Susan struggled to make herself audible over Lydia's passionate percussion. "I know this is an odd time to call with Ringo banging away upstairs."

Anna laughed, released her carrier bag, which she had been gripping so tightly it had indented a red line across her palm.

"But I don't like to interrupt your work, and I know you usually run errands at this time of day."

"Yes," Anna replied eagerly. "Can I get you anything at the shops?"

"No." Susan drew a deep breath. "I called just now because you wouldn't be writing, to thank you for taking Lydia to the theatre."

"We had a super time," Anna said.

"I heard. I was a little jealous."

Silence on the line. How could she respond?

"Sorry, love, I'm a tough old cow, too abrupt at times. Maybe it's being a solicitor. Anyway, I felt so mixed that night—watching you and Lydia, who appeared truly gorgeous without those baggy, ripped jeans I can never get her to part with. Watching the two of you setting out on the town. I always looked forward to her teenage years, when we could become real friends. I was determined not to be one of those rigid, menopausal mums."

Anna listened nervously, marveling at her two months of pointless discretion, during which she and Susan might have had real conversations.

"And I guess that's one fate I'm about to avoid."

"But you . . ." Anna began to protest, fixed on that ten percent.

"Anyway, cancer helped me cut through the shit. I called to thank you and ask a favor at the same time."

"Yes," Anna said tentatively. Then, "Sure."

"There's a performance at Lydia's school."

"Right," declared Anna, "she's been talking about it for weeks."

A long sigh on the other end. Then a sob.

"Oh, I'm sorry," Anna fumbled, "I didn't mean . . ."

"No, not to worry." Susan pulled herself together. "We just have to get on with this. Anyway, I have plenty of other friends I could ask, but Lydia feels you're 'her' friend, really her only adult friend—and I was wondering . . ."

"Of course, I'd be glad to go with her," offered Anna, embarrassed that it had taken so long to pick up Susan's meaning.

After hanging up, she remembered that this was to have been her London weekend. Well, Esther didn't seem all that busy. She'd call and rearrange for sometime next month, before her flight home.

THE PERFORMANCE of light classical and popular music was enthusiastically received by parents, siblings, teachers, and a group of seniors from a nearby retirement home. The brass section was especially strong.

Confident of her unbiased opinion, Anna told Lydia on the walk home, "Your percussion solo was the highlight—the way you brushed those cymbals, firmly but softly—just lovely."

"Cymbals and symbols," Lydia mused. "Maybe that's why you liked it."

"And," Anna smiled, "that riff you did on the big drum—"

"It's not called a riff." Lydia cut her off sharply.

"Well, that sustained beat on the—"

"You're not my mother, you know!"

Hurt, she told herself that Lydia's mood had nothing to do with her. The girl was enduring an almost impossible ordeal. Anna walked more slowly, surveying the greening grass of Princes Street Gardens, the floral clock, the statue of Walter Scott inspecting all the passersby. Finally she said, carefully, "You have a wonderful mother in Susan."

"She *looks* like a mother," Lydia burst out. "Taller than me, with big, floppy arms. You're so tiny, like a doll, *très petite.*"

Anna recalled Lydia's earlier use of the term, in a tone of curiosity rather than derision, last month. She looked up at the sulfur streetlights, noticed how they seemed to warm the shop-window displays.

By the time they reached their turning to Broughton Street, the girl was strides ahead of her. Anna remembered her own ragged anger when Mother was dying. She would find herself going deaf in the classroom, honking madly in a small traffic jam on Hennepin Avenue, assaulting Stephen with long silences. Maybe that's why he needed his nationwide tour with Edie, the perfect cat. Now, in the warm Edinburgh night, she stood by the statue of Wellington, sobbing into the feet of the Duke's horse.

Lydia must have looked around, the way a dog does, walking her humans, just to check. Suddenly the girl was throwing her strong drummer's arms around Anna and crying, too. "I'm sorry, I can be a bitch. Mum says this all the time. 'Lydia, it's not the mean old world rattling against you. You're too young to be such a bitch.' She's right. I'm sorry, really sorry."

Anna sobbed harder, hanging on to Lydia, crying and crying for the girl, for Susan, for her own mother, for herself.

"We'll catch a chill from all these tears," Lydia said finally. "A wee thing like you, who knows what kind of constitution you've got?" She grinned provocatively.

Anna smiled back, and they finished their walk in silence, holding hands.

THE MORNING AFTER she returned from Esther's, Anna sensed something was very wrong. None of the usual sounds were heard—toilet flushing, Radio 4, Radio I. She picked up the phone to call upstairs.

Then she saw Lydia leaving the house at her regular hour with a school bag. Just her imagination, surely, thought Anna. Lydia wouldn't be going to school if something were really wrong. Still travel-weary, she forced herself on the morning's walk.

The Botanics were almost too hot. While she was in London, blossoms had dropped from the apple and cherry trees, and this morning, when she looked closer, she detected small fruits swelling against the branches. The tulips, too, were disappointing—petals faded, dry, darkened, blown away. Hurriedly, she walked to the beech hedge. Of course, the magnificent brown and gold had disappeared into a twenty-foot wall of terrible green.

Anna wasted the morning unpacking her weekend case. She couldn't focus on work. The London trip had been too long a distraction. Oh, Esther had been nice enough, more interesting than she had expected. We all grow up, Anna reminded herself. And when Esther saw her off at King's Cross, Anna heard herself inviting her only cousin back to St. Paul. On the five-hour train journey, Anna hoped to accomplish some writing—at least the letter she owed Mrs. Penny—but she felt too exhausted for anything besides staring out the window and drinking quarts of putrid railway tea. Could you get a tea hangover?

She was all set—blotter cleared, vase of flowers catching sun from the open window, desk lamp at medium setting. Still, nothing came. She put her head on the desk and several hours later wakened to a door slamming upstairs and a reassuring thumping and shuffling. Then she heard it—yes, Susan's voice. So she *was* OK. A great, unacknowledged ache lifted for the first time in four days as she admitted that she feared Susan would die while she was in London. She had to remember what she had said about being a tough old cow.

Anna waited for the drums. All she heard was clomping feet and murmured words. She had brought them small gifts from England—a CD of Max Roach for Lydia and some bath salts for Susan—but now didn't seem the proper moment, so close to dinner hour and in the midst of Lydia's musical block. She'd visit Susan tomorrow, once Lydia had gone off to school.

After her usual round of errands, on the spur of the moment, she decided to have dinner at a little Italian café. The house had felt so heavy over her all day. She bought a *Scotsman,* sat in a corner under good light, ordered half a carafe of chianti, and settled in for a cozy meal. Picking at her food, ignoring the paper, she puzzled about why she had become completely preoccupied with the neighbors. Fond as she was of them, she had to get back on track with the book. In two weeks, summer school began.

The ambulance arrived just after 2 A.M., siren blasting, lights flashing outside her window. Anna rose, threw a coat over her nightgown, fumbled for her shoes, and raced out the door, up her steps to the pavement. She watched the paramedics carefully transporting Susan down her long stone stairway on a white nylon stretcher. The material seemed so flimsy, as if it might rip under Susan's sturdy body. Anna's next thought was Lydia, and she peered in the front doorway to find the girl standing under the arm of an aunt. Once Susan was situated in the ambulance, Lydia and the woman followed. Susan observed the girl's composure as she stomped down the steps in her raggedy jeans, an anorak tossed over her sweatshirt.

Lydia turned toward Anna, a blank look in her eyes.

"Shall I come?" asked Anna.

The aunt looked at her curiously. "They said 'only family.' I'm sorry, love."

Anna stared at her, one of the sisters who had flitted in and out these past three months.

"Good luck, sweetheart," Anna called softly to Lydia.

The girl nodded—exhausted, stalwart—looking through her, up toward the closed front door.

A FORTNIGHT LATER, Anna stood in the stairwell, carefully patting soil into the red clay pot, then nestling the budding white and purple petunias into the dirt. With an old watering can, she lightly sprinkled the pot to keep the flowers moist for Lydia's return.

As she swept up the remaining soil, Anna wondered how her young friend was doing in Airdrie with all those loving aunties. She had so hoped the girl would be back from the funeral before her plane to the States. But what could she do? No way to cancel her flight, because as it was, she would be arriving a day before summer term. She checked her watch—an hour until the taxi. Her flat was vacuumed and scrubbed—she'd accomplished this much faster than she had expected. After a dreary week of packing and mailing home books, she gave her formal reading at the Overseas Club. The presentation was sparsely attended, but courteously received. (She thought she might have been more successful with a good backup drummer.) These last few days had been too quiet for writing.

From inside her flat, a ringing. Maybe Lydia calling to say good-bye? She herself had no way to reach the girl. Why would auntie have given her phone number to the renter?

Breathlessly, she picked up the receiver.

Esther—dear, decent Esther calling to say farewell, *bon voyage.* To say she'd see Anna in St. Paul.

Anna had hoped to invite Lydia to what the girl laughingly called "The Tundra." But everything ended so suddenly. She could write, but how much would a traumatized kid remember about one of the many downstairs tenants in her life? Anna studied the golfer's hole in the rug.

As she replaced the receiver in its cradle, she remembered the girl's footsteps and the first bang and thump of drumming. Cymbals and symbols, she smiled, taking a long breath and wondering if she could ever write in silence again.

On the desk, Anna placed the CD with a card for Lydia, then walked outside to retrieve the plant, thinking how much the sight of pansies and daffodils had meant to her on that first miserable night in her garden flat. She had never found out whether the gift had been from Susan or Lydia.

One more inspection of her briefcase—ticket, wallet, passport, and an almost-finished manuscript.

The knocking startled her. Taxi drivers were so courteous here: they never honked from the curb. Sentimentally, she had imagined riding with the same old man who had delivered her in April. He would pretend to groan at the weight of the old grey elephant, and as they drove through elegant New Town, he would ask about her writing, demand to know if she had read all those books she brought.

She apologized to the new cabbie about the heavy bags.

He shook his head. "My job, Ma'am."

Picking up her briefcase, she followed him, locking the door from the outside, then kneeling down to slip the keys through the mail slot. As she did so, she took one last sliver of a glance at her writing respite. She could see the CD, the card, the clay pot. She could almost hear the drums. Surely Lydia would return before the flowers needed watering.

What She Didn't Say

I ROCKED ON HER FRONT PORCH, BREATHING IN FAMILIAR SCENTS OF ROSES AND honeysuckle, swatting away the mosquitoes and no-see-ums, sipping at warm iced tea. Absently, I straightened out the skirt of the pretty lime dress I had bought especially to wear for Grandma. She'd gone to bed an hour past supper, after being reassured five times that I didn't mind sitting alone. *Not at all.*

I should have come down to see her last July. And the July before that. But college summers are designed for earning next year's tuition. And those short vacations between jobs and school seemed marked for adventure, not for visiting Grandma in the hot and buggy Blue Ridge Mountains. I was finished now—at least until I decided about grad school. Dad voted for law; Mom had no opinion. Lately, I was dreaming about architecture—the pleasing aesthetic of all those straight lines: squares, rectangles, triangles leading to houses, schools, theatres. After graduation, Mom phoned me in Boston and said her mother's hip was mending nicely. (The old woman was tougher—and braver—than any of us.) What she didn't say was—a trip to Grandma was long overdue.

Days were peaceful at Grandma's; they bestowed quiet of a degree I never found during college. Amazingly, Grandma seemed the same as ever, maybe a little creakier, a little more melancholy. After what she'd been through I didn't expect her to have the same wide-open heart, but I felt right at home, welcomed and loved in a way I found nowhere else. Tonight I studied different shades of green, visually untangling the vines and trying to identify the wildflowers. The long moan of a freight train brought it all back. I remembered being bored here as a girl. *And happy.* Each of my summers—from age five to seventeen—Mom and Dad drove Sara and me down from Washington, leaving us with Grandma for two months while they got on with their hectic office jobs and took a two-week vacation by themselves. "To rev up our romance," they explained once we were in our teens. Despite our embarrassment at their corniness, we were grateful they loved each other, given how many of our friends had broken families.

A beige pickup snaked down the narrow road, the driver raising his hand in greeting. I waved back automatically, then recognized Mr. Handley. Grandma's "young grocer" had gone all grey, a different man entirely from the guy who used to practice pitching with my sister each evening. After dinner, Grandma and I would play rummy, listening to the whish and smack, whish and smack of the baseball from Sara's mitt to Mr. Handley's larger, older, louder mitt. When dark arrived, she would slip into the house and emerge carrying a cake or pie, whatever she had baked that afternoon.

Sara always got the biggest slice, because she was a "growing athlete," and even in those days I had to watch my weight. You'd think Grandma might have questioned a young girl's passion for sports, but she adored the Olympics on TV and declared she was looking forward to Sara carrying that torch one day.

I loved Grandma's baking, but didn't mind the smaller slice. Oh, maybe I minded a bit—that and all the attention Sara got. The hopes pinned on her. Mom and Dad believed in low-key parenting, yet they did buy Sara's sports gear, did attend her track events when they could. Soon I surrendered petty jealousy and happily joined the fans. Running was her forte, and I loved the way she glided out early in front of the others, holding her place confidently, breaking the ribbon. She looked as if she would run forever.

Those summers not only gave me time with Grandma, they were also when I got to know my sister. Although she was just a year younger, I never saw Sara at school. She lived in the gym and I hung out in the library. So each July, as I watched Dad load our red and turquoise boxes in the car, I began to smell the gingerbread and honeysuckle and Grandma's wild-rose toilet water and the sweaty leather of Mr. Handley's mitt. I could feel the first evening cooling and hear Mr. Handley's precise assessments of Sara's developing fastball.

My red wooden travel box was filled with dolls and their elaborate wardrobes until I was seven; then I started to pack books there because Grandma's local library was too small for my appetite. Sara's turquoise box contained board games for a few years before she discovered sports, and then she would stuff in a football, a basketball, mitt and baseball, running shoes. Of course we must have packed a suitcase of clothes, but all I remember are those two wooden boxes and how they used to rattle against one another on the ride from D.C. to Coldwell, as Sara and I teased and bickered in the back seat. The drive home in August usually felt more serene, because we had run out of things to argue about, because we had become tentative summer friends, and because I, at least, felt sad about the way we would soon grow apart during the school year.

Tonight, I noticed that the early July light went on forever in these mountains. I stood and stretched, weary of the warm iced tea and the memories, and headed down the road. Shivering at the rumble of another train, I pulled my green sweater close. Lawn ornaments were always popular among Grandma's neighbors. Now they proliferated in front of the newer prefab houses as if they'd come for a convention. Granite lions, wrought-iron horses, plastic geese and parakeets, papier-mâché deer. Mrs. Brandon still had the silhouettes of a cat sitting atop her mailbox and a dog barking up the side. The black paint was peeling from Fido's tail.

As I walked west along Horsehaven Road, blue-grey peaks in the distance, the number of houses dwindled. Here, the high grass was grazed by goats and sheep and cows. Some parcels weren't up to much more than being open land. You never saw this kind of emptiness in Eastern Massachusetts. Not emptiness, I reminded myself—counting the hickory trees and the walnut and maple and oak—rather "openness." I never noticed trees in Boston. I noticed cars and billboards and deadlines. Filled with longing for those summers of aimless reading in the luxuriant countryside, those Julys and Augusts spent half-listening to the slow conversation of Grandma and her friends, I marveled how childhood monotony metamorphosed into dreaming. The dreams leading me to college. First in my family to go. I was heading to grad school, a profession, a life of possibility; but would I ever again find such rich, safe openness?

Many late afternoons, Sara and I walked this back road to stave off our hunger. We tried not to anticipate another delicious supper of black-eyed peas and ham, or fried chicken and mashed potatoes. How could our frozen-fish-stick-and-Sloppy-Joe mother possibly be the daughter of this great Southern cook? Go figure. During one hike, we found ourselves in Fordley, poking around the old Baptist graveyard. On our way out, Sara noticed a white sign on the wooden gate. "No Trespassing after Church Hours." My sister never missed a beat. "I'd guess that's when most people *do* their trespassing." We didn't stop laughing all the way back to Grandma's.

There were some things you didn't dwell on. That's what Mom said whenever I tried to talk about Sara and why she did it, about what *I* could have done to prevent my beautiful, talented nineteen-year-old sister from jumping in front of a freight train. We weren't a family of talkers. Mom's silence asked, what was there to discuss? No note.

No explanation. No sense. For a while, I insisted she must have tripped and fallen from the overpass. *No* one bought this explanation about our agile Olympian. Mom still kept Sara's photos on the mantle—senior prom, state track meet, high school graduation. Yet she never talked about her younger daughter after the funeral. Maybe Mom's approach was best. Maybe my urgent need to know "why" came from vanity—the belief that as her older sister, I should have seen this coming. Was it the sports pressure? Did she want more from my unforthcoming parents and me? Was she suffering from some mental illness? Around and around I went, propelled by the conviction that I needed to learn something from all this pain. Didn't our postmodern theory prof teach us to dismiss the arcane assumption that every narrative has a point? In ending her story, Sara had changed mine forever. It had taken me two years to let go of the "why," years when I couldn't possibly visit Grandma.

As I passed Mr. Handley's brick house, a mockingbird flitted before me. Nearby, I could hear a magpie. Yesterday I had seen three cardinals in the morning, deer and possum in the evening. Boston had what? Pigeons? Crows? There must be other birds, perhaps along the Charles. I'd look closer next time I jogged by the river.

The biggest puzzle was why she chose to do it *here*, why she drove down that July to see our delighted grandmother and went out the next morning to leap in front of a speeding train. She must have known Grandma would have to clean up (as she always had, putting away those baseball cards and mitts and hats in the turquoise box each summer). She must have known Grandma would be called to identify the body, phone our parents, live the rest of her life amid shame and sympathy in this small town.

Light was dimming, and I heard gunshots in the distance. Never wear green strolling on a country road, Grandma had instructed us. My pace quickened toward the sunset and the summer home of my girlhood. (None of us cried at her funeral; public weeping wasn't in the family repertoire.) Now the lightning bugs were blinking—great moon-sized ones glowing behind bushes, around the almost indistinguishable lawn ornaments. Bats sailed from shadowed rafters.

———

I WOKE BEFORE DAWN, lay in bed half an hour, reaching for sleep. Never was I awake before Grandma, and this gave me my first good idea in two days.

At seven, when she normally rose, I knocked softly on her door.

"Yes, dear?"

Her voice was strong, wakeful, blessedly familiar.

"May I come in?"

"Certainly dear." Then a worried sigh, "Is something wrong?"

"Surprise!" I held out a tray of toast and jam and orange juice, and tea brewed as strong as she liked it.

She smiled up at me through sleepy eyes. "Why, how lovely. Thank you."

I grinned back, setting the tray on her oak bedside table.

The room was lush with roses. A new toilet water, I assumed—until I saw the blowsy white flowers, open and opulently fragrant, standing in a tall vase set on a box by her window. A battered turquoise box.

She followed my glance, then locked eyes until both of us verged on tears.

"I found it in the cellar last summer," she said, sitting straighter. "It's such a cheerful shade of blue. Or green, I could never tell which. Bluish green. A youthful color. Well, I just brought it upstairs to keep me company."

Always Avoid Accidents

WALTER SHARMA ARRIVED EARLY AND ASSUMED HIS FAVORITE SEAT IN THE LAST row of the auditorium, on the right. He would have a good view of the audience and the speaker. An historian this time. Talking about American politics in the 1970s. Just up his alley. And to think he might have missed the lecture if Goyal hadn't told him at the canteen. Did he not inform the dean's office time and time again to put him on the invitation list for visiting scholars, especially Americans? Like so many other things in this dilapidated country, his request had been neglected. Efficiency was simply not an Indian concept. Ignore the petty irritations—he shrugged and straightened the collar of his blue work shirt, still in good shape since all those years ago in Missoula. The Americans knew how to make things, and how to make things happen.

The dimly lit hall was filling with a predictable cast: Goyal and Asnani and Nahar from History. Chawla and Patel and that new Miss Nair from Politics. The gangling graduate students, who looked both resentful and scared. Had not Walter explained to them, over and over, the value of international perspectives? Had he not told them—briefly and modestly—about his seven years in the U.S.? Ah, to these provincial children, Calcutta and Delhi and Mumbai were imaginary horizons. His colleagues, too, suffered limited ambition and sometimes claimed to be too busy for foreign lectures. Alas, they hosted only three or four visitors in the course of a year. Asnani resented cultural imperialists from the British Council and the American Center, yet he seemed happy enough with the Canadians, ever since his son began flourishing in Toronto.

Still muddled by pointless annoyances, he almost missed the arrival of Dr. William Stone, Professor of History from Warren University in Michigan.

Professor Stone was younger than Walter expected—in his forties at most—so for him the 1970s truly were history, rather than the drama

Walter experienced directly. Walter and Asha—yes, Asha savored those years as much as he.

His application to graduate school had been accepted with some delay. Professor Sanders had written back that he was older than most students, but he had stunning test scores and he wrote beautifully. From the minute he arrived in the Rocky Mountains, Walter felt appreciated in a way he never was in India. Walter rose to the top of the Modern Poetry Core: Marianne Moore, the Beats, Elizabeth Bishop, Robert Lowell. His critical work revealed an original brilliance. He even published some of his own verse in local literary journals. The department offered him a junior faculty position. Asha was already using her new American counseling degree at a local high school. But the passionate righteousness of the Civil Rights and Anti-War Movements fired their own idealism. They would return home to help build the New India. Thus he made the fateful decision of accepting a post in this remote hill station.

Walter felt his resistance to Professor Stone's youth ebbing because the man spoke in an eloquent English one did not always find among Americans. And he had a command of his subject. *Walter was pulled back immediately to those evenings watching the little black-and-white TV in their studio apartment. Watergate. The Plumbers. Endless testimony. He and Asha were fascinated by how deeply the Americans believed in a discernable truth and an exercisable justice. Body counts every night on Walter Cronkite. Then the surrender to Hanoi. The jumbled administration of Gerald Ford. And the long, bleak night of the Iran hostage negotiations.* Professor Stone perceived it all leading inexorably to Ronald Reagan's election. Perhaps he was right; after such chaos, people sought cheerful, commanding father figure. That's not how Walter had analyzed the man, but by the election, he and Asha and little Ashok were settling into these legendary foothills, nostalgic for Missoula friends—and yes, for some of the comforts—but eager to share the privileges from their foreign educations.

The discussion period was predictably dull. Inane questions about the two-party system. And the significance of Nixon's trip to China. Walter waited for three questions before raising his own. Best not to go first, because your contribution could get lost. On the other hand, you shouldn't wait too long, because Goyal might adjourn the session early. Last year, Walter himself had hosted a professor of English literature from Berkeley, and everyone agreed it was one of their best events. Even two graduate students asked questions.

Now he rose from his perch at the back—one's voice could be better heard if one stood, and visitors often had trouble understanding Indian

English, even his English, if one were not loud enough. "Dr. Stone," he began.

Heads turned. Dr. Stone looked Walter directly in the face with one of those American expressions of frank curiosity.

"How do you think American involvement in Vietnam and subsequent withdrawal (he knew enough not to say "defeat") influenced ensuing U.S. policies toward other Asian countries?"

"A fascinating question," Dr. Stone declared before launching into a lengthy, technical response about distinct theatres of engagement.

Walter found himself a bit lost, but then he wasn't a scholar of history. He did appreciate the visitor's erudition, a godsend in this backwater. Yes, now it was settled; he would invite Professor Stone to dinner tonight. Having traveled abroad himself, he knew the pleasures of a home-cooked meal in a distant land. Goyal would be planning to dump the poor fellow at his hotel. When he had told Asha this morning that he might bring home an American, she was delighted and sent him off with a long grocery list.

————

AFTER FETCHING Asha's vegetables, Walter picked up a bottle of the best Indian gin. Americans loved gin, he recalled: dry martinis and tall, frosted glasses of gin and tonic. Then he got on his scooter and zigzagged through the late-afternoon traffic. Really, the pollution was getting ridiculous— even up here in the hills. You used to be able to see the Himalayas on bright afternoons. Now sunlight, interacting with ubiquitous carbon monoxide, created the most disgusting haze, like film on teeth that hadn't been brushed for a day. Suddenly—out of the sky—a lorry careened forward, impelling Walter over to the pavement. He stepped quickly on his brake to avoid hitting an old man. Out spilled the cauliflower and peas and potatoes. Hurriedly, he collected his groceries and proceeded with caution back into the noisy traffic.

On the drive home, he dredged up details about Michigan. The Detroit Tigers. The Ford Motor Company. A border with Canada. Great Lakes. Definitely Lake Michigan. But also Lake Superior . . . or was that Wisconsin? He always mixed up those Midwestern states. Perhaps Professor Stone had visited Missoula. He and Asha loved to reminisce about Montana with American visitors. Each year, they received Christmas cards from four old friends there. Walter's mood improved as he rounded the corner to Vasant Road.

Asha's yellow roses were doing nicely, and the purple pansies flourished by their door, distracting one's eye from the peeling paint and broken step. Over twenty-five years they had lived in this house, the university promising them a more suitable one nearer the campus for over a decade. Now he was certain that when he retired, he would still be afflicted by the leaking water tank, the cracked windows, and the temperamental toilet.

Asha opened the door as he detached himself gingerly from the scooter. He could feel a huge bruise on his right leg from that lorry incident.

"So late you are. And I am more than ready for the *gobi* and the *aloo*. Did you find the chutney, both the tamarind and the mango?"

"Yes, yes," he laughed. "Hold your horses." The American idioms returned at moments like this. "Professor Stone isn't due until 8 P.M."

She hurried the groceries into the kitchen and called over her shoulder. "The toilet. It's acting up again. Will you see what you can do? Thank god Ashok and Anita are out of station, or this would be a rare chaos tonight."

Passing Ashok's closed door, he thought how much he enjoyed the company of his bright son and cheerful daughter-in-law, but the new baby—as adorable as he was—made it difficult to read or even mark papers at home.

Nothing did he hate more than reaching his hand into the cold, wet tank of their ancient toilet. Only water, he knew, yet it seemed unclean. In Missoula, they would have called a plumber, who would have billed their landlord. In America, there was always someone who fixed things within a day or two. Here, the university bureaucrats behaved as if it were a privilege to rent one of their crumbling abodes, which left no one to ring except Shiva or Ganesh or Krishna.

The hors d'oeuvres were set on the coffee table: peanuts and almonds in a painted bowl bought at a Blackfeet powwow; a silver tray of pimento cheese on Ritz crackers. Their old neighbors, the Jordans, sent them an "American Care Package" every year, and they saved many goodies for special evenings like this.

Walter arranged the gin, vermouth, and tonic, catching sight of himself in the sideboard mirror. The modified cowboy shirt with its mother-of-pearl buttons still fit him well. He decided against the bolo tie.

Asha looked more relaxed now as she appeared from the kitchen in her new yellow *salwar kameez*. A lovely woman with just a few threads of silver in her curly black hair. He sometimes wished she would wear the pretty skirts and dresses she had brought home from America, but she felt conspicuous in them here. In *was* easier for men, he reckoned. No one expected him to wear a *kurta*.

"You look like you are seeing a ghost," Asha laughed.

"I am seeing the beautiful bride I took to America," he smiled wistfully—a bit seductively, he hoped.

"I was hardly a bride, already the mother of your son. You know, sometimes you sentimentalize those years in Montana."

"What do you mean?" he demanded, struck to the core, for he thought they shared his happy dream. "Was it not the best time in our lives?" His heart was racing as if he had discovered an intruder in the house.

"Our lives aren't over, Walter. Yes, yes, they were good days. But who knows our karma. Maybe we will go back."

Walter smiled, relieved and gratified that as they lay in bed together at night, they were still dreaming the same dream.

"But where is Mr. American Historian? Already I am thinking he is half an hour late."

"Patience, dear. You will sit and have a martini with me?"

"No, I will stand and watch over our dinner so that it doesn't dry out. Who do you think you are? Cocktails! Dean Martin?" she teased.

Dean Martin, that reminded him of the records. He pulled out a couple of Andy Williams and Dean Martin seventy-eights. While his American classmates listened to Bob Dylan and James Taylor, he developed an odd taste for romantic crooners. Now, cheered by the familiar music, he flipped through an atlas. Michigan. Yes, on Lake Superior, Lake Huron, Lake Erie, Lake Ontario, *and* Lake Michigan.

Finally, a knock. The bell had been broken for years. Asha emerged from the fragrant kitchen, whisking imaginary wrinkles from her clothes. Walter straightened the cuffs on his shirt and, as she approached the door, noticed his right leg aching numbly.

There stood Professor Stone, holding a bouquet of sunny roses, sputtering apologies. "The driver couldn't find your place. We've been riding around. I'm so sorry."

"It is *we* who are sorry," said Walter. He stuck his head out the door, searching for the idiot driver, but he had already vanished in shame or delight with his stupendous fare.

"Please come in," he enjoined the American, glad to discern that the guest was an inch or two shorter than himself. "We do have many visitors." Walter tried not to sound defensive. "The taxi company knows us. He must be a new cabby. From Bihar. We have a lot of Bihari refugees . . ." Tripping over his words, he remembered that regional or ethnic discrimination was highly incorrect in American circles. As well it should be. "I shall call the company myself for you at evening's end—but may that be a long while from now. Come, come, make yourself at home." He couldn't offer a ride back to the hotel on his scooter, an unwise conveyance for foreign visitors.

"I did get to see a lot of your beautiful town." He took a seat on the rattan chair. "The profusion of flowers, the stately trees, the views of the Himalayas. Wish I had brought my camera tonight. So what does it feel like to live in Paradise?"

Walter, who hadn't seen the mountains for months, was distracted, wondering just how far the taxi had gone.

More alert to social graces, Asha passed the hors d'oeuvres.

"How about a drink?" offered Walter. "We have first-rate gin. May I make you a martini? Perhaps a double after that treacherous odyssey. Or a gin and tonic?"

"Thanks, no," smiled Professor Stone. "I'd love a glass of mineral water or juice."

As Asha served the juice, Walter poured himself a long gin and tonic. He never drank unless they had a visitor, but it had been a wretched day with the traffic accident, the broken toilet (Oh, that didn't bear thinking about), and the egregious taxi delay. He would sip slowly, the alcohol making him fitter company.

"I never realized how tucked away these hill stations were," Professor Stone (who wanted to be called "Bill") was saying.

"Yes," Walter nodded sympathetically, "it's an arduous journey from the airport—three-and-a-half hours."

"But *so* interesting how the towns and foliage change as you go up, up, up on that winding, dipping road."

Walter felt a little queasy, recalling the back seat of the crowded airport van. Perhaps he was not drinking slowly enough.

"Yes," agreed Asha, "I sometimes think I'm riding into heaven."

"Exactly." Bill thumped the table with his big palm.

Curiously, Walter watched the table's left front leg, which had been repaired last week after one of Baby's somersaults.

"And the road signs." Bill was warming up.

Truly, the man's loquacity didn't require alcohol, Walter marveled.

"'One Blunder and You Go Under,'" he reminisced. "'Slow Drive—Long Life.' 'Always Avoid Accidents.' We'd do well to post some of those signs on our interstates."

"The sign I noticed when we returned from Missoula," Walter said, "was 'Lane Driving is Sane Driving.'"

They all laughed. The room fell silent, and Asha again passed the hors d'oeuvres.

"We lived in the States for seven years," Walter tried again.

"Oh, yes?" Bill asked politely.

"From 1970 to 1977," Walter expanded. "That's why I found your lecture so illuminating. I did my Ph.D. in Missoula."

"Oh, really?" Bill's voice was curious. "Missoula . . . I'm not sure . . ."

"The University of Montana in Missoula. In the Rocky Mountains."

"Oh, yes, yes, of course, beautiful country. I'm from the flat Midwest, myself. Big sky, big lakes, but not much contour to the land. That's why I'm so taken with your Eden here. This must be a prized posting. Imagine, the Himalayas at your doorstep."

Walter was tempted to look out the window, for it had been such a muggy afternoon, with no vistas to speak of.

Asha excused herself to the kitchen.

Walter slightly increased the stereo volume.

"Dean Martin . . ." Bill shook his head in amusement. "One of my Dad's favorites. Did you get that in the States?"

"Yes," Walter acknowledged, then cleared his throat of a peanut skin.

When she called them to dinner, Walter was extolling the seriousness of American students—their eagerness for class discussion, their carefully crafted critical essays.

"Say, this is delicious," Bill exclaimed. "The *aloo gobi* is wonderful, *and* the *muttar paneer.* Martha and I have a favorite Indian restaurant in Ann Arbor, but the food is nothing like this."

Asha beamed.

"We enjoyed the casseroles in America," Walter reminisced. "Lasagna. Macaroni and cheese. Baked spaghetti."

"Baked spaghetti, really?" Bill grinned.

Walter poured himself another drink, ignoring Asha's disapproving scrutiny.

"Yes, the potlucks," Asha declared. "So friendly and full of surprises. So much your people do with Jell-O—all those different colors—some molded with fruit, others with carrots or celery. And the holiday picnics. Memorial Day. Fourth of July. Labor Day. Potato salad. Pickles. Corn on the cob."

Walter nodded, waiting his turn. "But most of all, it was the teaching and the collegial relations I enjoyed. We could have stayed. We often wish we had."

Bill looked embarrassed. "Well, maybe you'll come back to visit."

"The airline expense," Walter sighed, in spite of himself. "The exchange rate!" Normally Walter didn't disclose like this; for some reason, he felt comfortable with Bill.

Asha relieved the tension by presenting a glistening *gulab jameen.*

"My favorite dessert!" exclaimed Bill.

"You have been to India before?" Asha asked.

"Oh, no, this is my first trip. But Martha and the boys are dying to come. I definitely plan to return."

"That's what we declared when we left Missoula," Walter said gloomily.

Asha shot him a look of caution.

He smiled from across the seas.

"Hey, I have an idea." Bill leaned toward Walter. "We have a new post-colonial studies program. Several good friends teach there, and every year they bring a visitor from Africa, Latin America, South Asia . . . well, anyway, it's not a bad deal. They pay a full Warren University salary, take care of the plane fare and all."

Walter was looking out the window. It got dark so early here—everywhere in the country, actually. In Montana, the summer nights lasted forever.

"I'd be glad to recommend you."

Asha's eyes lit up. "Well, that's very thoughtful."

Walter remained silent.

Asha tried again. "It is generous of Bill. We'd be very interested, wouldn't we?"

Detached, Walter said, "Oh, yes," as if speaking down a long tunnel. "Very kind."

"Your vita . . ." Asha could hardly contain her anticipation. "You keep copies here?"

"In the office," Walter snapped, then softened. "May I post it to the address on your business card?"

"Sure, sure," said Bill. "The more I think about this, the more likely it sounds. We haven't had a visitor in literature for several years. If it's easier, you could send the vita over as an attachment."

Walter was feeling very sleepy. He remembered this "can do" mentality of Americans, how it used to stimulate him all those years ago. He couldn't bring himself to tell this nice Bill that he didn't have a computer, that his university hadn't discovered the joys of e-mail or the funding for it. "Post will be easiest, thanks."

As Bill's taxi pulled up, he fondly thanked Asha and Walter. "This will be great. We can invite you to dinner at our place. Martha will love meeting you."

"Thank you," answered Asha shyly.

Walter was happy to have Asha speak for them.

"And thanks again for the roses," she grinned.

After clearing up the kitchen, she joined Walter in the living room.

He was listening to Andy Williams now. "Moon River" had always been a favorite.

"So I guess I'll be wearing those skirts and dresses you like pretty soon."

"Hmmmm," Walter sighed.

"Well, aren't you excited about the chance to go back?"

Walter was engorged with sadness for the Rocky Mountains, for the Himalayas.

"Well?"

"We can't go back."

"What do you mean?"

"I don't know that postcolonial nonsense. I teach Plath, Moore, Bishop, Ginsberg . . ."

"But surely you could design some different courses, read some new books. You're always complaining about how stale you feel." She studied his face anxiously.

"Besides, Michigan isn't Montana," he said sharply. "Do you know how flat the Midwest is? Do you really think you'd be happy there after over twenty years in the Himalayan Foothills?"

"You're kidding," she said. "Gin sometimes gives you a funny sense of humor. Gin and American visitors."

"The hour is late," he sighed, grateful that soon they would be snuggled in their old bed, dreaming together.

Cocktails

PEOPLE THINK IT'S STRANGE WHEN I CALL HER MY KID SISTER. AFTER ALL, WE'RE celebrating her sixtieth birthday. The nurse counts six candles, offers her shocked congratulations before disappearing. Actually, both of us look young—fiftyish—thanks to Grandma Loretta's bone structure and somebody's genes. Even now, as June's dark hair vanishes into grey like Mary Queen of Scots.

We laugh at the nurse's reaction once the door clicks shut.

"People seem more scared of age than of death," June says, blowing out the fire, deftly removing the candles before slicing us each a large chunk of chocolate-chocolate torte.

WHEN JUNE STARTED to eat again, after the last chemo subsided, I brought brown rice and broccoli to the hospital. I know all the delis because June has traveled to Chicago for treatments, and the hospital is in my neighborhood. For three days, I brought delicious smoothies made from organic carrots.

"Stop! Stop!" she demanded. "I want jelly doughnuts, a Reuben sandwich with the fat left on, a dry martini."

June's always had a zest for life. Mom used to say, "a talent for disaster." Since I'm four years older, I was expected to be sensible and rein in my vivacious sister, walking her home from school, sitting on the aisle seat, protecting her from strangers when we took the bus to visit Auntie Eileen. And—as June got older—keeping an eye on the boys. Always gorgeous, she set her sights on a Hollywood career. And a house overlooking the Pacific.

"*DELICIOSO!*" JUNE EXCLAIMS as she digs into the birthday cake. "You've always been a wizard at finding desserts, Lucy. Remember that raspberry cheesecake you bought for my fourth wedding?"

I laugh. "I was looking for something *nontraditional.*"

"And what did you ask for this time? 'Deep-shit chocolate' for a cancer patient?" she cackles.

I love that cackle, love the bright irreverence in her eyes. I didn't always enjoy the trouble she caused, or the rescuing she expected. A shoplifting charge in ninth grade. ("Oh, Lucy, Dad will *kill* me. Could you just go to Mr. Simpson and tell him I'll *never* do it again?") Two abortions before the end of high school. Her calamities invariably occurred in winter, maybe a psychological reaction to darkness, dampness. By the time summer came, we'd talk about that year's disaster on the bus to Auntie's. From her window seat, she pointed out odd license plates, pretty farmhouses, junk-cluttered yards. Each July, I tried to believe that she was starting afresh.

"Really, Luce, you've done a star job with this birthday—the cake, the luscious satin bed jacket. When I get out of here, we'll go to Davard's—my treat—order chateaubriand and champagne."

"Sounds good," I say, aching to cheer up this sterile room. But flowers are verboten—potted or cut. "After the cord-cell transplant, they say you'll be out in three or four weeks."

She sits up straight, which I know is painful, and raises those hairless, yet wildly expressive eyebrows. "You make it sound as if I'm in prison."

"Well?"

"Prison's worse. The food. The noise. The 'toilet facilities.'"

Eighteen months for a few bad checks. She could never balance her accounts. Nothing I could do about that one. Happened right after her second husband's car crash. Nothing you can do about black ice in February. Left alone with three kids at twenty-five—that's hard on a person.

"Oh, I almost forgot." I pulled out a wrapped box from my carrier bag. "I have another present."

"You spoil me." She puts her hand on her heart, over the embossed rose on the birthday bed jacket. "Already I feel like Carole Lombard."

I had debated about the rose on the pocket—ornate and sentimental to my eye—but June was a romantic, and this was her day.

"'It's just a *wee* thing,' as Auntie would say."

"So am *I* these days." June winks. "Chemotherapy was not my choice of weight-loss programs."

She's trying too hard, which is how I know she's hurting.

"Do you need more meds? Shall I call the nurse?"

"I want my other present!" When she laughs, I see my five-year-old sister.

June rips the fancy wrapping and picks up a little mechanical toy—an egg balanced on a metal wheel, which is driven by a lever. She studies the gift. "Virtual breakfast?" Her voice is annoyed, disappointed.

"Press the lever there," I instruct.

June bursts into loud laughter as a fuzzy yellow chicken pops up from the yawning petals of the plastic egg.

"Which came first?" we ask in unison.

Auntie Eileen always sent us home with riddles, and we both took determinedly opposite positions on this one. June insisted on the chicken. I voted for the egg.

She hunches there in bed, as January flurries drift past her window, pressing the lever back and forth, back and forth. "This is good for my fine motor skills," she grins. "Much more fun than that hard rubber ball Dr. Park gave me."

———

TWO MORE ROUNDS of chemo before she'll be ready for the transplant. She ages ten years in these weeks.

Her children come to town in ones and twos. It still puzzles her why they're not closer to each other. After their topsy-turvy childhoods with different stepfathers, I'm amazed the kids are in touch. Kids? Sam is thirty-eight.

Myself, I'm relieved she has daytime visitors, because I work at the bank until five, and—well, she needs more than me.

Will is a tonic. He adores his mother. A more dubious prescription is the twins' visit the following week. Sarah and Sally have always argued, and June blames herself. If only they had been identical instead of fraternal twins, she says. Her fault as the chicken, of course. By month's end, Joel has come up from Indianapolis, and Miranda—a miniature June if there ever was one—from Los Angeles.

Finally, finally, the lab report shows that the chemo has zapped all the malignant cells. Killed quite a few healthy ones too, it seems. But June remains game. Wants me to decorate the room for "T Day."

Taking a personal leave from work, I bring in blue and green crepe paper and party hats for the collection of stuffed animals sent by kids, by friends. She insists I make a tiny hat to be worn by the chicken when it pops out of the shell.

Not much to a cord-cell transplant actually—just another plastic bag tied to the pole by her bed, dripping into one of many tubes in her perforated little body. She has shrunk even more in February. Lost muscle in her arms and legs. Her head looks as if it's getting bigger. During the kids' visits, she wore scarves. They irritated her scalp, so I told her not to bother for me. She did look more in proportion with a scarf. Anyway, she's wearing a party hat today—a dark blue cone with silver stars. A magician's hat: I thought we could use all the help we could get. The sun comes out, melting some snow around her windowsill. We decide it's a good omen. The procedure is over in half an hour; then we toast with chocolate milkshakes.

I look down at my thighs. It must be said that while she's losing weight, I've put on fifteen pounds sharing the forbidden foods of girlhood.

The next evening I find her reading a fashion magazine, a feature on bald actresses. She knows the wardrobes and biographies of people I've never heard of. "See? All I need is a little makeup, and I'll be ready for the Academy Awards."

"Well, if you recover as quickly as they're predicting, we could go to Hollywood in late March. The bank owes me vacation time. We'd get a nice motel. Visit Miranda. Go watch the stars saunter into the theatre."

"Sure, Lucy," she winks. "You book the tickets and I'll design our gowns."

I wink back. There's something in her voice—something detached that I don't like at all. Still, the days are getting longer, and as the dark winter eases away, my hope expands.

"Three birds this morning," she says, a little woozy. "What are they called? The black ones?"

"Crows? Or bigger? Ravens?"

"Never more."

"Pardon?"

"Quoth the raven . . ."

"Oh, right, your high school speech prize." Everyone had high hopes for June, with her looks and her personality and her mellifluous voice. "TV anchor," Mr. Chambers advised. "Broadway!" Mom declared. "Hollywood," decided June, heading west. As luck would have it, she stopped short of California: Milwaukee, where she was discovered by her first husband—not a movie producer, but a landscape gardener with a bad temper.

The conversations unravel like this in late February. We start talking about a news item or last night's TV soap and wind up in a fragmented memory. She needs more mental stimulation than I am capable of after work. And now that she's getting well, the kids have all returned home to their families and jobs.

"GREAT NEWS." Dr. Park comes in one evening. "All your cancer cells have been replaced by healthy cord cells."

As he talks, June dozes. "She'll be dancing in a couple of weeks."

"A good thing, too," I say playfully, "because she has a date with Tom Selleck for the Academy Awards."

Dr. Park cocks his head curiously. "Oh, yes, we'll watch for June on the TV."

A code alarm sounds in the corridor and he rushes out.

June opens one eye. "Tom Selleck? Anthony Hopkins or nothing."

"I understand Hopkins is very shy."

"They're never shy with me for long," she moues. Then coughs.

"More morphine?"

She nods. I press the buzzer for the nurse, who explained earlier today that the chemo kills natural bacteria and often provokes these throat infections, even as a person is recovering from the cancer. I shouldn't keep her talking.

While we wait for sardonic Gretchen, our favorite nurse, she picks up the chicken-egg gizmo. "Did you know that Harvey, in the seventeenth century, was the first person to speculate about the chicken and the egg in scientific literature?"

I laugh, shaking my head at her eclectic store of information.

She tries four times to press down the lever. Her face morphs from fascination to frustration. Still she tries, and finally succeeds.

June is recovering, I tell myself. Today was just a dip in energy. Soon she'll be fine, ready for the flight.

The morphine works quickly and she's snoring, head back on the pillow, mouth open an inch, right hand still clutching the chicken-egg.

I pick up a book and find myself staring at superclean hands. So strange to wash with disinfectant soap, to leave my worldly coat and briefcase in a locker before entering June's sterile environment. I feel as if I'm in astronaut training.

The book is about Chicago architecture—something my son Brendan sent, remembering how his father and I liked quiet Sunday walks among the handsome downtown buildings. He would have been as proud of Brendan as I am. Charles's heart attack ten years ago—that's my only life regret. He had so much to give, so much to enjoy. Otherwise, I've had a lucky time—luckier than June's: happy family, a steadily rising job at the bank, a nice garden. A relatively uncomplicated life. Truth is, I lack June's imagination.

I've tried to cheer up the antiseptic cell with photos of her children, pictures from our own girlhood. And the kids have come through. Miranda sent the white teddy bear, Will the silk flowers. The twins brought a good CD player. But I ache for signs of life—blossoms, a parakeet, goldfish. Outside her window, I want something besides snow and sleet and hardy crows. Yes, yes, I'm grateful for the vigilant antideath weapons—the metal stand holding IV bags, the electronic monitors. What bothers me most days is that damn erasable white board, with the names and phone numbers of me and the kids and her primary physician. It's so essentially temporary, and you know the day she leaves, they're going to get a wet cotton cloth and wipe her away. At night I fantasize about taking a pen knife and carving, "June was here."

———

ON SATURDAY MORNING, I arrive a little late. June is miffed until I tell her I have two surprises.

She tries to guess which hand they're in.

Then I show her: our plane tickets to L.A.

She looks puzzled, sits a bit straighter as if to speed blood flow to the old brain.

I wait.

"You're kidding." Her voice is incredulous, maybe a little irritated. "You're still on this Academy Awards kick. Lucy, how could I possibly?"

"Oh, we wouldn't really go to the theatre entrance—that would be too chaotic." Too contagious, I think. "But I have a reservation at a nearby motel run by Brendan's college friend. And I thought it would be fun to watch it there on TV."

Do I sound desperate, or just silly?

"Luce, honey . . ." Her eyes are wide and over-bright. Have they installed a new drug in one of the bags? "The Academy Awards are just three weeks away."

"Yes," I answer hastily. "Think of it; there we'll be, watching the program on a warm balcony, sipping martinis and—"

"No, Lucy." She shakes her shiny head.

"Oh, once you're out of here, Dr. Park wouldn't be checking your teacup any more."

She starts to protest again, then suddenly asks, "Lucy—you ever get really angry at me over the years?"

I stare at her.

June swallows and winces.

"More morphine?"

"No, I want to stay awake for this." She picks up her toy, trying unsuccessfully to roust the chicken.

I reach over to help her and realize that this is beside the point. Morphine, all these drugs impair motor coordination. The chicken will be a regular pole-vaulter by the time we get to California.

"Well, if your throat hurts, we shouldn't talk."

"But you can talk *to me.*"

"About what?"

"Anger." It's in her voice. "I must have royally pissed you off sometimes."

"That's normal sibling stuff," I try.

"No, Lucy."

"OK. Sometimes I resented all the attention you got from Mom and Dad. And how I covered up for you, bailed you out. Yeah, I got angry, occasionally. I told you then."

"And . . ."

"But that ended years ago."

"Look around," she shrugs.

"Well, this—how could I be mad at *this?*"

She stares at me. At the tickets on the nursing tray. Out the window at the snow sailing from the grey sky.

"I mean, I *am* mad about this. This cancer. This medieval medical torture. I'm bloody mad."

She holds out her hand. "So am I."

I move my chair closer, embrace my disappearing sister, and we cry together. I am surprised, relieved, by June's weeping. Then, in a ridiculous panic, I worry about these tears, about her losing bodily fluids—wonder how long it will be before my sister vanishes altogether.

Gretchen arrives with the next round of meds. "Ah, a wet weep is good for the soul, but don't soak the sheets. We only have a few more days allocated for you. Dr. Park thinks you'll be dancing down Michigan Avenue next week."

"Next week?" I ask excitedly.

"Tuesday, he predicted."

"That's wonderful, isn't it, June?"

"Yes," she smiles, fiddling with the toy.

The nurse and I watch, fixated, until she pops out the chicken.

"Next Tuesday." The small success with the lever has cheered her. "Then it's on to Hollywood for my belated screen test."

She falls asleep soon after the new morphine starts to drip. I tiptoe out. June will need new clothes—several sizes smaller—for the California trip.

———

DRIVING HOME from the dress shops, I remember I've always been impatient. Hardly the guardian angel June imagines. The truth is, if I was angry at June for anything, it was for not being the friend I wanted as a girl. And what a pain *I* must have been to her: older sister, straight shooter, successful student. The only wild thing I ever did was to drop out of Northwestern to marry Charles. Yes, well, I had hoped for more from her after Charles died. But she had several families of her own by then.

Now it looks as if we have a chance at friendship. I'm loosening up. Take the California tickets. I wouldn't have been that impetuous twenty years ago.

I almost pass the expensive florist shop near my house. Impatience makes me buy the coral lilies. Too early in the season, I know. But they'll be pretty on the oak table when she comes home. In the dining room, I arrange them in my favorite glass bowl.

SHE SLEEPS THROUGH most of the next two visits because of the throat pain and the morphine. I leaf through the magazines I've bought for her. Skim interviews with this year's nominees. Then I return to Brendan's book, think maybe I'll take a night class in architecture this fall. June might enjoy that, too. I'm hoping she'll stay on in Chicago. Certainly there's plenty of room in my old house, and June loves the garden.

The damn lilies: no matter what I do—clip the stems, change the water, add flower food, move them near the radiator, away from the radiator—they just don't open up.

One morning I awaken from a dream that the glass bowl has turned into June's bald head.

WE ARRIVE EARLY at the airport. I've always been wary about plane travel, and today especially, I want to make sure we get good seats.

The lines are interminable unless you're one of their gold-card flyers. As we wait, I chat with a student from the Art Institute who's going to L.A. for spring break.

The clerk studies both tickets. She says June needs to be right there in person to collect her boarding pass, to answer the questions about who packed her bags and has anyone given her anything to carry on.

I explain that June needs rest after a long hospital stay.

The clerk sees a woman in a wheelchair. "What the hell," she says, "she looks pretty exhausted."

I get just what I want—a window seat and the one next to it.

During boarding, the disabled passengers enter with the gold cards. I wait for our seats to be called.

Once the plane's hatch locks, I buckle a box beside me into the window seat, then toss my sweater over it.

WHEN I THINK BACK on her death, I still ache for a catharsis, an epiphany. But there wasn't much time. They phoned me at 3 A.M. I pictured the night nurse finding my name and local number on that erasable board. They said she was failing fast, from a sudden heart attack. Completely unexpected but not unprecedented. Well, leave it to June. When I arrived, the room was alive with blinking lights, whistles, beeps.

I took her hand.

She opened her eyes halfway. "Sorry, Lucy," she started.

"Hush, sweetheart. Don't talk. Your sore throat. Save your breath."

"I love you," she said.

"Oh, June, I love you, too."

And then something faint. Later, others said they couldn't catch the words. I did.

"Now you get the window seat."

⌒

WELL, MAYBE NEXT TIME. First, I'm taking June to L.A., where Sam and Miranda and I will scatter her ashes in the Pacific, as she asked in the will.

The flight attendant is taking drink orders.

"Two dry martinis—straight up, please."

"A double?"

"No—two, please. Two glasses."

"Whatever."

I lower June's tray next to mine, sighing as the martinis are served.

We are above the clouds now; sun drenches the window seat.

They Burn Witches, Don't They?

ON THE TRAIN HOME TO LONDON, I TRIED TO WORK. THERE WAS PLENTY OF LIGHT and I'd got a table to myself, but I couldn't concentrate. I turned to the newspapers, yet after a few paragraphs, found myself gazing out the window. My mind kept sweeping back to the long, eerie weekend in St. Andrews.

First off, before you get the wrong idea, let me say that I don't believe in spirits, witches, ghosts, that sort of thing. I've always been a political, pragmatic person. Working-class lass turned solicitor. Rational. Logical. No airy-fairy stuff. Yet every time I looked at this picture in the old tin frame, I wondered if Miss Mack *didn't* have some kind of supernatural powers, the way she appeared in my life on and off. Well, if she were a *spirit,* she would have been a *witch;* she was just the sort of independent woman extinguished by the *Malleus Maleficarum.* No, I reminded myself— that was all centuries past. This was the 1970s. Besides, they burn witches, don't they?

MISS MACK DIED at fifty-eight. Hypothermia. Ridiculous in our civilized society, not to say our socialized National Health Service. There was no excuse. No reason she should earn only £14 per week. No reason for her to live in such a hovel. It wasn't as if she were alone. She had a brother in Cupar and a sister right here in St. Andrews. Four or five nieces and nephews scattered around this part of Scotland. And my old friend Rosemary upstairs.

During the three-day weekend, Rosemary told me that Miss MacGregor visited her for a cup of tea every Saturday at 4 o'clock. Never more than one cup, and usually no biscuits. She didn't want to impose. She was cordial but formal like that. A cup of Queen's Blend, a nice chat about

Rosemary's current ghost story or the latest celebrity at Miss Mack's hotel, and she was usually away in forty-five minutes.

Rosemary never visited downstairs, although she would have enjoyed watching Miss Mack's TV set, or simply sharing conversation on cold, damp nights. God knows, there are enough of those murky, desolate winter midweeks in St. Andrews. Rosemary never went down, though, because if loneliness troubled Miss Mack, it also provided her with her last sacred source of control from the world which already knew too much about her. Besides, she knew the woman would be tired on weeknights. Each Sunday, Miss Mack stayed in bed all day and nursed her bronchitis, reviving herself for the following week.

Miss Mack worked ten hours a day at the Four Woods Hotel—sometimes longer if there were a tournament. All her life she was a poorly paid housekeeper, at schools and hotels. But ten hours a day for £14 a week!

This is where I came in. Those were the heady days of equal-pay consciousness, and Rosemary thought that I—as a semi-well-known activist solicitor—could threaten the management. It *would* have been a classic test case. Not only was Miss Mack being paid £6 less than the male custodian, but *he* was significantly under minimum wage. I think I could have done something for her, but she died the day before I arrived.

Rosemary said she found the body after a day of complete silence from below. Miss Mack lay in bed, huddled under the comforter. The hearth was swept clean. Her coal drawer was empty. Weather had been fierce, but she must have been pretty weak to pass in one evening like that. Of course, Rosemary had been worrying about the woman for ages.

"Oh, sweetie!" I hugged Rosemary. Searched around for cups and tea. Sat listening to her shock, her grief.

As she talked, I kept thinking that if I had only come earlier, I could have done something. (I'd been planning to visit Rosemary ever since she moved back to St. Andrews to study women spirits.) Immediately it was clear that we wouldn't have the kind of reunion I anticipated, but at least I could serve as company and some solace to my childhood friend.

After Rosemary finished the story, we went out walking. We made a strange pair—rakish and squat—me all the thinner from tension at the office, and Rosemary spread all the wider from her Fife bread. (In fact, with this new girth, she reminded me of Mags, our favorite school porter.

But we'll return to her later.) First, Rosemary took me to the street where the troubled spirit of Cardinal Beaton paces in the dark. Then we ambled down to the cathedral, where at midnight an icy hand greets yours through the graveyard wall. Then past St. Rule's Tower, from which a student jumped—or, as Rosemary insists, was pushed by a ghost—six weeks before. Together we reminisced about our old haunts, places where we conspired to escape the predictable futures of St. Leonard's girls. Yet all afternoon, we were trailed by Rosemary's memories of her spinster neighbor.

Every time we sat down for a cup of tea, Miss Mack reappeared.

Rosemary kept reminding me that she was neither old (I just cannot accept that middle-aged people die of hypothermia), nor a spinster. Fifty-eight that month, Rosemary said, and she told me all about Miss Mack's marvelous, brittle sense of humor, quick and irreverent. Her family, it seemed, were tenacious Papists since Jacobean times. And she had that Catholic passion right down to the roots of her red hair. Rosemary said that although she had grown gaunt, and her skin had paled in recent years, her hair remained the color of harvest flames. Miss Mack let go of the Church after she married. She could have used her married name—Mrs. James Anderson—because she never followed through with the divorce. Rosemary didn't know much about the story, just that the woman liked being called MacGregor, "Miss MacGregor" or "Miss Mack."

I thought I should catch up on some casework while Rosemary attended the funeral. Since my mission to help Miss Mack was moot, I could make use of the time. But Rosemary asked me to go with her. And actually, I found the story about this stranger's life and death oddly compelling.

The day was wet and windy. Many people came to pay their last respects. Mainly workers from the hotel, Rosemary whispered to me. Even the Stewarts stopped by in their Jaguar for the actual interment. Miss Mack's employers remained discreetly at the back of the crowd. Her sister wore the hundred-quid beaver coat that Miss Mack was given on her wedding day, but had later discarded in favor of a thin, green raincoat. The grave's edge was lined with plastic lawn to protect mourners from mud. A priest intoned prayers that Miss Mack had long neglected. Still, Rosemary said, the woman wouldn't have minded a religious service if it comforted her sister.

Perhaps it was the priest's sonorous formality. Perhaps it was just that the mourners were uncomfortably close to that age when such rituals become premonitions of their own funerals. Everyone seemed distracted. I noticed several people looking over their shoulders. Rosemary explained they were probably anticipating James Anderson. The golden boy still lived in St. Andrews and apparently had remained a constant, if ethereal, presence in Miss Mack's life these last twenty years. Although he didn't appear, Anderson was the main topic of conversation at tea and scones after the funeral. Perhaps people were relieved to talk about the living, Rosemary explained in a charitable disposition. On the way home, she said she was in no mood, however, to stay inside. So we went for a long walk around St. Leonard's School.

It's not something I admit often—having attended the most proper girls' academy in Scotland. I have tried to escape that henhouse everywhere from Essex to Tangier. But there are moments when I know I am indelibly a St. Leonard's girl. Like Rosemary. Perhaps that's what holds us together, despite her vegetarian mysticism and my agitprop earnestness. I shall always love Rosemary because I have seen her strength tested—against Mrs. Cowan in early-morning class after a breakfast of salty oatmeal water.

"Do you remember that confrontation with Mrs. Cowan when we were eleven?"

"Twelve," she said, as we wandered toward our old dormitory.

"I can see you now, wee Rosemary, insisting that you *had* seen the mutilated nun in the corridor. No quantity of chill glance from Mrs. Cowan could bring you to reason."

She shrugged, looking very much like the small, plump, determined girl. "I did see her. It was that simple."

I nodded. "Tell me the story again?"

"According to what *some* folk call a "legend," but is actually a true story, a beautiful young nun was lured into romantic attraction to a passing nobleman. Despite frequent invocations to the Blessed Virgin, her lust increased. As penance and protection against further temptation, she hacked up her face and chopped off her eyelids. Now she paces the damp corridors, lifting her veil to night visitors, affirming the tale."

"Right," I said, remembering how we used to whisper the horrid fable to one another before falling asleep. Actually, this is one legend I almost accepted, if only because I admire Rosemary's showdown with the dour Mrs. Cowan.

But I had advised Rosemary that it was frivolous for a talented feminist writer to waste her time writing a book about witches and spirits.

What about abortion rights and access to childcare, here at home? What about the economic struggles of women in Africa? Over the years, she just ignored my orthodox secularity, and we stuck to more earthbound conversations. But that Saturday after the interment, partially to get Rosemary's mind off Miss Mack and partially because of the funereal atmosphere, I became sentimental enough to remember my own school ghost story.

Rosemary suggested we stop for tea at a tiny caf we frequented as girls.

"Fine, fine," I said, preoccupied about how to begin this story without sounding as though I'd lost my grip.

I found us seats in a corner booth and studied the familiar menu.

"Come on, come on," Rosemary cajoled. "You promised a story."

One sip of that stewed tea and I was away. "On an afternoon, the year before I left St. Leonard's, our hall porter, Mags—you remember her, Rosemary?"

"Slightly. You were her favorite. I think because you were a scholarship girl from a home not too different from her own."

"Anyway," I shrugged, "she often popped by my room when she finished washing the floors. I did enjoy her meaty Fife language after the affected drawls of my teachers. But on this particular day, she wore a raw timidity, her face drawn pallid against the scarlet hair. She told me a story about visiting the church to light a candle in front of the Virgin for a blessing on her forthcoming wedding.

"Congratulations," I began, but she stopped me dead.

"Och no," she said fretfully. "I dinna ken, but every time I lit the candle and knelt down, it blew itself out. I looked 'round for a prankster and there was none. I looked for a draft and there was none. Finally, after six snuffs, I got up and left, putting tuppence in the poor box on the way out."

"Mags seemed to recover just in the telling, and she didn't mention the incident again before the end of the school year." I ordered another cup of tea.

Rosemary listened, rapt.

"Mags came by my room often to have a good laugh about the posh wardrobes of the rich girls. Or about men. Mags was hilarious on the subject of useless men. Was the blond, handsome bloke she had found any different? she asked herself. Worth trying out at least, she decided. And he was buying her a fur coat to keep her warm in case he left her. How odd, I thought, but just listened, as you do at that age. Mags insisted she'd be back in the autumn, as she wasn't going to be a pampered bride. When she left, I thought to ask her new name, and then realized I didn't know her maiden name. She'd always been 'Mags.' Simply 'Mags' to the girls of St. Leonard's."

"She didn't come back, though, did she?" Rosemary asked.

"I never saw her again. Except one evening, when I caught sight of a pale woman at a turning off the High Street." Even as I told the story, I trembled at this dramatic memory. "I shouted, 'Mags!' but the figure scuttled away."

As we finished our tea, I realized it wasn't much of a ghost tale—only twenty years old, the reappearance of Mags being so sketchy, all the subjects being alive—yet it distracted Rosemary momentarily from her grief as it brought forth other tales from her sizeable collection.

The cold, misty weather continued, but we were warmly dressed. She guided me around the old castle grounds, speculating on the spirits captured in the Bottle Dungeon, where men had been confined in the darkness of their gradually blinded eyes.

"What happened to the women prisoners?" I asked. "Did they burn them indiscriminately?"

"A lot of them," sighed Rosemary.

We walked out along the pier, disdainful of the passing undergraduates in their crimson robes. And, although our reunion should have been claimed by school gossip or our mutual political concerns, the conversation kept returning to the dead neighbor.

Strangely enough, I was the one who revealed Miss Mack was an alcoholic.

Her brother-in-law, Arthur, had spent Saturday afternoon clearing out the flat. First, he found a bottle of unopened wine.

Then, in the storage closet under the stairs, I discovered a sweet green sea of empty bottles. Dozens of bottles. Medium dry sherry. Neatly stacked, not one of them broken.

Everyone stood around the cache, marveling at how she could have afforded all that drink on £14 per week. Not impossible if she ate her meals at the hotel and kept the fuel box low all winter. She had no entertainment expenses. The Saturday tea was the only socializing she'd done for years. A strangely reclusive woman for someone with such a sense of humor.

"If I'd known about the drinking"—Rosemary was on the verge of tears—"I would have tried to do something."

Arthur shrugged in disgust.

Miss Mack's sister, Jean, bowed her head sadly.

Arthur, a kind-faced dockman with a Burntisland accent, told Rosemary to take her pick of Miss Mack's furniture. He said Miss Mack—or Margaret, as he called her—"would want it that way."

Upstairs, Rosemary dithered with me about whether it would be greedy to ask for the TV set. It was only a black-and-white, after all—six years old and, she understood from Miss Mack, slightly astigmatic.

On Sunday morning, we ate breakfast overlooking a bonfire.

Arthur did most of the work—piling threadbare tea towels on stacks of *Women's Own* magazines and dozens of plastic milk bottles.

Miss Mack's sister held a laundry pole and poked languidly at the flames. She roamed about the wee garden looking confused. Occasionally, Arthur came upstairs with a relic revealing something more about Miss Mack.

"An electric blanket," he declared, shaking his head. "Still in the box. Never been touched. Can you beat that? And a brass kettle that looks like it's been around for fifty or sixty years."

"At least a hundred," declared Rosemary. "My mum has been watching the auctions for something like that."

"Then why don't you take it," he said, "for all your kindness."

"Oh, I couldn't," said Rosemary. "It's worth at least forty quid."

"That's the least of it," he grunted. "She had an old oil lamp and a Chinese fire screen—family heirloom sorts of things that my wife thought were lost years ago. I don't know, maybe it's because she was adopted that she didn't pay them any mind."

"Miss Mack, adopted?" Rosemary was astonished.

"Yes, when she was a lass of nine or ten," Arthur explained, then blushed as if he'd betrayed something unsavory about his sister-in-law. "But my wife says she became just one of the family, fit right in." He leaned heavily on Rosemary's counter. "Now it's just beginning to register, how much we didn't know about her. And what we could have done if we *had* known."

We were looking down into the yard at Jean, a stocky woman blurred between fifty and sixty. She held the beaver coat close around her. Every step was a numbed drudgery as she carried a pile of cards to the pyre.

"That'll be the valentines," he told us. "She never sent them and she never let go. Lived her life half in terror, half in hope of seeing that demonic bastard on the street."

"That's one part I couldn't understand," said Rosemary. "Why didn't she move? Once she told me she was offered the head-housekeeper's job at the Caledonian in Edinburgh."

"Aye, but all she knew," he said, "her family and that, were around here in Fife."

"Surely she was a young woman when he left her," said Rosemary. "She could have started a new life."

"Instead," Arthur spat, "she froze herself to death."

After an embarrassed silence, he walked downstairs, outside to his wife, who was sitting on a turquoise vinyl kitchen chair, poking aimlessly while large paper ashes flew about, mingling with the grey in their hair.

The grief was wearing heavy on me, even though I hadn't known the poor woman. Clouds and mist had entered the flat; it was going to rain inside any minute. So I agreed with alacrity when Rosemary suggested a walk in the Boar Hills, which I hadn't visited since school.

The place still looked the same, with the exception of a few new caravans. We meandered along the stream, past small farms and hulks of flour mills and myths about vanished monasteries, walking, walking down to the ocean. Despite the bitter wind, we sat for half an hour on the beach, resting against the rocks, watching the North Sea waves.

Rosemary led us back a different way through the wheat fields to another of her ruins: a convent where all the nuns had been burned at the stake. Local villagers—with due trepidation about the penance meted out for unholy trespassing—had avoided the buildings for two centuries. Then, in recent years, some Scottish-American Masons bought the convent land for a convention center, intending to use as much of the original structure as possible. Twenty-four hours into the restoration, lightning set fire to their lumber stocks. For the next eighteen months, the Americans failed to attract local labor, and finally they deserted the project. Rosemary said the nuns had been a contemplative, agrarian order. No one had recorded the charges that brought them to the stake.

Back at the house, Jean and Arthur were piling sweaters on the fire: aqua, mauve, and orange orlon melted into each other, creating a sickening stench.

Rosemary suggested that they take a break. She would bring down tea for everyone.

"Aye," Arthur groaned. "We're nearly finished anyway. Maybe you'd like to come have a look at the furniture."

After tea, I wandered Miss Mack's flat, feeling more and more the voyeur. Yet he insisted that Miss Mack liked all of Rosemary's friends, and that I, too, should select a memento. Wind whipped through the dormer of the plain little parlor.

Jean held herself tightly in the fur coat.

We all crowded around the small grate, trying to warm ourselves on the coal fire.

Rosemary rose abruptly—determined, I guessed, to break the maudlin spell. She began to forage through the furniture.

Suddenly, she spotted a pottery jug pushed back on a high shelf. She had to stand on a kitchen chair to climb on the counter to reach the jug.

"It looks like Minton," she said, with what could have been heard as crassness but was simply astonishment. Carefully, she handed me the precious jug.

Jean nodded—out of resignation or recognition, I couldn't tell.

"Holy Mother!" exclaimed Rosemary. "It's loaded with matchbooks. 'The Ermentrude, Crammond'; "The Sea Witch, Berwick'; 'The Three Maries, Portree.'"

"Aye," nodded Arthur. "They were a queer thing to collect, all right. Especially for someone scared out of her wits about fire. That's why she couldn't be buried with the rest of the family. Refused to be cremated, you know."

His wife managed a reproving glance.

Arthur was furious now. "All right," he said. "All right for her in Cloud Cuckoo Land. But it's her family that'll have to cope with the stories. She had no need to live like this." He shook his head bitterly. "If only we had known."

We all watched him cautiously.

Jean started to cry.

He grabbed the jug from Rosemary, stepped out the front door, and tossed its contents onto the smoldering bonfire. Flames seared up from the old matchbooks for a minute or two; then the slow, steady smoking resumed.

His voice lowered. "She did that every holiday for twenty years—every February—that's the only time the hotel could spare her. She went to some damp seaside resort and played Bingo with the other old maids."

"But she wasn't an old maid," I said impulsively. "She was only fifty-eight; she was married."

"Married to the Devil," murmured Jean.

"She was separated," added Rosemary gently. "In this town, a single woman with that hanging over her head might as well be a nun or a witch for her chances of finding company. All she can do is wait to die."

"Or commit suicide!" he declared. "You can bet she did just that. Out of spite. People remember her for her quiet, wry wit, for her hard work at the hotel. But to the family, she was just a burden."

Jean shook her head, at Arthur, at Miss Mack, perhaps at both of them.

"You'll be in for a shock when you read her will in the *Citizen*," he continued. "Miss MacGregor left several thousand pounds. Have a look." He pointed his blunt finger to the table. "The bankbook is right there, next to your friend."

Rosemary removed the book from a pile of documents and photos.

I picked up a photograph in a shilling tin frame. The familiar face turned my hands to ice. Now I realized why I felt Rosemary's grief so strongly. *I* had known Miss Mack; *we both had,* in a different life.

Rosemary exclaimed over the deposits—six quid out of fourteen a week.

Jean spoke up. "Peggy was saving it against her old age. She was that afraid of being left poor and alone."

I continued to stare at my old friend.

Arthur cleared his throat. "That frame will no be worth much, but you can take it, lass, if it strikes your fancy."

"Actually," I managed, "it's the photograph."

"Oh, yes," he nodded. "That'll be the only likeness of herself she kept. She threw away the later ones we had made for her from family Christmases. In fact, she started acting so queer altogether that we stopped inviting her on holidays. Because of the children, you understand."

He reached for the photo. "She had this one taken just before the wedding. By god, she was a changed woman in recent years. See?"—he tilted out of the glare of the overhead bulb—"See, it says, 'To Jamie, all my love, Mags.'"

"Mags," I repeated numbly, turning to Rosemary. My friend was still absorbed in the amazing financial revelations.

"Yes, 'Mags'—she would never let us call her that after he left. He'd been partial to the name. Didn't want her childhood 'Peggy' either. So, she became 'Margaret' to family, 'Miss Mack' to Rosemary and other young folk, 'Miss MacGregor' at work."

Misunderstanding the look on my face, he said, "You go right ahead and take the frame for your boyfriend's photo. We'll no be wanting the picture. Heaven knows she's in the albums at home, and they provide enough unpleasant memories for poor Jean."

I slipped the picture in my handbag, meaning to show Rosemary later.

We started to shift the furniture.

Arthur took the TV set to an old people's home.

Rosemary got the jug and the kettle.

Suddenly noticing the time, I made a quick farewell to everyone and raced to catch my train.

ON THE RIDE HOME, I tried to work out a way to tell Rosemary that Miss Mack was our Mags, from school. But I knew that this would make her feel worse, and Rosemary was always a sensitive soul, given to self-recrimination. By the time I reached King's Cross, I realized this wasn't her sort of ghost story. She mightn't even believe it—because they burn witches, don't they?

All the Way

The self-defined, astride the created will . . .
At worst one is in motion; and at best,
Reaching no absolute in which to rest,
One is always nearer by not keeping still.
                        —*Thom Gunn, "On The Move"*

WILD PURPLE ORCHID, VIBRANT GERANIUM, WHITE AND PINK HAWTHORN, unruly bushes of valerian. Ahead, our lane is misty, spring fragrant. Mid-May, yet redolent soot thickens afternoon air. Coal fires are outlawed now, unless you win a dispensation for your ancient stove. So much has changed. England truly has become a green *and pleasant* land, with the welcome comforts of central heating, good European wines, and sunny Mediterranean veg on every high street.

I enjoy coming back here, and I'm grateful to my grad school friends—Lisa, Theodore, and Muriel—for providing the excuse. Long ago, the four of us bonded under Dr. Nigel Jeffrey's goodwilled and absent-minded tutelage. Despite Professor Jeffrey's inattention to registrar requirements, and with the grace of his generous mind, we all achieved good degrees in British literature. But we were young adventurers and ignored Dr. Jeffrey's scholarly trajectory.

This coastal path through Cornwall has long been a dream of mine. Pirates. Mermaids. Shipwrecks. Nothing that romantic so far, but we have walked on sandy beaches and rugged cliffs. We've struggled through brambles and blackthorn. Theodore has lectured us about the declining Cornish economy, the debilitating downturn in fishing, tin mining, granite quarrying. I keep expecting to spy Eeyore in the gorse. Instead, I glimpse the occasional stand of yellow daffodils and narcissus.

Muriel and Theodore taught in Zambia for fifteen years after grad school. Lisa went back to Toronto, got interested in bodywork, and became an inspired massage therapist. I returned to Oakland, took a job at Laney Community College, where I abandoned Chaucer to teach remedial writing. For a while we lost touch, but five years ago, when Theodore and Muriel returned from Lusaka to teach at Exeter University, we began these annual walking trips.

The first reunion took us back to the South Downs, near Sussex, where we excavated graduate school memories and took a detour to visit Dr. Jeffrey, happily retired to his cluttered library overlooking the sea. Having rediscovered each other's company, we spent subsequent summers on uncommon ground—Oregon's high desert, James Bay in Canada, the mountains of Northern Scotland. This year, it is the Cornish coast. Each trip has two requirements: we walk a lot during the day, and we have a splashy dinner each night. Lisa, who recently started writing a food column for *Toronto Today,* is our infallible diviner of restaurants.

Last night, in the dining room of our small harborside hotel, we ate looking out on fishing boats, gray stone houses, and a large white building with a thatched roof. Virginia Woolf set *To the Lighthouse* in Cornwall, I recalled. We listened to moaning foghorns and barking seals. Barbara Hepworth created some of her wide-eyed, huge-hearted sculptures here.

Sussex stole my cultural virginity: there, I recognized my deep provincialism and grew interested in history before 1492. Eagerly, I practiced being a real English person before accepting myself as indelibly American. But a different kind of American now. With Theodore, Muriel, and Lisa, I traveled through Europe and the Middle East. Each of us discovered something vital about ourselves in each other's potential. We were tied together by a sibling resistance/submission to the authorities of our generation. We smoked our first pot together, saw our first opera, danced to the new music of reggae.

Muriel has been promising mountains all morning—mountains and the seventh-century priory by the sea, a shrine to St. Francis of Genoa. That's where Theodore and Muriel were married after Lisa and I returned to opposite ends of North America. We have come to Cornwall this year for the coastal path, for the priory, and for their marriage, which is show-ing some strain—although being authentic English people, neither men-tions the trouble. Their interests have shifted, creating huge questions about where and how to live. Theodore, now permanently drifted from lit-erature to history, is tied to Southern England for his research. Muriel aches to travel, to explore the larger world to which our once-restless Theodore introduced her.

I almost went to Zambia with Theodore, but Muriel married him instead. You might think it strange to go on a second honeymoon with your former boyfriend and the roommate who stole him, but over time I've grown very happy with my life in California. Lisa worries about me, says I should find a good partner, like her love, Marilyn. Muriel also scolds that I don't have to be alone. But I'm hardly alone. I adore the sweet nephews I raised after my sister died. I have close friends. And my students. Once I decided that I preferred teaching to scholarship, I began to love my life. Now that the boys are grown, I relish the freedom to walk around the apartment singing loudly, bothering no one. How ironic—Muriel worry-ing about my singleness while I fret about her marriage. During the last couple of days, I've sensed that Muriel is expecting something significant from this visit to St. Francis's shrine.

It has to be said that Muriel believes in God. She expects their mar-riage to be renewed by a return to the priory. All morning, she has been reminiscing about the healing well next to the church, the sarcophagus of St. Francis on the right side of the sanctuary, the handsome altar of pol-ished local granite, the beautifully groomed graveyard. It's a little creepy how many small details Muriel has retained.

She also recalls the woman caretaker who lives next door in the former manse. A holy woman, Muriel says, who listens for the voice of St. Francis every night. Twenty years ago, she urged the newlyweds to come back and visit. Now Muriel hopes that the woman—who would be in her mid-sev-enties—is still alive.

If Muriel carries heavy expectations, Theodore is relatively carefree, savoring this ramble in the sweet Cornish countryside. The mind of our ragged, middle-aged academic is on history of a more ancient sort. Or on birds. Chewing wild mint, he names them: razorbills, kittiwakes, shags, guillemots. Lisa says he is beginning to look just like Dr. Jeffrey.

Fog still, on our third day. I listen to the sea below, swelling, crashing against an invisible beach. Here we are, on the edge of an ocean which separates my two lives. Plymouth is just sixty miles along the coast. I picture the *Mayflower* sailing tentatively toward the Atlantic, pilgrims reluctant to leave behind that last glimpse of land, but bravely proceeding through a gray unknown. Sailing, bobbing, rocking, day after day, ignited with faith, guided by Providence. Me, I believe in luck, not providence, and know they're not the same thing.

Muriel and Theodore are in the lead. From this distance of five yards, they might be the newlyweds of twenty years before. Slim, dark-haired, gregarious people. Their jeans are slightly looser these days, their windbreakers brighter in dramatic turquoise and purple. (What *was* the attraction of that seventies army-surplus gear—drab yellowy greens and browns?) Perhaps a flattering contrast to the natural plumage of our youth. Today, Theodore wears an expensive camera around his neck, and Lisa carries a nifty set of miniature binoculars, but they are unmistakably my old friends. The very same people.

"The mountains should be just over there," Muriel calls back to us. "They're jagged, three peaks, heavily forested," she continues, as if guiding the sightless, which—given the fog—we are.

"St. Francis climbed those mountains barefoot for penance every spring." She drops back, talking to Lisa and me.

Now penance is one expression of humility I've never understood. In my eight-cylinder Catholic childhood, I preferred good works to suffering-for-the-sake-of-it, and always thought there was something sadomasochistic about all those crucifixes. So many useful ways to subsume your ego—bandaging the wounded, mopping up after floods, chopping vegetables in a soup kitchen. What a waste of a good able body to walk up a mountain barefoot.

"There's a wild rose that grows up there," Muriel explains. "White, with a speckled red center. They've named it Francesca."

God forbid a male rose—Frank or Franco or Frankie? I tell myself to cut the sarcasm. This place is important to Muriel, also to Theodore.

"How do you know all this?" I ask.

"We learned a lot that first time; Theodore was a history buff even then." She peers toward the invisible mountains. "And last year, I read a great book about the village."

Muriel describes the area's development by the Brythonic Celts, who went to Cornwall, Wales, and Brittany in contrast to the Goidelic Celts, who settled Scotland and Ireland. Celtic saints, she explained, held closer to early, communal notions of Christianity. The representative from Rome brought hierarchy, bureaucracy, institution.

"That's why St. Francis was beloved. Unlike the other Vatican emissaries, he respected local culture and practice."

St. Francis of Genoa. Why have I never heard of him? It's vaguely frightening at my age to come across a new saint.

Birds caw and honk from a near distance, perhaps perched on a small rock island or promontory. Gulls and cormorants, most likely. I love to watch the black and white dance of those shore birds. Through the fog, I try to imagine it now.

Tonight, we follow Lisa to Smuggler's Cove, dressed in our slightly-better-than-hiking-gear dinner attire. The charitable description is that we look clean, but a little wrinkled. Each woman wears black, accented by a scarf or necklace. Theodore sports a red Aran sweater. Lisa has a talent for finding chefs who combine artistry, "health consciousness," and just enough self-indulgence. We have nothing to worry about (in this case nothing to gain rather than nothing to lose) because we will walk off potatoes and lamb and chocolate tomorrow. It's as if dinner is the reward for walking. And walking—particularly in the lusciously fresh mornings—is a pleasurable recompense for eating.

At Smuggler's Cove, we find a corner table with a view of the sea—a potential view, for the night is misty. The bottle of Australian Sauvignon Blanc makes a promising start. Lisa recommends their special: crayfish served with boiled red new potatoes, and leeks lightly braised in garlic and ginger. I follow her suggestion. Muriel wants grilled bream. For the third night in a row, Theodore asks for crab.

"When I discover a good thing, I stick with it." He winks lovingly at Muriel.

Muriel changes the subject. "I don't suppose early pilgrims ate very well."

"Depends on what you mean by well," Lisa answers, biting into a butterless hunk of sourdough rye baguette. "Probably not so fancy, but I'm sure they enjoyed themselves. People generally bring bodies on pilgrimages.

Not all those travelers were ascetic. Think of the Wife of Bath . . ."

"Right," Theodore laughs, pouring everyone a second glass of wine. "Depends what you mean by pilgrims. You think those sultans from Qatar and Kuwait and Dubai leave their silver teapots behind on the way to Mecca?"

"And," Lisa adds, "Richard the Lionhearted brought his chef along on the Crusades."

"You wouldn't call the Crusaders pilgrims, would you?" I ask.

Muriel nods. "Raping and pillaging aren't exactly spiritual practices."

"One person's pilgrimage is another's invasion," I point out. "The Indians learned that once those nice, pious people disembarked from the *Mayflower.*"

"All pilgrims are after something." Theodore gulps his wine.

"Theodore, that's so crude," Muriel says. "What about Fatima? Lourdes?"

"Yes, there too." He leans toward his wife seriously. "Supplicants ask to be delivered from arthritis, tuberculosis, cancer. They pray for an end to Communism. All pilgrims want something."

"Leeks braised in garlic and ginger." I swerve the conversation to safety. "Remember our grad school dinners—beans on toast?"

"Chips on chips," Lisa grimaces, "garnished with vinegar and salt."

But Muriel won't let go. "Maybe Theodore's right. Don't we all want something from this trip?"

"Well, I don't know about you lot," Theodore says abruptly, "but I want my dinner."

At this point our lithe waiter, far more elegant than any of his guests, appears with four beautiful steaming plates.

We all admire the individual and collective "presentation." Our appreciative silence is a sort of nouveau grace. Are middle-aged people drawn to food the way young people are drawn to sex? Is there more god in food, or in sex?

Theodore orders another bottle of wine.

"So, what's the plan for tomorrow?" Lisa wants to know.

"We'll make it to the priory before lunch?" I ask, incredulous how eating has become a major preoccupation.

"Oh, no, it's at least six hours to St. Francis's," answers Theodore.

"Five or six," says Muriel.

"Definitely post-lunch, then," decides Lisa. "On the way, there's a nice little pub—sixteenth century. Local ale on tap. And I've read they do a lovely smoked eel."

We all laugh—at Lisa, at our appetites, at the reprieve from examining the purpose of this pilgrimage.

Next afternoon, the fog gets dangerous. Our path closely skirts the cliff, and it would be so easy to lose footing. But we stick to this trail because hikers have been eroding the land by walking cross-country. I watch Theodore's wobbly gait and wish he hadn't ordered that second pint at lunch. Of course, he's a grown man, and I should mind my own business. So I think back on the sturdy ceiling beams in Lisa's pub. The others pronounced the eel delicious. I took their word for it, thoroughly enjoying my Stilton salad.

I'm not cold this afternoon, despite the mist. The air is warm, propitious; our pilgrimage feels dreamlike in this vaguely etched landscape. We have lapsed into companionable silence, and my mind returns to last night's conversation about purpose. Somehow traveling (planning, remembering, as well as actually journeying) promises to make me a fuller person, part of a larger world. But I also wonder if I'm caught in an unalterable rhythm, moving continually, going nowhere. Has travel become a habit? Of course, there are good reasons to go specific places—as Lisa and I did to study English literature in England. As Muriel and Theodore did, to take skills to a developing country. On this trip, Lisa is writing her food articles. Theodore is researching his book. Muriel is saving her marriage. And me? I don't know. I have no goal. No gift. No god.

Adjusting my pack, I walk faster. At breakfast this morning, we troubled the line between being a traveler and being a tourist, concluding that the difference was one of depth. (Tourists skimmed the surface, Lisa said, and brought back trophies, souvenirs. Travelers made progress, Muriel decided, had adventures, asked questions, started friendships, returned with intentions.) Travel. Travail, I think now. Yes, it has some thing to do with effort, with work, with learning. It's easier to be surprised in a foreign place, to have your assumptions shaken. Perhaps easier to locate an essence of self when dislocated from the familiar.

This is what Muriel wants for Theodore. She isn't traveling for herself (to revisit the church or to find the holy woman), but rather to reawaken

Theodore's sense of adventure. How tricky; he wants to settle down, just as she's found momentum. Muriel expects Theodore to remain the peripatetic man she married, and Theodore wants a middle-aged wife to join him tilling their abundant garden.

I understand them both. If I were a true friend, I would wish that each got what was necessary. But I don't want them to split up. I want them to be Muriel and Theodore as they have been for twenty years.

"Damn, damn mist," Muriel says. "It could be so beautiful: the foothills, the mountains. Acres of ferns. A forest leading up to the summit."

"Pretty this way, too," Lisa says sincerely. A North American, she has no need of miniature British mountains. "And the air is so soft. Great for your skin."

"Here," I call, pulling out my camera. "We'll take a picture of this place. Maybe you'll finally see how lovely it is when you're leafing through the photos back in Exeter."

An old man appears, followed by an adolescent boy, walking the path from the opposite direction. Courteously, they hang back so I can snap the picture. We haven't met many people on the trail, because May is too misty for timid hikers.

"I don't know," Theodore teases. "Is this a tourist's snapshot or a traveler's record?"

My friends arrange themselves. Fiddling with the camera, I realize I can't get in all the background with the strangers waiting there. So I wave them to pass. What's the point of having a group portrait with other people in it? Of course, Chaucer adjusted the record: there were other people on that road to Canterbury he edited out. He made up the whole thing.

As they pass in front of us, Muriel asks, "This is the way to the Priory of St. Francis, isn't it?"

I stare at her. We checked Theodore's Ordnance Survey map just five minutes before. Is she losing faith?

"Yes, yes." The boy stops. He looks at her with pale blue eyes. "Just along the path. Perhaps a kilometer further."

For some reason, I glance after his companion—a bald man in a brown coat who has moved down the trail, almost out of sight.

Merrily, Theodore, Muriel, and Lisa wave to the young wayfarer and then pose themselves artfully on the side of the trail. After my shot,

Theodore hands me his elaborate camera. Unfamiliar with it, I take a while to find the focus. Once I do, I see my three old friends lolling together on the side of a mountain. Click.

A jagged, heavily forested mountain.

"The sun!" exclaims Muriel, swiveling around. "How wonderful. The mountains. At last!"

Yes, much as she has described them. Gracefully formidable, a landscape of green and brownish pastureland. Old mountains. You can tell by their rounded shoulders. And above them, mist rising to reveal a bluing sky.

In the near distance, off the trailside, stands a Celtic cross—round head on a skirted body. I love the pagan shapeliness of these crosses—half human, half god, strong graven images.

"Not far now!" Theodore says excitedly. "Remember, we took this path—from the other direction—the day before the wedding?"

"Yes." Muriel is almost inaudible. "I said farewell to my single life here."

Lisa busily identifies the newly visible flowers.

Bluebells.

Bell heather.

Wild yellow iris.

Under sun, this is a different country—crisp, cheerful, textured. I lag behind, aware I don't want to reach our destination. This is what we came for—the promise. Here we are in the sunshine, surrounded by Muriel's mountains, Lisa's flowers, Theodore's birds. The rest is unnecessary, a possible disappointment—or something worse.

Lisa, Muriel, and Theodore fairly prance onward. Sun casts its propagating shadows, so that ahead of them walk three additional pilgrims—larger, darker, ghostly disciples of St. Francis.

The small stone church is a miraculously preserved pre-Norman building. Lisa inspects an ivy-covered well. Muriel guides us around the well-tended graveyard. A modest manse, seventeenth or eighteenth century, stands just outside the church gates. Discreetly, Muriel scans the windows for sight of her holy woman.

Conducting us to a tall, cylindrical building, Theodore explains this is a dovecote—or *ducut* in Scotland. I've never seen anything like it. Inside the ancient stone structure are dozens of cubby holes where doves nested. An abandoned post office, with letter boxes vacant for centuries.

"How did they use them?" Lisa wants to know. "Did the doves serve as carrier pigeons? Pets?"

"They were food," he answers abruptly, in a voice I have come to identify as "male shocking female with brutal reality." Brothers talk like this to sisters. Cowboys to saloon girls. But I've rarely heard this side of Theodore.

"How did they catch them?" I wonder. "Bows and arrows? It was too early for shotguns."

"See that rope there?" nods Theodore.

I can hear him explaining these cold facts to his bride twenty years before. Lisa and I nod. Muriel has disappeared.

"They'd tie a large stone on the end and swing it around in a spiral. Then they'd make a noise and the birds would flutter around. Some would get knocked to the ground; they were dinner."

A semivegetarian, I understand why my preference in monks has always run to the Buddhist variety.

I should join anxious Muriel in the church. First, though, I'm drawn back to the graveyard. Time has worn names off most of the pocked granite headstones. Some are still readable—"Robert Harrison, Beloved Husband of Verity. Father of Thomas and Samuel. 1737." "Margaret Ann Fraser, Devoted Wife. 1865." I remember Dante's visit with the shades, and I want to ask Robert Harrison and Margaret Ann Fraser just how devoted, how beloved, they felt in life.

Inside, the ancient church reveals centuries of wear and repair and accommodation. An Elizabethan altar rail. Seventeenth-century baptismal font. Bright Victorian stained-glass windows, almost cartoon-like in their color. The sarcophagus of St. Francis rests against a wall at the right of the sanctuary. On the left, under rainbow light washing in from a high window, is the simple statue of St. Francis. He looks almost contemporary, somehow familiar, and I remember my sixth-grade holy card collection— serene saints holding crucifixes and spiked wheels, surrounded by flowers or birds. Francis is represented here in a dark brown cloak, shiny head, enigmatic smile, open palms, bare feet. Beneath the statue, a large glass vase offers sprays of red and white roses.

I can only take so much holy before I start to feel closed in. I have to get away before one of the statue's blue eyes winks at me. Yes, I do retain some childhood delight in the elaborate: sheen of gold vessels, splash of vivid vestments, secretive aroma of incense. But if I stay too long, the guilt and fear of an overserious Catholic girlhood will suffocate me. I might as well be in the ground with those old bones of Robert Harrison and Margaret Ann Fraser.

Muriel, head bowed, kneels at the altar rail.

Theodore and Lisa, having made an even quicker tour than I, are already out the sacristy door, standing on the stone steps, chatting in the benevolent sunshine. I join them.

"Oh."

The three of us turn toward a handsome woman, holding a dog.

"Good afternoon," Theodore greets her cordially.

"Hi," Lisa says, "Are you the caretaker?"

Muriel will be so disappointed that her holy woman has gone. Probably we trod over her grave this afternoon. She won't appreciate this stylish replacement in her turquoise jacket and skirt, carefully made-up with mascara and a flattering shade of rose lipstick.

Gently, she sets down the long-haired dachshund.

"This is Maggio," she says—then, laughing at herself, adds, "And I'm Mary Eglantine."

We introduce ourselves.

"I'm not really a caretaker. Don't do much. Just freshen the flowers, open and shut the church."

"Oh, if you're closing up, I'll get my wife."

"No, it's fine. Nice to see people using the place. We've had so few visitors this week, because of the fog."

"We saw a boy and an old man on the trail," says Lisa.

"Yes, of course, they come every day."

Muriel joins the circle.

Mary Eglantine describes how she has grown up here, how her father was the parish's last regular pastor. "I used to pick mushrooms as I walked across that hill to school. And berries on the way home."

Muriel stares at the stranger; then her face lights up. "Do you, did you, have an older sister, who was caretaker before you?"

Mary looks puzzled. "No, I was an only child, I'm afraid. And, as I was telling the others, after Father died, I stayed on here alone—well, with Maggio's mother and now Maggio, and of course with St. Francis—for twenty-five years." She fingers a red and white enamel rose pendant, hanging from a gold chain.

Staring closely, Muriel inquires, "You never married?"

If Mary is taken aback by this rather un-English question, she reveals nothing beyond a rueful smile. "No."

"And you've been tending the church alone?" Muriel persists.

Mary nods, then asks, perhaps to elude Muriel's intensity, "Are you two American?"

"I'm Canadian," Lisa says quickly.

"I'm from the U.S.," I nod.

"You wouldn't be from Hoboken by any chance?"

"Hoboken . . ." I pause. "New Jersey? No, I live in California. Why Hoboken?"

"Well, the voice passed on last night, and I was rather hoping for someone from Hoboken."

I glance from Mary to Muriel and back again. Holy, holy, holy, let's get out of here.

"Oh, The Voice, right!" Theodore exclaims.

My allergy to the mystical is really kicking in.

Theodore interprets. "Frank Sinatra died yesterday. I saw the *Guardian* headline."

"Oh, yes." Mary blinks back tears. "When I was growing up, he was my idol—ever since the Tommy Dorsey days. Those eyes. That smile. I bought every record. Then he went into films. *Reveille with Beverly, Till Clouds Roll By, On the Town.*" She takes a deep breath. "And my favorite, *From Here to Eternity.* I must have seen that five times."

Politely, Theodore keeps pace. "I understand he was called 'The Master of Timing.'"

"Absolutely," she declares. "And nowhere was this more obvious than on a live stage. I had the thrill of my life twenty years ago. Took a train to London and heard him at the Palladium."

"That must have been something." Theodore nods intently, perhaps to distract Mary Eglantine from Muriel's baffled face.

"Wonderful, beautiful. Although he deserved better than that Palladium dump. And London—suffice it to say, I've never felt the need to return to that filthy place."

"This must be a sad day for you," Lisa murmurs.

Muriel has turned back toward the church. Perhaps to compose herself, perhaps to rage at whatever gods remain for her.

"Indeed. But really, last night was the hardest. Getting the news over the radio all alone—well, with Maggio of course, but no one else to talk to."

I hope Muriel is all right; I'm afraid to look at her.

"But do you know what I did? Well, it was a warm night—unusually warm, despite the mist. So I came out here and sang. Yes, I sang 'Fly Me to the Moon,' at the top of my lungs."

Lisa is kneeling on the paving stones, scratching Maggio's tummy as she listens.

"You can do that sort of thing out here," Mary smiles. "No one around for ten kilometers."

I gather courage to glance at Muriel and I find her looking at Theodore.

Lisa hums "Fly Me to the Moon" quietly to Maggio.

Looking *into* Theodore. Wife and husband bathed in each other's grins, arms comfortably around one another.

Clearly we are all charmed by Mary. Charmed to speechlessness, but no matter. Mary has saved up her conversation for the pilgrims.

("What a lovely story," I can hear Muriel say over the lobster bisque tonight.)

Mary Eglantine notices that I am the only one still making eye contact, and she puts a hand on my shoulder as she continues, confidentially: "Singing is a kind of prayer, I've always believed. I sang 'In the Wee Small Hours of the Morning,' and that made it a little easier."

I am smiling now, happy to be here with my friends and Maggio and the caretaker. I'm on the verge of asking Mary Eglantine if she would give us a rendition of "Strangers in the Night."

The Fall

YOU'RE TELLING A JOKE TO YOUR NEW FRIEND, SUDHA, WHEN SUDDENLY you are down on the pavement. From here, Delhi feels like an enchanted world, blinking and swirling and beeping around you. Horns. Voices. Music. Swish, swish—colorful saris. Down here you are a noncombatant. For the first time in three months, you realize you're exhausted.

"Oh, dear, are you hurt?" cries Sudha, extending her hand. The glass bangles tinkle, like cool water trickling down her arm.

"Sorry. Yes. A little," you mutter, rising tentatively. The right foot is fine. The left clearly sprained. Please god not broken.

"Can you make it to Chitra's place? We're almost there." Sudha is kind and practical. One minute of lying on the pavement is OK, but more time would be pressing our luck on this hectic crossroad of commerce and transport.

"Thanks, I'm fine." So American, you think: *Can do.* Nope, can't do everything, you realize, hobbling alongside her, trying to summon up the punch line from before the fall.

Inside the small apartment, fragrant with dinner spices, Chitra offers ice for your foot, vodka for your nerves. Then she serves delicious *dahl* and *raita* and *brinjal* and *sag paneer.* Soon you are laughing. You have forgotten the foot. Almost. As for your poise, you released that years ago. Poise and pride don't travel well.

Together, the three of you gossip hilariously about certain mutual colleagues at the Center. You eat more than you imagined possible. The evening is *that* delicious.

Next morning, they each phone, within five minutes of one another. "We are going to the doctor."

Ah—you thought you'd carried it off last night, wincing only when you ducked into the taxi.

———

THE THREE OF YOU sit on beige plastic chairs beneath languid ceiling fans in a storefront chemist's shop.

Also waiting are an elderly grey-skinned woman, two thin men who look as if they share the same headache, and a pregnant teenager. Passersby carry shopping and laundry and long garlands of sunny marigolds. Each patient spends about five minutes with the doctor.

Meanwhile, Chitra and Sudha chat about taking you to India Gate when you are well, to a dance performance at Treveni Kala Sangam. Each of them apologizes for Delhi's every-which-way pavement.

"No," you declare. "This could have happened in Paris or New York. I'm just a klutz."

A *klutz?*" puzzles Sudha.

The doctor appears in a beige cotton coat. He nods directly to you. "Please, this way."

You're grateful for his good English because your Hindi is still about as clumsy as your walking.

Sitting across from the perspiring middle-aged man in his closet-sized office, you watch a gecko climbing over a two-year-old wall calendar bearing an attractive picture of throbbing blue Krishna. The trash container is an old cardboard box.

Dr. Kapur invites you to sit on the examining table, on the same sheet used by the previous graying, sore, aching, pregnant patients today—and for who knows how many weeks before. You think about the HMO clinic in Dayton—colorful mobiles hanging from the ceilings, the racks of news magazines, the diverting aquarium. Where would Dr. Kapur put an aquarium?

With exquisite tenderness, he examines your foot, clearly familiar with the universal order of cartilage, bones, tendons. You would trust this quiet man with brain surgery. Well, maybe in a different building.

"Nothing broken," he almost smiles, and scrawls a prescription. "Anti-inflammatory cream," he advises. "And an Ace bandage."

In Dayton, they would have insisted on an x-ray. You'd be driving all over the city with one good foot. Waiting for hours. Filling out insurance forms. His consultation costs $1.15. The prescribed cream is ten cents.

As you leave, Chitra and Sudha are relieved, but still solicitous.

You wish you could recall the punch line to yesterday's joke; that would reassure them that now you really are OK.

The plastic chairs are claimed by new patient patients.

———

MONDAY, YOU LIMP around work in your bright pink Ace bandage. Alarmed people ask what happened.

They apologize for the shocking state of New Delhi sidewalks.

Colleagues—even the ones you were catty about the other night— squabble over who will carry your briefcase down the long dark corridors and up the flights of broken stairs.

You think back to the shiny, convenient offices at home, where safe, efficient elevators open to brightly lit hallways. And you wonder if you have to go back.

Three Women by the River, at One Time or Another

ELSIE JOY PIPER, AGED 24, FROM SOUTHERN OHIO. YOU CAN TELL BY HER MIDDLE name that they expected something from her, for her. In the 1870s, that might've been finishing high school. Or becoming a milliner. But for Elsie Joy, it meant marrying Nelson Piper and heading West on the Oregon Trail.

Maria Lourdes Ortega. *Her* middle name predicted miracles. I love the Spanish pronunciation—"Lourdes"—with its round and cornered letters. Richer than the brusque French "Lourdes," where the liquid of the first syllable dries out in the quick exit of the second. I suspect Maria Lourdes was the first park ranger in her family. The newspapers last week didn't say that, but I'm fairly certain.

Patricia Helen Buckley. Helen, of course, means "light." Not sure if my nursing brightens the ICU; there's a lot of competition from those blinking colored balls. But light needs fuel, so I enjoy these weekend trips to state parks—sometimes camping overnight, sometimes, like today, just picnicking and poking around.

Elsie Joy Piper, 1850–1875, passed on giving birth to her daughter, Eleanor Ruth Piper. Right here on this riverbank in Idaho. You can't tell me that child had an easy life: Ruth, the follower. But it's really for Elsie Joy I'm here, and for Maria Lourdes. I've read about each of them.

Three bullets in Maria Lourdes's beautiful head. A sniper disappeared into the brush. One of a series of female park ranger homicides in the tri-state area, according to the article—the suspect a tall, bearded white male between twenty and forty. (Maybe poor, grief-stricken Mr. Piper stayed behind to haunt his wife's grave all these years?) The newspaper and radio keep warning women not to visit the park alone.

Cheerful, bright afternoon—the dry air welcoming after a rainy May that seeped into too much of June. Unusually wet for the high desert. Peaceful here at a picnic table by the river. Silent, except for the electrical sizzle of bees and the drilling of hummers around the pungent sage. Those flowers look blue or lavender to me, not really *purple,* but perhaps Western myth requires *purple* sage. I'd like to ask Maria Lourdes.

I unpack my turkey on high-fiber bread and a bag of midget carrots. Maria Lourdes probably never had to worry about weight, running around acres of parkland all day. Her specialty was rare desert plants. The Sunday paper said she liked long-distance bicycle holidays. And Elsie Joy probably ate what she could get—whatever dried meats remained from Ohio, whatever her husband Nelson could shoot or trap.

EARLY THIS MORNING, when I drive into the park, the director of the little Oregon Trail museum here is surprised to see me. They haven't had many visitors since the shooting. She assures me the exhibit room is safe, that the Park Service has sent an armed guard. The lady asks if I'm an historian, and I say yes. Several years ago, I learned that they let historians into secret rooms in these regional museums, then show you documents, journals, letters. So I've had a wide-ranging career teaching at Vanderbilt, the University of Colorado, and—why not—Berkeley.

She presents Elsie Joy's diary, a red leather-bound book with yellowing pages. I must sit there two hours reading about the farewells in Cincinnati, the exciting first week of their trip, group calamities of broken wheels and sick children and fierce weather. Their journey west went much slower than expected. Elsie Joy never dreamed of giving birth until they were safely in Oregon. I wonder what new world she anticipated. Did she believe the ocean would really be pacific? Had she heard about the giant trees? Did she reckon the edge of the continent was some kind of culmination? Elsie Joy's keen eye is evident in her descriptions of elk, buffalo, wolf, bear, heron, and flowers for which she had no names. In another life, she might have been Maria Lourdes Ortega.

Finishing up in the museum and promising the director—another Patricia—to send a copy of my article, I collect my backpack and head down toward the river. Patricia comes running after me, heaving with warning about last week's sniper. Perhaps she forgets we discussed him when I arrived. The murder of her friend Maria Lourdes has traumatized her.

Respectfully, I listen, then say I'll be fine—that I'm meeting friends at the river for lunch.

Patricia looks around doubtfully.

"They're late," I shrug.

A van full of visitors pulls up, and excited, she excuses herself to greet them.

———

THESE SANDWICHES AREN'T BAD if you add tomato and a wave of mustard. The carrots are sweet and crunchy. I raise my water bottle to Elsie Joy and Maria Lourdes. Like Patricia, they're worried about my being there. Alone.

"But I'm not alone," I grin.

Maria Lourdes laughs.

She understands, I think, why I've come.

"So you know all about *us*." Maria reaches for my water, takes a swig. "What's your story?"

"Next time," I say, looking at my watch and calculating the drive back to Twin Falls.

Elsie Joy tries again: "This is not a safe place."

"We'll change things," I say, wondering why the blood coursing through my veins grants me any special wisdom or power.

They watch me.

"We'll change things," I repeat.

That's something all three of us have believed at one time or another.

Vital Signs

THEY ARRIVED IN THE FULL HEAT OF A LATE AUGUST MORNING, HIGH-SPIRITED children released from an overlong car journey. Matsuda navigated the turquoise Camaro swiftly along the dirt road, and they alighted in a cloud of golden dust. Felipe first—Felipe always first—bouncing toward me, grinning in his campy, flirty, I-know-you'll-always-love-me way.

He was right about that love, but I practiced dignified affront. "Fourteen hours late?" I called archly. After all, it was my fiftieth birthday, and this celebratory weekend with best friends had been shortened half a day because—well, I could just guess—because Felipe was late for a dead-line. Or he forgot to pick up his special birthday shirt from the cleaners.

He won, of course—right arm around my waist, the other switching sun hats with me—cooing, "I get to try on the crown, don't I? Since my birthday is in a couple of weeks. I have to see if I like being fifty!"

"And if you don't?" I laughed between his kisses.

"Hey, hey," called Eleanor, extricating her long legs from the back seat with Hepburnesque grace. "You can't start the party without us." She looked especially trim in her white T-shirt and little red shorts. In my next life, I resolved, I would be lanky.

"That's right," Greg grumbled, combing sweaty black curls behind his ears. "We may have traveled economy, but we count too." How had they persuaded Greg, who always got carsick, to sit in the back?

Matsuda, Felipe's new boyfriend, stood by the purring Camaro, watching us curiously. A red baseball cap shaded his eyes, a long dark ponytail looped over the back strap.

I hadn't seen my friends for six months. Now that we lived in different parts of the country, at each reunion I found myself looking cautiously for evidence of aging. Yes, I was a little obsessive; fifty was still young these days. Young middle age. These people—"The Symposium," Felipe mockingly named us years ago—meant more to me than anyone in my life. The Symposium and my partner, Victoria.

We had met in our late twenties, seasoned citizens of a troubled world we were determined to change by teaching in the Oakland high schools. All of us were active in our union, but we each wanted more than that— a place where we could talk about issues personally, worry out ethical questions with rigorous, good-humored friends. And so, once a month we met for a potluck dinner and serious discussion about literacy outreach to parents, the value of compensatory education for gifted kids, the socially weighted definition of "gifted." The five of us were in our prime—professional, political, sexual.

Over the years, some of us came out; some got married, unmarried, remarried. Andrew and Greg became parents. Everyone went into therapy. I could never find the language to describe our relationship. Years before, we had abandoned the identity of discussion group. Although we still loved to argue megapolitics, these days we also talked job security, health difficulties, hairstyles, and mortgage payments. If the word weren't so overused, I'd say we had become a voluntary "family."

This morning, my first reaction on seeing them was relief. I had begun to worry when they didn't arrive for last night's dinner. It was a three-hour drive north from the Bay Area on sometimes twisting, difficult roads. (Then, early today, there was that fiery sunrise, an overbright red blur slashing across the new sky . . . Sailor's warning? Did it apply to highway driving?) Silly to fret, I could see that now, as they stretched their legs, admired the view from our ridge, and ambled around the new deck.

Strangely, it had been ten years since we had all spent a weekend at this particular place, a small parcel of Mendocino hill country Victoria and I used as a summer retreat. I'll never forget that July weekend when they helped build the cabin: everyone had a good time; some were more skillful carpenters than others. Greg was a natural at roof shingling. Felipe, who suffered vertigo, spent his time hammering down the kitchen floor. (He did such a dreadful job that we had to yank out most of those nails the following Monday, after the gang drove back to the Bay Area.) Today, Felipe's first destination was the kitchen, where he enthusiastically admired his fine craftsmanship.

After bagels and fresh ground coffee—their offering for being so late—we walked around the land and I showed them sleeping quarters. I always feel more comfortable as a visitor once I've met my bed. Eleanor was happy to camp on our couch. At the bunkhouse, Felipe and Matsuda would stay in the big room; Greg took the loft with a view of Cow Mountain.

Andrew and his family would stay down the hill. Most of the other members of our land cooperative, except for Rosemarie, were away this week. So we could put up Andrew, Kimiko, and the boys at the big cabin by the pond when they arrived—*if* they arrived—tonight.

"Of course they'll arrive, Maryann," Felipe laughed at me. "Where does a small, skinny person find the energy for all this silly worry? After twenty-odd years, you're still waiting for us to be on time, *amiga.*"

This was meant to be the perfect weekend, a triumvirate celebration of fifty. Oddly, we were all born within a month: Andrew first, me ten days later, then Felipe—late of course—in mid-September. He joked that we were triplets, separated after a very arduous labor in which the mother of us all birthed Andrew in Boston, me in San Francisco, and then had the good sense to retire to Merida, where she raised Felipe, the most well-adjusted sibling. We had planned the party for years.

"Fourteen hours late." I widened my eyes, hurt as well as pissed off.

"Ah, but weren't we worth waiting for, butterfly?"

We would eat lunch under the oak in the dappled sunshine. I unfurled the canary yellow tablecloth—a fifteenth-anniversary gift from Victoria—which glowed even more golden in this bright afternoon against the rolling Mendocino hills. Yellow jackets hovered around a decoy plate, interrupting us only occasionally with a low buzz—café conversation from a distant table. I inhaled well-being, friendship, and glorious late-August heat.

Lunch, catered by Felipe and Matsuda, wasn't what I had pictured. As they unpacked salami and cheese and iceberg lettuce and sliced white bread, Victoria gave me one of those "Relax, it ain't in your control" winks, and I returned to my nascent practice of tranquility. The sandwich was a fine guy meal; I sneezed at the familiar taste of Dad's favorite horseradish mustard.

The geographical "where" of the Symposium had become trickier to identify over the years. Only Felipe was still teaching high school, still evangelizing physics to Oakland teenagers. Eleanor now traveled the country as an education writer. Diplomatic Greg worked at the school board. Andrew became a super-canny consultant in online educational materials. Much to my surprise, I had turned into a professor of education in Seattle, where I had been lucky enough to meet Victoria. Felipe joked that while the rest of us launched into larger worlds, he had no imagination, no ambition. In truth, I believed that Felipe kept teaching because he was the best one. (What did that mean? How could you say someone was the most generous? The most compassionate? All virtues were circumstantial, temporal. Maybe I was simply saying I loved him the most.)

Above us, Spanish moss drooped down from the knotted branches of the live oak. Eleanor and Greg were arguing about Jerry Brown—a debate they might have finished years ago if the man didn't continually reincarnate. Felipe was asking Victoria about her Saturday choral group. She had a beautiful voice—a big woman's voice—but long ago traded in concert dreams for a job as a school counselor and Saturdays singing with her friends. The table became cluttered with bottles of Pepsi, Corona, Calistoga water, Handley chardonnay; a vat of mayo; a bowl of fragrant, sweaty blackberries. Matsuda seemed distracted, twiddling his ponytail, looking off toward the western hills; did he know the weather blew in from that direction? I should have tried to bring Felipe's new lover into the conversation, but I wanted to sit back and watch my old friends. Our charmed weekend had begun; we ate too much and caught up on gossip and laughed at Felipe's ridiculous jokes. Eleanor passed out photos of our Thanksgiving gathering. Greg showed pictures of his son's high school graduation. Young Jonathan was starting Berkeley this week, in a physics honors program recommended by Uncle Felipe.

As we cleared the table, Felipe suggested casually, "Hey, Maryann, let's go for a walk after lunch."

Sure, I nodded, taken aback because usually, after a midday engorgement like this, we'd all go hiking together.

To shake a vague uneasiness, I thought back to their Christmas visit long ago, when I was finishing grad school in Minneapolis. We all walked *across* frozen Lake Calhoun, Felipe playing a queenie Jesus, sashaying on the solid water. Thought back to the August we stayed at Eleanor's family cottage on the Jersey shore, taking long rambles every afternoon. But there would be no invigorating communal hike this afternoon; everyone was finking out. Matsuda wanted a nap. Greg needed to finish the *Times* crossword, and Eleanor had some last minute galleys to review. Each slipped off, promising to do dishes later.

The dishes, that's what clued me in. Every family had rituals, and doing dishes together was ours. We had all survived enough childhood kitchen fights to have a firm regimen. One scraped, one washed, two dried, and one put away. Everyone had a task. No coffee, no walk, no future until the dishes were done.

ALONE NOW, FELIPE AND I sat across from one another, listening to the lonely wind riffling through golden grasses. Even the bees had left. Felipe fiddled with his thread bracelet; I now recalled a matching one on Matsuda's tanned wrist.

"All right," I said, picking up a blackberry. "Tell me what's going on." Had he been fired for rabble-rousing at school? Was he finally making progress with the Merida project?

Anxiety rarely visited Felipe's sturdy face. I noticed his hair thinning on top. Lights of silver winked from the beard under his full, mauve lips. I searched his brown eyes and saw my friend of twenty years ago: Felipe suing the school board for tracking black students into industrial arts. Felipe confiscating half a dozen guns from Asian gang kids in his neighborhood and then absent-mindedly leaving the arsenal in his trunk for six months. Wonderfully fierce Felipe battling homophobic Proposition Six and, winning that round, initiating a Gay Pride Week at school. This was familiar, smart, whimsical, maddening Felipe.

Felipe facing a terrible change.

Ragged breath reached my lungs.

"I have some bad news." His voice got louder. "Maybe not bad"—the words faded in and out—"just a little hard."

No longer could I see his face. I struggled to keep myself warm and steady, hands gripping the sides of the picnic bench. A bleating noise threatened, louder and louder in gaudy colors.

"No, no," I heard myself ranting. Of all my friends, Felipe would remain safe from HIV. Since two negative tests (the second just to check the first) ten years ago, I had relinquished fear. We were dealing with a community pioneer, who chaired the mayor's AIDS Education Board.

He reached for my fist, which was slowly pounding a blackberry into the gold tablecloth.

"It's all right," he said gently.

"No it's not," I spat back. "It isn't true. Not now. There's a mistake."

"I've had three tests," he shrugged.

"Well"—I gulped hot, dry air—"you'll be fine, of course." I raced ahead—simultaneously by myself, away from Felipe, and ushering him with me to safety. "With the protease inhibitors. It's just a chronic illness now."

He shook his head—sympathy, fatalism in sad, dark eyes.

Jays barked from a tree near the ridge.

Ashamed of how I ripped the story from his telling, I allowed my fingers to relax in his and we held hands as the purple juice seeped along random threads of the linen cloth.

"Matsuda's T-cells," he explained with relief, "are much better, responding to the cocktail. Last test, there was no HIV detectable in his system."

Wind shifted, and I noticed early fog rolling in, imagined how it had started at the coast an hour ago. He was telling me that his new boyfriend of six months had got bored with safe sex. Turning the pale green ring around his finger, Felipe said they were theoretically monogamous, but that it was tough on Matsuda to be the twentyish lover of a middle-aged man, especially of someone so preoccupied with work and politics and . . .

He registered my incredulity, stopped.

Goosebumps on his solid, muscular arms. Was it going to rain? No, I wasn't cold. He shivered.

"Shouldn't you get a sweater or something?"

He smiled—fondly, wisely, older than I had ever seen him. "A nap," he answered. "I'll just lie down for a while."

"Yes, yes," I encouraged. "Rest, it's the fastest route to recovery."

Before I could feel foolish, he said, "I love you."

"I love you too, Felipe."

BACK IN THE CABIN, I stared out the window at the ghostly moss—tawdry Christmas tinsel rusting in the late-summer fog.

Suddenly, a knock at the door. Greg and Eleanor peered through the back window.

I opened the door and we hugged. Then, in sighs and silence, we washed the sticky lunch plates. The aroma of horseradish mustard and lemon Joy pervaded the close air of our small cabin.

Eleanor stepped back from the sink, snapping her dishtowel. "I think we're being too WASP about this."

Greg sniffed in agreement.

I waited, drying spots off the glass pitcher.

Eleanor was waving those long, graceful arms. "We're all just taking the news politely. He wants to tell us individually, discreetly, and that's the end of that. On with the party!" Her voice rose. I always admired the quick swell of Eleanor's anger. "He wants us to move along with the weekend . . . argue about the fall elections . . . plan the dinner menu."

"So what can we do?" Greg's face was drawn. The quietest and the most observant of us, he was also the most practical. Here, however, he looked lost.

I had almost forgiven his lie about the crossword.

Eleanor paced back and forth to the window. "This isn't just Felipe's news. It belongs to all of us."

"It's Felipe's life," I said, "Felipe's—"

"Now don't even start thinking that," she commanded. "My father treats lots of HIV, and he swears by these new drugs."

I wondered if the whole weekend would be like this—all of us arguing the same stale, desperate reassurances.

"Well"—Greg swallowed his familiar impatience with Eleanor—"it's mostly *his* news. His and Matsuda's."

"Matsuda!" Eleanor declared. "It's so creepy to have him here this weekend. I mean after what he did to Felipe."

"Felipe would say they 'did it' together," I objected. (Why did we call him Matsuda? I wondered. Because Felipe did. Roy, Ray; once I knew his first name.)

"Don't give me that 'luck of the draw' shit. Matsuda lied. He was screwing around and promising Felipe he was monogamous. I feel like shooting the little teenybopper."

Was he a teenybopper? No, he was twenty-three or twenty-four, almost the age we had all been when we first met.

"No weapons!" Greg raised his hand. "Felipe threw out the guns he confiscated from the kids six or seven years ago."

Eleanor and I laughed half-heartedly.

We agreed to tell Felipe we were worried, that we loved him—not only individually, but as a group. None of us was maudlin enough to say "family" out loud.

"At dinner," Greg suggested. "After the second glass of wine, we'll bring it up then. We'll be brief, but clear." I watched Greg returning to his comfortable, competent skin.

Hard to say much more. We were all so shaken by the news. Each of them left for a solo walk.

A FEW MINUTES LATER, the phone beeped. Andrew ringing from Corning. He, Kimiko, and the boys *were* making progress on their way south from Mount Shasta. Originally, they had planned to come for lunch, but I felt no irritation. (Safety, that's all I cared about. *When* didn't matter. Just four safe people.)

"We'll arrive by 6 P.M., easily," he said. "Meanwhile, do you want any olives?"

"Olives?"

"We're sampling at the Olive Pit," he rasped loudly over the background noise. "And we thought we'd bring an hors d'oeuvres tray. Nuts, artichoke hearts, and—what do you want—kalamatas? niçoise? Moroccan?"

"T-cells," I spit into the phone, careening suddenly from rage to grief. "We could use some T-cells."

"He's told you?" Andrew's familiar voice softened.

I sobbed. Finally.

"That's it," he said. "Cry. You never let go." Behind him, I heard a dinging cash register, voices murmuring through brine and oil.

I couldn't stop.

He waited.

"This is a ridiculous phone call," I inhaled, pulling myself together.

"I love you," Andrew said.

I broke down.

DESPITE THE DARKENING CHILL, everyone remained determined to have a proper country Saturday afternoon. (Autumn already? I wondered.

Sometimes fall came early in Mendocino, but I prayed for the weather to cheer up.) Eleanor, training for a marathon, declared she would go running in nearby Hendy Woods. Felipe was resolutely refreshed from his nap and decided to accompany her.

As they drove toward the gate, Greg, Victoria, Matsuda, and I walked downhill to the pond. Too cold for swimming, but we could bird-watch, read, talk.

One toe in the pond, Matsuda deemed the temperature perfect.

This strong, muscular young man cut through the water like a dancer, gracefully sidestroking to the distant cattails. Back and forth: crawl, breast-stroke, dog paddle. We watched, mumbling plans about dinner, when to light the charcoal. Greg closed his eyes, seemed to nap. Victoria took my hand, and I stared at the crimson of her whimsical manicure, teasing her about turning into a lipstick dyke. Lovely hands, one of the first things I noticed—her firm gentleness. I used to believe self-sufficiency was the noblest virtue, but now I wondered what I would do without Victoria's wackiness and practical intelligence.

Matsuda lifted himself from the water, nimble as a silkie, dried off, and stretched out on his towel, eyes closed. Like all silkies, a creature of mysterious powers.

Since I had been reading, it took me a while to register the noise. Victoria was already waving to Rosemarie, who ambled down the hill, almost keeping pace with her wonderfully silly dog, Kipper. Tensing, I glanced at the innocent sleepers. Years before, when we first bought the acreage with three other friends, Rosemarie argued for preserving it as women-only land. Eventually, she compromised, allowing men on week-ends and special occasions. This was both a weekend and a birthday, so what was I anxious about?

Victoria squeezed my shoulder reassuringly, then called, "Rosemarie! Terrific! Come meet our friends, Greg and Matsuda."

Of course Victoria realized we had all mellowed over the years. Even Rosemarie had invited her uncle last summer. She probably wouldn't even notice Victoria's femme fingernails.

Kipper, the West's most elegant cocker spaniel, bounced toward us in a jingle of tags.

I grinned at this flurry of brownish blond curls. Such a welcome con-trast to dour, practical Rosemarie.

Greg and Matsuda nodded hello.

I scooted over, remembering how she enjoyed afternoons reading by the pond.

Book in one hand, towel in the other, she stood peering into the green water. "Do you mind if I swim?"

Greg and Matsuda shrugged at the unnecessary question, and it took me a couple of beats to realize Rosemarie hadn't brought a suit. Ordinarily we skinny-dipped in the pond. Maybe Rosemarie had forgotten this was a guest weekend. Maybe she didn't care. The guys wouldn't know that Rosemarie was not only suitless, she was also breastless, having made a courageous recovery from a double mastectomy two years before.

I twisted through embarrassment for the boys, anger at Rosemarie, admiration for Rosemarie, a pang for Felipe. Patched grey and white and darker grey, the sky closed in on us.

Kipper sniffed intently around the base of the old willow. Greg asked Matsuda computer advice, and I wondered how he could converse so civilly with Felipe's potential murderer. The afternoon was spinning fast and slow.

A maverick wave of sun cast Rosemarie's long shadow across the yellow grass. She was a tall, fit woman, big-boned, and I was touched by the puckering flesh in her thighs and a faint purple varicose streak in her right calf. I almost missed the moment she pulled off her T-shirt and deliberately poised herself to dive into the murky water. Greg glanced away, but Matsuda's face was observant. Her chest was flat, slightly concave against the sturdy ribs, and the scars were, as always, smaller than I expected—the right one virtually invisible, the left one red against pale Danish skin. Matsuda studied Rosemarie's long, balletic arch into the pond and followed the passage of a spectral green mermaid until she surfaced at the cattails. Another shape-shifter.

"Nice dive," Matsuda nodded.

Victoria smiled. "Yes, she captained her college swim team."

At the sight of Rosemarie floating, the dog barked, jumping jerkily at the deck's slippery edge.

Rosemarie yelled inaudibly from the cattails.

Greg reached over to calm Kipper.

Rosemarie shouted louder. "Don't let her too close to the edge; she can't swim."

This was the tension breaker we needed, and the four of us howled at the notion of a cocker spaniel, this natural-born water dog, unable to swim. Maybe Rosemarie was developing her own weird sense of humor after all these years.

Kipper quivered with excitement at her friend's voice and our fits of laughter. Suddenly, propelled by her own giddiness, she skidded and flew into the pond.

Rosemarie screamed. "Save her! Save her, someone; she can't swim!" Stroking frantically toward the dock, she screamed, "Somebody, help!"

Kipper's sweet face wrenched with panic. She practiced some primal paddling instinct, clearly losing.

The next sound: Matsuda crashing into the water. He dove precisely, yanking a terrified dog by the scruff of her neck.

Rosemarie had made it halfway across the pond. This must have been happening very fast, but I felt frozen in slow motion, imagined us back in wintry Minneapolis, Lake Calhoun cracking, all of us falling in, slipping down, down.

Matsuda's long black hair sprayed across his face as he struggled to stay afloat with wiggling Kipper. Pressing toward the dock, he treaded water, finally managing to hand the sad, wet dog up to me. A minute later, Rosemarie reached the ladder.

She leapt on the dock. "Thank you, thank you," she shouted down to the grinning St. Christopher. "You saved her!" Rosemarie lifted the dog from my embrace.

I was grinning, too—then saw spots of blood along my forearm where I had held Kipper, noticed a rusty screw protruding slightly from one of the dock boards. My blood? The dog's? Matsuda's?

"Naughty, naughty dog," Rosemarie lectured Kipper, who had run off to the safe grasses, nervously shaking dry. Pulling on her shirt and shorts, Rosemarie hurried after the dog, then turned back. "Thank you, thank you!" she called to Matsuda.

He smiled.

I could see Felipe loving the sweetness in those shy eyes.

Her voice scratched through the warming afternoon, high and fast. "Ridiculous, really—a water dog who can't swim. Maybe it's why I love her."

I rubbed my arm. The blood was gone now.

Matsuda nodded gently and waved to Rosemarie.

FOURTEEN YEARS BEFORE—maybe fourteen and a half, because it was a winter night—we were sitting in a secondhand hot tub under the bay tree in Eleanor's backyard. There we were, pretending to be unselfconscious about our naked bodies, all of us looking up to identify constellations, making up names for unknown ones, whispering about our futures. Felipe spun fantasies about his Yucatan summer program for East Oakland kids. Greg toyed with running for State Assembly on a radical schools platform. Eleanor was going to found a magazine for activist teachers. I was newly in love with Victoria, and together we planned to work a year in Chile. Another year in Tanzania. The night sky grew more brilliant as we argued means versus ends, long- and short-term commitments. Everything was possible; all we had to do was choose.

FELIPE APPEARED as I rooted beneath the deck for briquettes.

Flushed, a little winded, he declared, "Great run! Three miles. Some serious hills. Frankly, I was kind of surprised I could keep up with Eleanor."

I grinned at the bloom in his cheeks. He and Matsuda ran off to buy wine for dinner.

Eleanor looked refreshed by her shower. "Let's start the artichokes." She took my hand, winking and waving to Felipe. "Washing, peeling, cooking artichokes takes forever."

Working at the sink, I listened to the water groaning from the outside faucet where Greg was taking a quick wash. Normally, our makeshift shower was one of summer's joys—standing there on a hundred-degree afternoon letting water clean and calm your body—but ablution was more penance than pleasure in this dreary weather.

When Eleanor's wet, sandy hair was slicked back, she always reminded me of a baby rabbit my brother raised. Soft, moist, vulnerable, and throbbing with quixotic growth. Any minute, the marathon runner and famous author would emerge.

It wasn't until long after the Symposium began that we realized three of us had suicide in our families—Greg's mother, Eleanor's sister, my little brother. Curiously perhaps, given all our other intimacies, we never really spoke about these deaths. People who haven't known suicide always wonder "how." Those of us who have suffered it are paralyzed by "why." We asked neither question, just nodded to that familiar expression of loss we recognized in one another. All that we shared was unspoken—sadness, guilt, cautiousness, a kind of elastic tolerance. Someday, I imagined, we would talk about suicide. Someday I'd forgive myself, my parents, for the disappearance of my beautiful teenage brother.

Eleanor scrubbed the artichokes vigorously. We always let her take charge of the vegetables; otherwise she would persecute us with detailed pesticide reports. I filled a big pot with water for the artichokes, squeezed in the juice of three tender Meyer lemons, and added a few garlic cloves.

"God, I'm glad we survived that run," she sighed. "I was terrified he was going to keel over. Those pills affect his balance. I just decided to quit once I was convinced we had put on a good-enough show."

I thought about Felipe's triumphant smile.

"What a relief to get him back in the car in one piece. Did he say anything about the run? Did he look all right to you?"

No, not all right. Jubilant. Exultant. "You put on a good-enough show," I said.

Her blond eyebrows lifted faintly over doleful eyes.

Artichokes prepared, she set upon the potatoes. I failed to persuade her you can't remove every nick of soil.

Into the salad bowl, I tossed fresh basil and arugula from Greg's garden, and veg we bought at the Mendocino Farmers' Market: shallots, green-red-orange peppers, seedless cucumbers, those little yellow light-bulb tomatoes.

"Hey, look what I found." Greg toweled his black curls with one hand and held out a brightly wrapped package with the other. "On the picnic table outside."

I could smell it from across the room: Rosemarie's famous dill wheat baguette. Still warm as Greg handed it to me. The card said, "For Matsuda and his friends, from Kipper and her friend."

"That was sweet of her," Eleanor said.

"You don't know," Victoria shook her head. "It's a bloody miracle."

"Matsuda, the miracle worker!" I sniffed.

"Let's just enjoy the bread," Greg cajoled. "And the evening."

I swiveled toward the counter to hide my tears, remembering Rosemarie's stalwart response to the diagnosis; her determined recuperation from surgery—all those exercises; then her passionate grasping at what life offered—taking kayak lessons, baking classes. The dill wheat was my favorite of her breads.

Victoria had almost finished preparing the green beans and cremini mushrooms, marinated in her garlic vinaigrette. Garlic—there was always *mucho* garlic in a Symposium feast—the key to our good humor, Greg insisted.

Almost dry now, Greg sat at the table, playfully lining up the six bottles of vino Felipe and Matsuda had brought home.

I could hear the wine mavens in our outside shower, whooping and giggling over the spray of hot water.

"Look," called Victoria, pointing out the bay window. "Look, sun!"

When I raised my head, the room had lightened in color and weight and spirit. We were floating.

"Right," I grumbled to settle myself, in no mood for a good mood. "Perfect timing: sunrise at 5 P.M."

"No, see!" she shouted through my petulance.

"Yes," declared Eleanor. "A rainbow—over the hills."

I walked to the back deck. "Hey, you guys," I shouted. "Hey, Felipe, Matsuda—a rainbow!"

Immediately, I felt foolish, interrupting their shower, childishly needing them to enjoy this—a goddamned rainbow—as if we'd all been astral-projected to Disneyland.

In seconds, they appeared on the grass, barefoot, towels around their waists, holding hands. Together, we watched the rainbow shimmering in the sky, reflected in the water. Buttery yellow, lime green, robin's-egg blue, lipstick pink, lavender. We named the colors. I peered through a translucent red at the stand of Douglas fir. We counted the bands—Greg saw seven, Felipe nine. Eleanor insisted there were really only three. The arch grew longer, stronger, stretching from the vineyard ridge to the far side of the valley. Carefully, I followed the silken trail. If I held my gaze, could I reach the end before any colors evaporated? I wanted my friends to come with me; surely, together we would make it.

Instead, I stood back, savoring their bickering laughter.

ELEVEN YEARS AGO, they all flew up to Seattle for Thanksgiving. "All" had a different meaning then. Andrew hadn't met Kimiko yet; Eleanor was married to Cecil. Often, in those early days, Greg's son Jonathan joined Symposium celebrations; but on this holiday, he was staying with his mother, as agreed in Greg's and Nola's tense but generally amicable custody arrangement. I was sorry to miss the boy, although perhaps at seven Jonny—or Jonathan, as he preferred now—was too old to be the Symposium mascot. That November weekend passed happily with our ritual rambles, vociferous arguments, high and low cultural forays, and elaborate homemade dinners. Especially during the pre-fat-and-fiber days, each meal was an extravagant cooking competition. Somewhere in the Pike Place Market, Felipe found a long blond wig. During our last night together, we lounged around the fireplace with chocolate cookies and brandy and coffee, taking turns fashioning the wig into coiffures for karaoke roles—Cher, Elvis, Bob Marley, Judy Garland, Aretha— brunettes all of them.

Late in the evening, my phone interrupted. It must have been ringing a long time because the nurse shouted at me when I finally answered . . . They didn't know much about the head-on collision: Nola was dead, and Jonathan remained in critical condition. We drove Greg to the airport and waited with him for a flight—any flight, any price—to San Francisco. Three hours later, they left, Felipe ushering Greg onto the plane. We would send their clothes with Eleanor on Monday.

Early the next morning, Felipe called to report Jonathan was pulling through, although his left leg was pretty shattered.

Greg had collapsed with exhaustion in Felipe's guest room.

———

ALMOST 8 P.M. and no sign of Andrew, Kimiko, and the kids. (Dear, distracted Andrew. Sometimes we called him Lucky Andrew, because, despite his career roulette, he always evaded disaster. Felipe thought luck came with his charming green eyes. When Kimiko first got pregnant, Andrew had no job. Then, just before Joey was born, he was headhunted for a hot position in computer consulting.) No telling when Andrew would finally pull up. We were all hungry and tired after a long day, so we lit the charcoal.

Of course, just as Greg lifted the perfectly cooked salmon from the grill, Andrew's forest green SUV crunched down the hill in the hazy evening afterlight.

Kisses. Hugs. The melt-in-your-mouth salmon was shoved into the oven to stay warm while we unloaded the car. Two little boys raced around the cabin, noisy as a gang of ten. Kimiko washed out a handkerchief spotted by Luke's bloody nose. From dark red dots on the cabin floor, I could tell the poor kid was still descending that mountain. The reel fast-forwarded: Carrying bags upstairs. Unveiling the olive tray. Pouring champagne. And finally—9 P.M. maybe—we sat down to the birthday feast.

Andrew and Kimiko entertained us with harrowing tales of backpacking with toddlers on Mount Shasta. Then we recited our stories: the long lunch, jogging, swimming, St. Christopher's rescue. Andrew raised a glass to Matsuda, the hero.

I told myself to relax—Felipe was right, we all survived on oxygen and chance. I concentrated on loving my friends, but couldn't stifle the vengeful wish that Matsuda choke on a fishbone.

Wine flowed. Felipe had good taste; god knew how much he had spent on this plonk. Of course, the food was divine—Eleanor's well-scrubbed, tender artichokes; Victoria's dream beans; Greg's masterful salmon, which was just a little dried out from its exile to the oven during welcoming ceremonies. Kimiko and Andrew had selected five types of specialty olives. The contest winner was a green olive stuffed with sun-dried tomatoes. Our moods lifted. It was possible to forget, for minutes at a time. And then, like coughing breaking the spell of a scherzo, Felipe's diagnosis erased my sense of well-being.

"Felipe," I heard myself saying. If I didn't do this now, I never would. Eleanor nodded encouragement.

Felipe cast me a warning glance, refilled his glass with dark cabernet, and began to tell a joke.

"Felipe," Greg interrupted, gently holding his arm.

Good, I thought; Greg, the diplomat among us, would be the best messenger. He had been especially close to Felipe since Jonathan's accident.

Silence.

As I waited for Greg's speech, I imagined Felipe raising his glass, consecrating the wine.

Actually, our friend looked cornered, angry—but grudgingly returned Greg's smile.

"Felipe"—Greg massaged his old friend's shoulder—"Maryann has something to say."

My courage almost evaporated, I made it brief and simple.

"Felipe," I sighed, "we have something to tell you as a group. I mean we're friends together—as well as individually." God, I was screwing this up, sounding like a TV therapist.

Victoria watched me closely.

"I'll make this short," I reminded myself. "We just need to say, we love you."

Felipe reached for Matsuda's hand.

The room was thick with wordlessness, not even a note from the children. I began to perceive Matsuda's bravery in facing this weekend, and to understand that Felipe might not have been able to come without him.

"Each of us. And all of us are here to do anything you need. And we won't do anything you don't want."

Felipe nodded. Enough. I could hear his unspoken protests of self-sufficiency. But he could no more talk than cut our ties.

"And," I continued, "we want to say we're sorry about the diagnosis. Diagnoses. Concerned for you and Matsuda."

Victoria wiped her eyes. Greg filled my glass.

Joey pierced the solemn quiet. "Cake, Mommy, didn't you say there would be birthday cake?"

We all followed Kimiko's firm instructions to eat another helping of vegetables before we even thought about dessert.

Felipe disappeared outside for his usual post-dinner smoke.

As they started clearing the table, I too slipped out.

He leaned against the redwood deck railing, staring into a landscape of fog. From our ridge, the valley looked like a foamy river. The bases of first-growth sequoias were so thickly veiled in mist, they might be a cluster of young trees caught in a night flood.

When he turned, I could see most of his face through the cigar smoke—the serious expression was hard to read.

"Are you mad at me?" I asked feebly. Not—How are you? May I join you?

His body was still; his eyes narrowed.

"Yes," he finally whispered.

I hung my head, warned myself not to dare cry.

He lifted my chin.

"And also, no," he said.

Felipe's arm on my shoulder, mine around his waist, we turned back to watch those treetops reaching through the fog. I breathed in the cool night, not bothering to look for stars in the overcast sky. We stood that way for a long time, listening to the frogs and crickets, inhaling musky smoke, letting the mist rise around us.

———

A VOICE SQUEAKED from the doorway. "Greg says to tell you we're all hungry for cake." Joey peered up at us with shy defiance.

"Oh, are we?" Felipe laughed and lifted the boy ceremoniously, a sacrifice to camouflaged stars. Joey giggled.

Felipe set him down and said, seriously, "Yes, some of us have come a long way for cake."

Laughing, we followed our buoyant messenger into the warm room, which seemed to have grown higher and wider in our absence.

"Finally!" Eleanor exclaimed. "You know, you can't put off turning fifty this way."

I shrugged, grinning.

Greg passed a cup of coffee and squeezed my hand.

Eleanor must have worked on the cake's design for a week. The 12 × 12 sheet was divided into three isosceles triangles. Andrew's section showed a family dancing around a computer. In mine perched a little country house. Felipe was portrayed as a teacher at the blackboard, singing. In the middle of all our lives stood three fat, garish pink candles, "5–0," flames screaming.

A round of "Happy Birthday." Clapping. Silent supplications from the honorees before we blew out the candles. Then, unabashed wishes from the others.

"I wish Luke's nose will stop bleeding by bedtime," Kimiko sighed.

"I hope the sun comes out early tomorrow," said Eleanor.

"I want some cake," said our little friend.

"About time!" Felipe stood and cut the first piece for Joey.

As Greg passed out the other slices of Eleanor's gorgeous cake, Victoria sang a sixteenth-century Italian birthday song her grandmother had taught her. I felt happier than I had all day.

"What's this?" A wail from the far end of the table.

Before anyone could answer, Joey was pointing accusingly to his father.

"Cake," Andrew answered, innocent, exhausted from the endless drive through bounteous California landscape with his two precious children. "Chocolate cake," he managed. "You love chocolate cake."

"This isn't chocolate!" Joey shouted. "I can't eat this."

"He's right," Eleanor struggled. "It's carob. I mean you guys have got so health conscious, I thought you'd prefer it."

Joey was bawling.

Greg tried gently, "It's delicious, Joey, really. And it's good for you."

"Ugh," he screamed.

Kimiko reached forward, stroking his hair, taking over from a depleted Andrew.

The child didn't want consolation; he wanted chocolate.

"I don't like things that are good for me!"

Felipe laughed the loudest. "I know what you mean, Joey."

⌁

ELEANOR GOT HER WISH; the next morning was brilliantly sunny, hot enough for swimming by 10:30 A.M. She, of course, went for a run. The kids loved playing with their parents in our battered, patched inner tubes. Matsuda swam laps. Greg sat with his feet in the water, finishing a mystery novel. Felipe stretched out on a purple flowered towel, working on his tan.

Felipe raised his head every once in a while, squinting at the kids and growling like a sea monster. They squealed with excitement, spattered him with water. All so normal, as if three of us hadn't turned fifty this year, as if . . .

Since Greg had a meeting in the city, we packed up and headed to the house for an early lunch. Matsuda, Greg, and Felipe took the lead, carrying the cooler and deck chairs and foam pads. Andrew hoisted Luke on his shoulders and held big Joey's hand.

Kimiko and I stayed behind, stacking inner tubes and beach balls. As she bent down to collect one of Luke's plastic frogmen, I noticed a trickle of red streaking along her right thigh. Another on her left leg.

I whispered, "Kimiko." Then, trying for Victoria's light matter-of-factness in the face of real life, "You're bleeding down your legs."

"Oh, Christ," Kimiko said, more irritated than embarrassed. "Since having the boys, my periods arrive without any warning." She cupped pond water and rinsed off her legs.

"We've got Tampax and pads in the privy," I offered.

"Thanks." She shook her head. "I guess I should be grateful—it's how/why we have Joey and Luke. It's a sign of life."

THE GRIZZLED SEA MONSTER had turned into a bucking bronco, chasing Joey and Luke around the table as Victoria finished lunch preparations. Then Felipe sank down on the couch, resolutely regaling us with a string of puns from his dreadful joke repertoire. The kids sat at his feet, swapping riddles with him. We finished the birthday cake for dessert—all of us except Joey, who had sworn to boycott carob for the rest of his long life. Greg started the dishes. Eleanor pulled out her electronic calendar and subdued the unruly mob into making definite Thanksgiving plans—her house in Berkeley this year. And was pumpkin pie acceptable to Master Joseph?

"Guys," Greg said with almost Monday-morning sobriety, "I have that meeting at seven tonight . . ."

Felipe roared loudly, prancing around Greg, wiggling his ragged tail and batting the air with menacing hoofs. Luke and Joey followed the bronco's lead, corralling Greg in a circle of neighs and whinnies and giggles.

MATSUDA HONKED THE HORN. Felipe and the kids snorted fiercely. Greg, Andrew, and Eleanor carried bags out to the car.

Twenty minutes later we were still hugging, pressing last-minute messages on one another. Greg ran back to the house for a missing thermos, Eleanor for her lost reading glasses. Matsuda straightened his backwards red baseball cap. Felipe closed his eyes momentarily.

Suddenly everyone was waving, a cluster of large and small organic pinwheels spinning. As they pulled away, Felipe jauntily tilted my sun hat over his brow. We were all shouting and blowing kisses. They disappeared into dust, the engine sound fading as they looped down far hills toward the gate.

———

"OH, NO," LUKE MOANED into the vacant afternoon. "I'm going to miss Felipe."

The adults looked from one to another helplessly.

"Don't worry," reassured his big brother, "he's not a very old horse. He'll be back soon, galloping the hills."

We laughed.

"Hey, Dad, how old is Felipe?" Joey asked. "The same age as you, right?"

"Yes," Andrew grinned. "Felipe is fifty this summer."

"*Fif*-ty!" Joey's face grew doubtful.

The road dust in my contacts was making me tear. I closed my eyes and saw Felipe's big smile. Oxygen and chance, I remembered.

"That's *oooold,*" said Joey.

"Not old enough," I called, doing my best to assume the spirit of a bucking bronco.

Acknowledgments

The author is grateful for residency fellowships at MacDowell, Yaddo, and the Virginia Center for the Creative Arts. I also acknowledge support from the McKnight Foundation, the Fulbright Program, the University of Edinburgh and the University of Minnesota.

Many thanks to the writers who gave me invaluable responses to drafts of these stories over a period of years: Margaret Love Denman, Heid Erdrich, Pamela Fletcher, Jana Harris, Lori Lei Hokyo, Helen Longino, Leslie Adrienne Miller, Scott Muskin, Martha Roth, Andria Williams, Lex Williford, and Susan Welch. I am grateful to Martha Bates, my editor, for her intelligence, wit, and literary commitment.

The following stories have appeared in journals or been broadcast (sometimes in slightly different incarnations):

"Back Home at the Driftwood Lodge," *Southwest Review,* Summer 2004

"Three Women by the River, At One Time or Another," *Ms.,* Fall 2003

"Percussion," *Prairie Schooner,* Fall 2003 (Winner of the Hugh G. Luke award)

"The House with Nobody in It," in *Telling Moments,* edited by Lynda Hall (University of Wisconsin Press, 2003)

"Cocktails," BBC Radio 4, 7 August 2003

"*Il Cortegiano* of Thomas Avenue," *The Georgia Review,* Summer 2003

"Always Avoid Accidents," *Ascent,* Winter 2003

"Veranda," *Southwest Review,* Winter 2002 (Winner of the McGinnis-Ritchie Prize for Fiction)

"Greyhound, 1970," *Puerto del Sol,* Summer 2002

"Vital Signs," *New Letters,* Spring 2001

"Abundant Light" (as "In Summer Light"), *Quarterly West,* Spring 2001

"All The Way," *Salmagundi,* Winter 2000

Michigan State University Press is committed to preserving ancient forests and natural resources. We have elected to print this title on Nature's Natural, which is 90% recycled (50% post-consumer waste). As a result of our paper choice, Michigan State University Press has saved the following natural resources*:

14.4	Trees (40 feet in height)
4,200	Gallons of Water
2,460	Kilowatt-hours of Electricity
36	Pounds of Air Pollution

We are a member of Green Press Initiative—a nonprofit program dedicated to supporting book publishers in maximizing their use of fiber that is not sourced from ancient or endangered forests. For more information about Green Press Initiative and the use of recycled paper in book publishing, please visit *www.greenpressinitiative.org.*

*Environmental benefits were calculated based on research provided by Conservatree and Californians Against Waste.